Rebecca

Beyond all Reason

Volume 3

A Novel

By

Stephen M Davis

Author Stephen M Davis was born in East London in 1957.

He was educated at Woodbridge High School, Woodford, Essex and St John Cass Royal School of Art, East London. He started writing seriously in 2009 once retired from Royal Mail.

First Published 2019

Typeset Stephen M Davis

Cover Design Stephen M Davis

Published by DMS Literary Publications

Author's website stevedauthor.wordpress.com

Setting – Modern Day

Follow Rebecca as she travels into the future and witnesses our planet devoid of human life.

She learns that mankind has been wiped out by its own relentless destruction of the environment.

Mother Nature though is thriving, albeit without mankind.

Rebecca now faces an epic voyage of discovery, which takes her right back to the "cradle of civilisation" where her story unfolds.

On her journey through the ages, she meets other time travellers of her making.

All though have failed to stop the unrelenting greed-clock from derailing humanity.

It now falls to Rebecca.

Rebecca - Beyond all Reason is my third novel in the Rebecca series. I have also written and illustrated a standalone light-hearted look at Rebecca's world.

Volume 1 in the series: Rebecca & the Spiral Staircase

Volume 2 in the series: Rebecca – a Way Back

Rebecca's Book of Fairies, Pixies, Elves & other Amazing Things

This novel is an illustrated storybook. A full colour chronicle, which is available in paperback and Kindle versions.

All books are available through Amazon.co.uk or Amazon.com.

All Books can be loaned through Essex UK Libraries.

A brief look at Rebecca & the Spiral Staircase, volume 1

Here is an insight into Rebecca's world, just in case you haven't read Volume 1. This introduction is a synopsis of *Rebecca & the Spiral Staircase*.

Rebecca's relationship with her 11-year-old brother, Tommy – who was forever kicking his football in her direction - was typical of most teenage brother and sister interactions. Rebecca shared a delightful, close bond with her mother, Elizabeth. Often though, she felt troubled by her mother's passive relationship with Rebecca's father, James. In particular, Elizabeth's inert response to James' Victorian marital attitude maddened Rebecca. On occasions, she would escape her frustration, and find solace in an imaginary world beside the Whispering Pond, which nestled in the grounds of the family home in Cheshire.

Just before Christmas, James announced he had bought a big old Gothic mansion up by the lakes for a bargain price. Outwardly oblivious to sentiments and feelings towards their present home, he informed everyone they should be ready to move soon.

Although Rebecca missed her old house, she quickly delighted in her new surroundings and set about exploring the vast grounds. Unbeknown to her, she had in fact arrived at her real home. Her imagination really kicked in when she found an ancient key and discovered it unlocked the door to a derelict summerhouse down by a lake. One day, when alone inside the summerhouse, a previously locked door opened, leading to a spiral staircase.

Taking to these stairs, she embarked on a series of journeys into the history of their old family house. Her first encounter was with a woman named Meredith in 1853. She was a troubled woman whose husband had a lover named Millicent, an unsavoury character, with a chequered past.

Rebecca challenged Millicent's unpleasant behaviour. She then set about showing Meredith an alternative approach to her marital situation, which helped Meredith resolve her issues.

Once back in her own time, Rebecca discovered by way of an old newspaper article Millicent had been shot to death. The report went on to say Meredith had been indicted for Millicent's murder.

Reading this article troubled Rebecca feeling powerless to do anything about Meredith's predicament. Having established a strong mother-daughter bond with this woman, Rebecca was certain Meredith was incapable of a murderous act.

Months passed without the door opening again, but when it did, she found herself in 1943. Here the mansion was being used as an orphanage for children evacuated from war-torn London. She soon learnt Judith, the lady of the house, was an outcast in her own home. Instantly aware of the bizarre similarities between Judith's life and Meredith's, she set about untangling this woman's relationship. Observing Judith's complicated plight, she drew upon her experiences from her previous trip and helped her towards an amicable resolution.

Back in her own time and with school finished for the summer holidays, Rebecca sat on her balcony sketching. For a couple of days, she felt an overwhelming pull towards the summerhouse. Having not been able to get Meredith's predicament from her consciousness, she wondered if this was the reason for this tangible, physical sensation. One particular day, unable to resist the call, she headed down to the summerhouse, and once again took to the stairs. This time, she found herself in 1911, where the family relationship was the complete opposite of her previous experiences. This time, the woman was a passive-aggressive who controlled all around her. With little to do here other than observe, she headed back to the summerhouse, wondering why she'd ended up in this era. Upon entering the summerhouse, she found a sixty-year-old suicide note written by Millicent. Armed with this note, she now knew why she'd arrived in 1911, and her next mission was to find her way back to Meredith.

Although her next journey seemed complicated and fraught with difficulties, she drew solace, now convinced Meredith's troubled spirit was leading her way. Assured by this belief, and going on a hunch, she followed her instinct. Armed with the suicide note, Rebecca found her way back to 1853 and thereby proved Meredith's innocence.

Attempting to return home, Rebecca found she'd travelled three months ahead of her own time. Here, she witnessed the aftermath of a tragic accident involving her mother. This time, unlike her previous adventures, she was invisible to all. Only able to stand, watch, and listen, she heard her sobbing father wishing he had taken notice of Elizabeth and fixed the heating boiler. Before returning to her own time, she concocted a plan that would convince her father to take action, and in so doing, prevent her mother's death.

The plan worked, and unwittingly she'd opened the door for her parents to re-establish their forgotten love, something Rebecca had always known was there. Reflecting on all that had happened over the last year, Rebecca believed Meredith had exposed this impending disaster as recompense for Rebecca clearing her name by uncovering the suicide note. She now felt confident Meredith had been her guardian angel throughout her journeys and believed her mission in all of this was to help Meredith's tormented spirit, which in turn led to her parent's rediscovered love. Sitting on her balcony, she again considered everything, and believing Meredith's spirit had at last found a resting place, Rebecca was certain her jaunts into the past were now over.

That indeed seemed to be the last of her journeys, as she suspected, and now entering her eighteenth year, Rebecca left home to take up residence at Warwick University. Returning home for the summer break at the end of her first year at university, she learnt her father had commissioned the rebuilding of the summerhouse. If there were any doubts before, with the old spiral staircase now gone, replaced with a new shiny one, she was sure her journeys were over for good.

During supper, her mother told her they had found four boxes in the summerhouse's loft during its restoration. With an element of apprehension, she set about exploring the contents of the boxes. To her amazement, the first box contained sepia photos of Rebecca with Meredith in the 1850s. With the nagging time-travel dream notion dismissed, she opened the next box with eagerness, only to find little other than some history relating to the house and its occupants. The third box, however, contained a letter from Meredith addressed to Rebecca. It stated that Rebecca's soul and spirit had always been present in this house. It also proposed Rebecca could manifest herself into previous eras, thereby seeing those worlds through her own eyes. Not only had this letter turned rational thinking on its head, but it had also conceivably opened a permanent doorway back.

Rebecca left box four unopened...

A brief look at Rebecca – A Way Back, Volume 2

Following on from the Spiral Staircase, Rebecca, having finished university tried to apply some logical thinking to her journeys into the past. Whichever way she looked at the events that lead up to meeting Meredith and beyond, there was no reasonable explanation for the phenomenon she'd experienced. With those around her now outwardly accepting her stories, abandoning their previous dream or fanciful story notions, Rebecca felt at ease talking of her time in the past.

After a few weeks at home, and annoyed with the rational, sensible thought process, which kept showing itself, she decided to go for a walk in the woods.

As she wandered down towards the area where her adventures had started, she kept thinking about the unopened fourth box. As much as her curiosity wanted to look inside, some odd emotion tucked away in her subconscious was telling her to wait. Meredith had suggested to Rebecca she would, in time, find a way to control her movements into the past and this was at the forefront of her thoughts right now.

As she arrived by the summerhouse, a tingling sensation ran up and down her spine, seeing her father had instigated a complete renovation. Gone were the old decaying veranda, the creaky door, and rather spooky spiral stairs. In fact, the spiral staircase, which served as her doorway through time, had been replaced with a sparkling new flight.

13

Well, that's the end of my time with Meredith and co she thought.

As she walked around outside, something was amiss, but for the life of her, she couldn't put her finger on anything. Unbeknown to Rebecca, as she had exited the shiny new summerhouse, she had somehow jumped through a time loop and was once again in the past.

This was the beginning of a new set of adventures for Rebecca. Amongst others, she helped Queen Matilda, a 12th-century Scottish-Queen escape the tyrants who wanted rid of her. She also journeys to 1623 when the old manor house she lives in was being built. Her mission was to stop plague-infested workers arriving at Liverpool docks, with a pestilence that would change her mother's existence. Indeed, every jaunt she ventured on would have a significant impact on her life or those dear to her. That was unless she could find a way to interrupt time and stop it taking an alternative direction.

Chapter 1 - Next Steps

At last, after weeks of reflection, Rebecca reckoned it was time to tell her future husband, Duncan, all about her journeys through time. Although she'd mentioned the concept a little in the past, she'd never gone into detail. She decided to start right at the beginning and the time she uncovered the spiral staircase, which led to her meeting Meredith in 1853. She then went through every episode, in detail. As she reflected on her time in the past, she was somewhat surprised, although nonetheless delighted, how well Duncan took all aspects in his stride. This was something that had been bothering her for a while now, and his total acceptance of all aspects of her story came as a big relief. She now knew she could share any further adventures with her husband to be, without fear of maddening questions, silly dream suggestions, or importantly a blinkered opinion.

After a very peaceful night's sleep, the following morning, she woke early. As she sat sipping some orange juice, it dawned on her she was just one week away from her wedding. Up and dressed, and with wedding arrangements scrambling her thoughts, she headed downstairs for breakfast. After some toast, she felt she needed a few minutes to herself, so told her mum she was going for a walk down by the lake.

'Are you okay, Sweetie?'

'Yeah, just fine, Mum, thanks for asking. Just need a few moments to clear my head.'

'Going for a chat with Meredith, perhaps about your wedding?' her mum asked and chuckled.

Rebecca shook her head and grinned. 'Not seen her for an age, Mum, and besides, I have you to talk to about my wedding. No, I just need a few calm moments on my own and sitting by the lake is the best place I know of.'

As she made her way down the now well-trodden path, she was picking up the shards of a familiar sensation at the back of her consciousness. Although she knew this type of emotion, she hadn't felt anything like this for months. Wondering what it could be, she sat on the summerhouse's veranda, looking out across the lake the way she had done so often in the past.

Over the next few minutes, every episode of her time in the past tumbled through her thoughts. Although she only recently spoke to Duncan about her journeys, right now it all felt as if it had just happened. As she was thinking about her time with Matilda in the 12th-century, she heard a particularly familiar voice from behind her. Expecting it to be her mother, she turned. It wasn't her mum at all. Instead, there was a young blonde girl, dressed in a grey all in one catsuit affair. Rebecca didn't initially recognise this woman, although there was something about her smile that was strangely familiar and particularly comforting.

Confusing her senses, she could recognise a captivating mixture of her mum and herself in all aspects of this girl's appearance and manner. There was even a bit of Tommy lurking somewhere, which made her smile. A little uncertain, although calm, she smiled back and said, 'Hello.' Not sure what to think or say, and where this might lead, she did know all too well from the past this could well be heading somewhere out of the ordinary.

'Hello, Rebecca. Please do not feel concerned, although I sense you are not. I am also Rebekah, although I spell my name the old way. I am Rebekah Fergusson, and your future forefathers orchestrated my visit with you this day. I am from four generations into your future. Your vision, receptiveness, and ability to speak to the world of your movements opened the door for our kind. As your dear Meredith told you, you are indeed holding the key, which will enable society to accept our type, and see us as the way forward. In my time, there are many like us, and we move between eras with ease. You and your future writings will open the eyes of all. We have watched your progress from afar, awaiting your readiness to step forward, and I am here to assure you each decision you make will be the right one. Trust yourself.'

Unsure what to say, Rebecca paused for a moment. 'You say four generations. By that, do you mean you are my great, great, granddaughter?'

She smiled and holding Rebecca's hand in a way that was oh so familiar, said, 'I am indeed your great, great, granddaughter. I am here for just a moment to suggest your focus should be to the future as well as the past. In time, there will be no limit for you. As your beloved Meredith said to you, "*Be safe, be well, be happy, and continue to remain true to your farsightedness.*" I must add, in time, there will be more for you, as there will be for your daughter, and onwards to myself. As you often do, you will sense a calling. You will be presented shortly with a mission. You must lead this forward. Time will not wait for me or indeed, others like me. You must make people listen now before it is too late.' She then turned, and in a breath, was gone.

Rebecca sat for a moment, and although her thoughts should have been scrambled by all this girl had told her, she felt composed and relatively peaceful. In fact, the more she considered this girl's words, the more comfortable she felt. What mission may lie ahead was the only aspect that was tickling her curiosity. She knew though, as always, this would unfold soon enough. One thing she'd learnt from all her journeys was to never think of what might happen, instead to be patient and trust in her judgement, something that had never let her down. Just as she was about to head back to the nonstop wedding arrangements, a thought occurred to her. This girl was her great, great, granddaughter, which suggested she would

17

have children of her own. Even though this should have had an impact, it didn't. Rebecca now found herself wondering if her experience with Etienne and having two children, albeit through the eyes of another, had somehow calmed her senses a little. Walking back towards the house, she started thinking about what name she would give to her daughter, even though she didn't want to, she couldn't help herself.

Arriving back home, she headed for the kitchen, knowing her mother was sorting out the seating plan for her wedding reception. Although a lot was going on in her mind, she felt able to put Rebekah's words, and the name choices, to the back of her thoughts and help her mum.

'Oh, hello, Sweetie. How was your walk down to the lake?'

'Good, Mum, thank you. In actual fact, it helped clear my head a little.' She then chuckled to herself, wondering just how her mum would react to hearing she would be a grandmother sometime in the future.

'Clear your head, how so, you're not having second thoughts are you? You know you can change your mind at any stage,' Elizabeth said, smiling, although Rebecca could see her concern.

'Not at all, Mum, I am fine. It's this nonstop sorting everything out. To be truthful, that cake brochure, with two million choices, scrambled my head, especially knowing I had just two days to make my mind up and well...' Rebecca sighed and then smiled. 'I am okay now, and that few minutes took my mind off things enough to help me refocus.'

'A chat with Meredith, by any chance?'

'Well, kind of, although she wasn't there today. I guess hearing my own words helped me if that makes sense. I talk to her sometimes, even when she's not there.' In the back of her thoughts, she knew this was neither the time nor place to tell her mother of the conversation she'd had with Rebekah.

18

'Well, I am here if you need to chat, and I promise you, your father and I are happy to take as much weight off you as you need.'

'I am honestly okay, Mum,' she said. She knew she had to now focus and stop allowing her thoughts to keep wandering back to her conversation with Rebekah.

Over the next couple of days, Rebecca remained focused, to the point where she started changing the seating arrangements, having done the same thing when she was kind of marrying Etienne in 1949. Even when that thought occurred to her, she stayed on track.

Two days before her big day, she was heading into Liverpool with all the important women in her life. Roxy and Sam, along with Elizabeth, had arranged the bride-to-be night out. When she arrived in a bar Roxy had chosen, she was shocked to see a couple of friends she'd gone to school with many years before. When Rebecca quizzed her mum, she said she'd kept their numbers from her 18th birthday party and was delighted they both still had the same numbers. Rebecca had a wonderful evening, although the following morning, she woke bleary-eyed having drunk too many fancy cocktails.

Chapter 2 – The Big Day & an Unexpected Step Forward

Rebecca woke early on the morning of her big day full of the joys of spring. Right from the moment Duncan asked her to marry him, she'd had no doubts. For sure, it was comforting knowing everyone was behind her, including Meredith's whispered support. Even so, she was happily making this step totally of her own choice and with no hesitancy or indecision.

With her hair just perfect, according to her mum, and dressed, she sat in the kitchen sipping some orange juice. She was two hours early and trying her best not to crease her dress while going over everything in her head. Having considered being fashionably late, Rebecca made a decision to turn the table, surprise everyone and arrive at the Church before her future husband. To add to this, she had already asked her mother to give her away, especially as Duncan had asked James and Tommy to be his joint best men. This was just how Rebecca liked it, and after telling Roxy and her mum, she wanted to go to the church early, she said, 'this way, that way or the Rebecca way.'

'Well, no change there then, Sweetie. We have grown to expect it the Rebecca way. I love and admire your style, and it makes me so proud to call you my daughter.'

'Thank you, Mum. I get my style from you, as does everyone in this family. Even Roxy says as much.'

'In fact, I should thank you. You have shown me it is okay to follow your dreams, even when others might frown upon them.' Elizabeth then seemed to think for a moment. 'What I mean by that is despite your time with Meredith being questioned you stuck by what you knew.'

'I hope so, Mum. Although it has helped me knowing you, Dad, Duncan and Roxy support everything I do. Then, of course, there has been Ruth and Amanda's involvement and their support. Hey, look where we are now. Right, the wedding is in an hour, and I am ready to go now, which should get us there thirty minutes early, and that suits me just fine.'

As she and Elizabeth opened the front door on a beautifully sunny Saturday morning in December, her mum said, 'Got to say, Rebecca, your choice of a vehicle is a picture to behold, and it sets off your red-rose bouquet and the red ribbon ringlets in your beautiful blonde hair.' She then picked up a leaflet from the back seat and narrowed her eyes. 'Rebecca, a 1940s Buick, in Canada Red. Is this choice anything to do with a certain Canadian chap by any chance?'

Rebecca smiled in a way that acknowledged her mother's question without answering it. She lifted the hem of her Victorian ivory white lace dress, adjusted the satin waistband, and climbed into the back seat. She then placed her 'southern belle' style hat on the front seat and beckoned her mother to sit next to her. 'Mum, I just love your dress. I know you weren't sure about wearing such a light colour, but I must say ashen pink suits you beautifully, and the fine lace picks out the colour even more so.'

'I must admit I do feel like the bride's mother. This Victorian journey is a lovely tribute to your girl Meredith. I hope she's there today, somehow, someway,' she said and gently squeezed Rebecca's arm. 'I love you, my daughter.'

With tears in her eyes, Rebecca turned to her mother. 'I love you also, my Mother. And thank you for what you said about Meredith. I too hope she is there to see my day.'

21

'She'll be beside you one way or another, Rebecca. This I know.'

'You seem so sure, Mum,' Rebecca said, both surprised and intrigued by her mother's certainty.

Her mum nodded, and said, we can have a chat soon enough when I will tell you more.

'Mum...'

'It can wait, Rebecca, let's focus on today.'

One thing Rebecca knew was when her mum didn't want to talk, she wouldn't. Even so, what her mum had just said started her curiosity racing. 'Mum, just give me a hint, please.'

'Later, I promise you.' She then pointed in front of the car. 'Focus on today, Sweetie.'

As Rebecca got out of the car at the front of the church, she took a deep breath. She then refocused her thoughts, straightened her dress and turned to her mother. 'Mum look what Father has arranged, although I am sure you had a hand in it,' she said, winking while pointing to the Gothic arch at the front of the old medieval church. She walked up to get a closer look at the ornamented gateway of white roses, interlaced with red ivy, which sent a shiver down her spine being scarily similar to the one Meredith's daughter had. She smiled inwardly certain Meredith was with her and reckoned this was thanks to her mum and dad for listening so carefully. She then paused for a moment to look, wondering how they'd managed to get it so perfect.

Her mum smiled, again squeezed her arm, and said, 'both your father and I arranged it as a tribute to your Meredith, and her daughter's wedding. When you described the scene to us, it sounded so wonderful, first chance I made notes. Just in case you know,' she said and grinned.

22

'I didn't know you and Dad had taken that much notice. I often ask myself if I go into too much detail. Clearly not,' she mumbled while pulling at her mother's little finger.

'Haha, far from it, because in those days, when I hadn't got my head around your journeys through time, it helped me stay on board by focussing on, and imagining the scenes you described.' She then smiled again and indicated towards the church.

Rebecca followed her mother into the church, greeted by several intakes of breaths, which although kind of caught Rebecca off guard, she had intended on taking an alternative standpoint, so was pleased with the outcome.

Once again picking up on this, her mum said, 'The gasps are because you look so amazing. You are the belle of the ball for sure,' She then squeezed Rebecca's hand, and whispered, 'stay focused, I rung ahead, and it's all sorted with the vicar.' She then took Rebecca's arm, just as her father would have done and led her down the aisle to a slightly jazzy version of 'here comes the bride.'

When they reached the altar, the vicar smiled and whispered, "The look on the faces of those who didn't know you were arriving before Duncan." He then smiled and said, 'God loves your way, dear girl.'

Rebecca beamed a huge smile as the bagpipers played outside, which brought back memories of Queen Matilda's entrance to Scone Priory. She then turned and couldn't help letting out a tiny happy sigh as Duncan entered the church appearing identical to Matilda's equerry, complete with the exact red and green tartan kilt. *Now Tommy would call that a hat trick* she thought, considering the white rose arch for Meredith's daughter, her Southern Belle bonnet just as Meredith wore herself, and now Matilda arrives at the party.

23

Shaking his head ever so slightly as he approached her, Duncan whispered, 'I guessed you would do something unusual, getting here before me indeed.'

Feeling remarkably relaxed around this man, she turned to the Vicar, and as she did, Rebecca's memory flickered to Etienne for just a second. Then, in what seemed like the blink of an eye, she was signing the register and turning to her mother and father with a contented smile on her face. She glanced at Tommy, poked her tongue out, before winking at Roxy.

As she was leaving the church to the sound of Chris Stapleton singing, Traveller, Duncan turned and said, 'love is the most precious thing, and we will always have that.' He then chuckled, and whispered, 'along with your journeys through time and this song is perfect. Did he write it for you?' He then shook his head and chuckled again. 'Traveller indeed you are.'

'Thank you for that, Duncan,' she whispered and smiled inwardly thinking how lucky she was.

She then glanced around the church, and as she did her mother, standing just behind her, lent forward, and whispered, 'she's here.'

Rebecca turned to her mother and still wondering about her comment regarding Meredith, mouthed, 'you better not keep me waiting. I want to know more and how you know with such certainty.' She then forced a mock frown.

When they arrived home, her parents had laid on the most lavish event, complete with a heated marquee in the garden, just like Meredith's daughter. During the reception, Rebecca quizzed her mother a few times about this secret she now had. In the end, though, getting nowhere, she focused her attention on Duncan and the other guests. This included ribbing Roxy who was spending a lot of time chatting to one of Tommy's teammates.

The following morning, they left for a honeymoon cruise to the East coast of Canada, a wish list for Rebecca, something arranged by Duncan in secrecy.

Upon their return, work on the summerhouse was near completion, turning it into a lovely home, complete with a beautiful kitchen and sumptuous bathroom. This was something both Rebecca and Duncan had wanted. Initially, Duncan joked he would love to live there as long as Rebecca didn't keep vanishing up the stairs. Although she'd smiled and nodded, in the back of her thoughts, she knew that was a distinct possibility. She also knew it was doubtful he would notice her gone as her previous experiences would suggest she'd only be missing for a minute or three, and besides, she was unlikely to go anywhere while he was in there at the same time.

They moved in the day before Christmas with a plan to cook for the family. Elizabeth, Roxy, and Tommy to some degree had secretly covered the summerhouse in decorations and adorned the outside with soft white lights, something Rebecca delighted in. Although Rebecca had never used a range cooker before, with a little help from her mother, Christmas dinner turned out brilliantly, in spite of the heating being a tad temperamental.

After Christmas, Rebecca settled into married life quickly. However, no more than a couple of weeks in, she began to feel a little fidgety and decided she fancied going back to work two days a week at least. Following a long discussion with her mother, who regretted stopping working the day James and she were married, Rebecca decided to speak with Duncan and her father about returning to work. Although they suggested she didn't need to work, both agreed, knowing Rebecca as they did, it was perhaps a good idea. So, it was amicably agreed she would restart at the end of January.

Working two days a week, combined with writing her first "fictional" novel *Days with Meredith* the days slipped into weeks, and before she knew it, the early signs of spring were showing.

Chapter 3 – Elizabeth's Secret

Sitting with her mum in the courtyard at the back of the house on a particularly lovely spring morning, Rebecca decided it was time to bridge something that had been nagging at her for months. During the last few weeks, she'd asked her mum several times how she could have been so certain Meredith would be at the church, each time without getting much more than a smile. Having gotten so little in the way of response previously, and seeing her mum was in a particularly bright mood, she decided to dig a little deeper.

'Mum, I know we've talked about this before, and each time you said you would talk about it when you're ready. It's just you are so certain Meredith would be at the church has been nagging in the back of my mind ever since. It struck me at the time that you knew more than you were letting on. To the point where when we came out, you seemed so certain she'd been there with us, how so?'

Her mum sipped her coffee, glanced at Rebecca, at her coffee, and with a thoughtful expression, looked across the yard. After a couple of moments, she glanced back at Rebecca and nodded. 'What I am about to tell you, I have kept in my inner thoughts since I was a child and have not mentioned it to anyone. Not even your father knows.' She then took a deep breath and again glanced around the yard, clearly considering what she was going to say.

Although Rebecca's intrigue was now at bursting point, she could see by her mum's expression that it was perhaps right to give her as much thinking time as she needed. She leaned across to her mum, squeezed her hand, and smiled.

'I am getting there, Sweetie.' Again, she averted her eyes. 'You have always understandably thought you inherited, if that's the right word, your time travelling gene from your father. What I am about to tell you may change that view, although you're going to have to be patient.' She then hesitated again.

Now with her thoughts like a flooded river, Rebecca could do nothing but watch her mum and wonder what was coming next.

Elizabeth turned to Rebecca, smiled and sipped her coffee again. 'Firstly, I must say I am sorry it's taken me so long to talk to you about this, especially as I annoyed you often when I suggested your journeys were perhaps dreams.' She shook her head, clearly a little uncertain. She then looked directly at Rebecca with a clear, oddly certain expression. 'When I was around six or seven, I experienced something similar to you, whereby I felt I had travelled back in time.' She took a deep breath. 'For me, it seemed like a dream perhaps because I was so young. Therefore, I put it to the back of my thoughts and got on with everyday things, like annoying my older brother. Something we have in common,' she said and chuckled, although it wasn't her usual chuckle.

Absolutely flummoxed, never in her wildest dreams did Rebecca expect these words to come from her mother's mouth, and so without thinking, blurted, 'what year did you travel to, Mum?' With her eyes widened, she held her hand up, unable to believe what she'd just said. 'Sorry, Mum, straight in, you know me,' she mumbled, and half grinned and grimaced simultaneously.

Shaking her head, she said, 'It's okay, and I am not really sure which year. I just knew it wasn't my time, and it was in the past. It was so fleeting it was easy to dismiss it as a dream.

That was until it happened again. This time, I was about ten. Upon my return, I knew for sure something very odd had happened, certain I had just been to Queen Victoria's wedding.' She again shook her head, as if she was unsure of her own words. 'Well, I best rephrase that. I was standing on a cobbled street, near to St James's Palace, along with thousands of people, watching from a distance.' Then in the blink of an eye, I was home. Now the thing is, three days later, I found some dried rose petals in my skirt pocket, exactly the same as I'd been throwing on the day of the procession.' She then breathed in and blew out slowly through her pursed lips. 'Another two days passed, and I was back again, this time standing with a woman.' She nodded, then delved into her handbag, and produced a small tan envelope. 'The woman told me to give this to my daughter and tell no one. I can tell you, at ten years-old it was hard to take on board.' She then opened the envelope and took out a small, frayed white hanky. With tears in her eyes, she handed it to Rebecca and pointed to the initial M in the corner. 'I am so sorry it has taken me this long to share this with you, my beloved daughter.'

With her head now jumbled between excitement and astonishment, she uttered, 'Mum, could it be?' She knew it had to be Meredith, recognising the M insignia as the same as the hanky she had. She knew without any debate that this was undoubtedly the same Meredith. Suddenly, as part of her brain felt a tiny element of uncertainty, this almighty bomb of realisation went off in her head. 'Mum, I get it. I really get why you considered my journeys were perhaps dreams. I am at a complete loss what to think. For some absolutely illogical and irrational reason, I am questioning the validity of your story. I can only apologise and suggest it may be because my Meredith was your Meredith too. Fifty years apart.' She then shook her head, both annoyed, but at the same time pleased, she'd had this light-bulb moment. 'It is so bizarre, I am looking at this hanky, which is identical to the one I have from Meredith, and yet my annoyingly obstinate rational university brain is telling me you must have dreamt it all.' She then nodded. 'Oddly, I am glad I've just had this moment of realisation because now I truly understand why you suggested my journeys were dreams.'

'Umm, I am not that old. Fifty years apart, indeed.' She then raised her eyebrows and smirked. 'It was nearer forty years, haha.' She then nodded. 'Yeah, it was your girl, Meredith. I talked to her for ages, and she told me all about you. The thing is she also said I must tell no one about my journeys other than you.' With her eyes filled with tears, she looked away. She took a deep breath and looked up, trying to force a smile.

'Whatever is the matter, Mum? I have never seen you look so upset.'

Again, Elizabeth took another deep breath and blew out slowly through her tightened lips. 'I was so excited I couldn't help myself and told my father all about my jaunt.' She shook her head and glanced away.

Trying to conceal her surprise, she asked as tactfully as possible, 'This is your real father, not your stepdad? Is that right?'

Nodding, with tears covering her cheeks, she said, stumbling through her words, 'he ridiculed me so much and beat me so hard, my mother took my brother and me to her mother's home that night. That was the last time any of us saw him.' Brushing tears from her cheek, she looked away, then looked back and smiled the only way she can. 'It is okay, Sweetie, no need to hide your surprise. For sure, I am upset, mostly with myself for waiting this long to tell you.'

'Mum, no wonder you never wanted to talk about my journeys. It all makes sense now.' Rebecca leaned across and squeezed her mum's hand. 'Did you ever tell your mum?'

Shaking her head, she said, 'as much as I wanted to, especially as I believed she knew something of my story from what my father had said. The thing is, she never mentioned it, and retrospectively, I understand why. I also think I was too scared to bring it up again.' She then nodded. 'I have carried this secret with me every day, waiting for the right time to tell you. There were times, I could have kicked myself for not mentioning it and thereby become an advocate for your journeys.' Then as if a weight had been lifted, Elizabeth smiled. She held Rebecca's hand and said, 'I am now ready to tell the world, and support you the way I should have through your every turn.'

'Mum, you have been there for me through every step, listening, even when you weren't ready. Your support has been in your own way, and it's a way I love. I am so not surprised I got the gene from you. I have met my future, get this, great, great, granddaughter, and she looks just like you.'

'You what, you met who, your great, great, granddaughter? Oh, my goodness, tell me more.'

'You know when I went down to the lake the other day, and you asked if I'd talked to Meredith, and I replied with a vague answer. Well, it was then, and now you know why I was so indistinct.' Rebecca spent the next couple of hours chatting with her mum all about their journeys.

'Okay, your father will be home soon, so can I suggest we tell him together about my time with Meredith? I am going to need your emotional support.

'Mum, it's the least I can do. I am so looking forward to seeing Dad's reaction. Just thinking aloud here, can we suggest I got my gene from both of you, which, thinking about it, I probably did.'

When James arrived home, and with Tommy being with the Liverpool team playing away at Stevenage in the FA Cup, they decided this was their best opportunity to tell him all about Elizabeth's secret.

Although he occasionally appeared a little concerned, his emotions seemed to be in response to Elizabeth's tale of suffering when she was a child. Most of the time, he seemed to take it in his stride, almost to the point where Rebecca found herself wondering if he'd known something of Elizabeth's story all along. No sooner Rebecca had this thought her father started talking.

'I have always suspected there was something there Liz, especially in the early days. Occasionally of late, again I have seen your reaction to Rebecca's stories and inwardly wondered if you knew more than you were letting on.'

'James, I'm sorry I haven't told you before, it is just...'

'Liz, let me stop you there. You have nothing to apologise for.'

The three of them sat around chatting until around ten pm. Soon after, Duncan returned home after a business meeting in Brussels. Elizabeth, James, and Rebecca had already decided not to tell him just yet, and so spent the remainder of the evening chatting about Duncan's trip.

Chapter 4 – A Rather Warm Spring

With everyone out for the day, Rebecca decided to go to the woods to do some sketching for an illustrated novel she'd finally started in earnest. As she approached her favourite area where she'd found the key under the fallen oak, fond memories filled her head. So, it felt just right sitting in the exact same spot. With recollections of Meredith cascading through her thoughts, mixed with the startling revelation from her mother, she suddenly became aware of the willows on the other side of the glade were covered in pussy willow buds. 'Make great pixie beds,' she mumbled, trying to focus her attention on Mother Nature in all her glory.

'What will?' a nicely familiar, but nonetheless, arm tingling voice asked.

'Ethernal,' she mumbled, feeling both calm and oddly goosy, having had only memories to hold on to for months.

'It is I, Ethernal your friend, Rebecca. How is married life for my intrepid, fearless girl, may I enquire?'

'You know?' she asked, a little taken aback, although strangely unsurprised.

'I would not be the one I am if I didn't know such things. I was at the first Rebekah's marriage to Isaac. Look it up on your fangled computing machine, and you will learn that marriage was four thousand of your year's past. I was at Matilda's and indeed your beloved Meredith's weddings, need I continue?'

She shook her head, somewhat bewildered by his words, but again unsurprised. 'Matilda and Meredith, I know, and love, Rebekah on the other hand. Is there something I should know?'

'Nothing to concern yourself with yet...' he then chuckled with an enchanting manner. 'Focus now. There are turns for you to follow, so go with your intuition, and look around for choices that must be made. For now, be safe, be well, be happy, and continue to remain true to your foresightedness.'

'Meredith said that to me, as did my great, great, grand...' before she could finish, she sensed he had gone. Turning her head slightly, she whispered, 'Have you gone?'

She didn't really know why she asked that, as she knew he had come and gone in a breath as he so often does. With his words resonating in her thoughts, she tried to focus on her sketching. Now fidgety, she decided to head back and research the 4000-year-old Rebekah he'd mentioned.

As she made her way down a now well-trodden route, she tried to lighten her thoughts by stopping to look at some late crocuses. As much as she loved these plants, and as always, was hopeful of spotting some young pixies playing thereabout, she couldn't see beyond Ethernal's words. Wandering, she tripped over a straying bramble creeper near the edge of the woods and scratched her ankle deeply on the horrid thorns. Smarting, she knelt to dab the scratch with her hanky. Noticing how deep the wound was, she decided it needed more than spit and tissue and so hurried back to the main house.

As she stood up, a wave of uneasiness came over her, making her feel particularly unsteady on her feet. She stood there for a moment, trying to steady both her composure and balance. With an abnormal amount of perspiration trickling down her forehead into her eyes, causing her to blink several times, she leaned her back against the wide trunk of an ancient conifer. A tad perplexed, unsure what was causing her unsteadiness, she now wondered if perhaps the scratch on her

34

ankle was worse than she'd initially thought. She bent over again and seeing the scratch, although in need of some attention, really wasn't that bad, and it probably wasn't that which was causing her shakiness. Then her focus switched to the bark on the tree she'd been leaning against earlier. Looking at it closely, she immediately knew something was amiss, not recognising it as the conifer she initially lent on. Glancing up briefly, she couldn't focus because of the sweat streaming into her eyes. Reckoning this tree needed a closer inspection, she held the trunk for steadiness and stood up. Just this action alone confused her further with the trunk feeling oddly spongy, and to some extent slippery.

As she stood there inspecting the sappy bark, a nigh on unbearable humidity and intense heat hit her bare arms and face. With a loud voice shouting and hollering inside her head, telling her something very odd was going on, she tried to regain her focus. Wiping the sweat from her eyes, and settling herself a little, she looked around and couldn't believe what she was seeing.

Glancing upwards, in place of the usual wispy pine branches, was an abundance of enormous palm-like leaves swaying randomly. Bizarre coloured creepers were clinging to the twisted branches that stretched out above her head almost spider-like. Finding it hard to take her eyes off these peculiar leaves, the likes of which her brain associated with the tropics, she again reached to hold the tree for steadiness as she tried to get her bearings. Reckoning she was on the edge of the woods, she glanced around. Where there would normally be a relatively well-manicured green, instead, stretching from the water's edge back towards the house was a fusion of waist-high ferns in a bizarre mixture of shapes. To compound her thoughts further, these plants ranged in colour from lime yellow, olive green, to an intense ruby red and every shade in between. No matter what she'd experienced during her previous adventures, nothing could have prepared her brain for this perplex cocktail of thoughts and emotions.

35

As she looked a little closer, somewhere in her memories from school, she recognised two of these ferns. Although her brain was a mishmash of feelings, she was certain one was a horsetail fern and the other a hares-foot fern. As she searched through her recollections of the subject, she was sure these plants were only found near the equator. With the palm trees and now these strange ferns, she was at a complete loss what to think. Carefully, she pushed her way through the ferns, heading to where she reckoned the summerhouse would be. After just a couple of steps, she felt something spongy against her leg. Looking down, she was astonished to see an unusually large mustard coloured toadstool the size of a dinner plate. She took two more steps, and this time, just to send her brain spiralling further, she came across an even bigger flaming red toadstool. Oddly, this one had aqua blue stripes running down the side as if they'd been poured from a jug.

She refocused and after wading through the ferns and past more oddly coloured mushrooms, she reached the edge of the lake. Seeing the water was a luminescent turquoise colour and covered as far as she could see with lily pads the size of a car bonnet left her confused, bewildered, and lightheaded.

Trying to regain her composure for the nth time and get a grip on the bizarre series of events, she wondered if she'd inexplicably journeyed to the Amazon rainforest or some such environment, because for sure, this didn't feel like home. That didn't fit though because glancing out towards a familiar shaped island, she was reasonably confident this was her lake, even though something very odd was going on. With perspiration running endlessly down her forehead and into her eyes, she looked over to her right, hoping to see the summerhouse.

With no sign of it anywhere, she knew with every step, she was heading further into the unknown. She stood, rooted to the spot for a few moments, looking and listening. The silence was alarming and compounding her already fragile consciousness. As the seconds turned into minutes, she kept trying to reassure herself, remembering all her other jaunts worked out fine. Just as she was gaining a speck of focus, an odd-sounding bird screeched in the trees behind her, spilling her nerves once again around her feet.

She glanced back to see where the noisy creature was and spotting a larger than average, odd coloured bird, flying away only served to heighten her emotions further. Although she'd reckoned a while ago, she was probably somewhere other than home, so many dramatic changes, the likes of which she'd never experienced before, and combined with the intense heat, was trampling down her ability to focus. To compound her mood further, were hints within her surroundings suggesting she may still be at home, albeit not the home she knew.

Now stood where the summerhouse should be, she scanned in every direction. There was not a sign or trace of human life anywhere, to the point where she felt as if she was on a planet devoid of humanity.

Considering Ethernal's words and that he had spoken of a Rebekah 4000 years ago, and relating this to all her previous journeys, which always needed her intervention, she briefly wondered if she was here to see what Earth would be like in the past if humankind didn't exist. She then laughed at herself for even considering such a daft idea.

'Is it?' a voice whispered.

'Who's there,' Rebecca blurted, not recognising the voice.

'Who I am, and where you are is of no matter. The time you are in does matter. We will speak again. Tread softly; be bold.'

She turned, and as she did, she kicked something hard. Bending down, and pushing her hand through the fern, she touched what felt like a large metal rail. Instantly the sensation of this object in her fingers reminded her of the first time she reached out and touched the spiral staircase rail. She pushed away the fern to get a closer look. If her senses were jumbled by the words of this unknown individual, now looking at a part of the rail from the new spiral staircase her father had installed pushed what little rationality she had out of reach.

With her thoughts in disarray, she decided to head towards the area where the main house should be. On her way, she kept stopping to look around, continually startled by odd coloured birds flying from one tree to the next. All the time, her thoughts kept jumping between her surroundings, the words, "the time you are in does matter," and trying to work out how the summerhouse could now be nothing but a wreck on the floor.

For a moment she paused and glanced back towards the area where the summerhouse should be, only to be dumfounded further, spotting a couple of enormous umbrella type trees standing hundreds of feet above the current tree line. She took a deep breath, trying to grasp some reassurance, hoping it would all make sense and there would be a good reason why she was here. Somewhere in the back of her thoughts, she clung to the belief that Meredith or Ethernal, or both wouldn't let any harm come to her. *They wouldn't, would they,* she thought.

The further up the slope she went, the further her senses jangled, spotting a peculiar looking, tan furry animal, the size of a big dog, running across an open area of grass. She paused again looking around, and as she did, an idea popped into her head that she might have jumped into the future. Thinking about it, it made sense and returned some kind of rationality to her thoughts, although she didn't know where this idea had come from. The question she now had was how far into the future she'd travelled if that was the case.

Unable to see a sign of the house, she carried on up the slope regardless, hoping it might be behind some tropical-looking trees that seemed to be covering the courtyard. As she grew closer, she realised the house wasn't there. Glancing back towards the lake to get her bearings, she stood where she reckoned the front door should be. As far as she could see in any direction were more waist-high ferns, ludicrously big mushrooms, and toadstools, all in a multitude of psychedelic colours. To add to this, many more bizarre animal-like creatures appeared and then vanished as quick, outwardly oblivious to her presence.

Once again, she stood still trying to apply some logical thinking to her surroundings and work out exactly what was going on. Now sure she had jumped some way into the future, what with the summerhouse a wreck, and her home on the face of it gone, she set about searching for a clue of sorts.

Chapter 5 – Remnants

With her fuel tanks almost empty and running entirely on a need to know basis, Rebecca headed over to where she reckoned the kitchen would have been. After a few steps, her foot slipped, causing the most irregular sensation with the floor feeling both soft and hard at the same time. Curious, she pushed back some fern to expose a weird-looking spongy moss covering the remnants of the Victorian mosaic tiles that once ran the length of her hallway. Seeing the floor in such a neglected, abandoned state, left her feeling quite emotional. While trying to regain her composure, Rebecca continued even though she was hesitant, not knowing what she might find next.

Stood still, she once more tried to convince herself there was bound to be a significant reason for her being here, and assure herself, as always, Meredith had a hand in this. No sooner she'd thought that, a voice from the depths of her brain suggested she should look to her left. Exhausted and uneasy, she glanced around unsure what she was looking for. The more she looked, the harder it was to see beyond the chaos. Then something to the left caught her attention, and through the dense undergrowth, she could just make out the shape of an oddly familiar sight. This triggered a weird sensation in her head, and she reckoned it was worthy of further investigation. With her eyes still jumping from one thing to the next, she pushed a pathway through the chest-high straw-like grasses. She then eased her way past some unusually large leaf ferns and a couple of bright yellow flowered cactus type plants. 'This used to be my house,' she muttered and forced a nervous laugh in spite of feeling both distressed and saddened by her surroundings.

Now standing by the object, she started pulling at a mass of spidery creepers. Little by little, she began to uncover what looked like the remnants of something that was becoming increasingly familiar. She took a sharp intake of breath as she pulled away more foliage to reveal amid all this chaos her father's old Victorian tallboy. It was something that had served her many times as an envoy and unbelievably, was still standing. For sure, it had seen better days, but it was something comforting from her world in the middle of this irrational, mad state of affairs. With it still mostly covered in strange coloured creepers, along with some eerily thick cobwebs, she set about completely uncovering this piece of home. Something wasn't quite right though in her head. For sure this cabinet was rock solid, but it was still made of wood, so how could it be here, through all this destruction and chaos. She nodded, now certain and somewhat comforted in the knowledge that Meredith had sent her here for a good reason. For a few seconds, she tried to understand how this bit of wood was in one piece when the three-foot thick walls around it had crumbled. 'Must be Meredith's handy work,' she mumbled, 'but how.'

She shook her head and again started pulling at the string-like cobwebs and horridly oily plants, all the time wondering just how far into the future she'd travelled. Gripping hold of an obstinately stubborn vine, she yanked hard, and as she did, one of the small doors opened. Although it was horribly dusty inside, she could see a rectangular object that was somewhat recognisable, but at the same time wasn't. Taking it from its resting place, she lifted out a metal box that was around six inches square. She laughed, recognising it as one of her mother's biscuit tins, which helped settle her nerves a little. She shook her head, wondering what it was doing in her father's tallboy. *Most irregular*, she thought, and flicked her eyebrows, muttering, 'enough of the speculation.' She then balanced the tin on the edge of the old cabinet and pulled at the lid without much joy. Then remembering her penknife, she eased it under the lid, and soon the box opened, albeit begrudgingly and with a horrid rusty groan.

Inside was an envelope made from an odd waxy material and although a little flimsy around the edges, it was reasonably sturdy. With curiosity now at a bursting point, and eager to open it, Rebecca felt strangely hesitant with an odd sensation in the back of her thoughts causing a little cautiousness. With narrowed eyes, she turned over the envelope not knowing what was causing her indecision. 'What,' she muttered, seeing her name, somewhat faded, written in her father's unmistakable handwriting across the back of the envelope. She took several deep breaths as she slowly opened the envelope and started reading.

My beloved Rebecca,

If you are reading this, then the mysterious letter that arrived at my office was unbelievably correct. It was addressed to me in strictest privacy. I was to tell no one of this letter, just forward it to you via your mother's cake tin and place the tin in my old tallboy.

So, hold your breath because you have travelled to the year 2938. Do not be alarmed, although, if I know you, I know you won't be.

The letter, as hard as it was for me to believe, was from your dear friend and guardian angel, Meredith. Evidently, it had been passed to her from a future ancestor who had travelled back eight centuries. By my reckoning, that would be from around 2800. I know what you must be thinking, although it is no stranger than this perpetual journey you are travelling.

Inside the letter, it contained details and instructions for this, your next mission. Mission is my word, it actually referred to it as an assignment, and I would suggest you could take what you will from that word. If you now go to the kitchen area and look for our fridge, and I was assured, like the Tallboy it would still be there, you will see inside the fridge another box, again with your name on it. Open it and take what you find into the sunlight. That is all I was told, and I can tell you, it left me feeling annoyingly curious. I must add, my curiosity was heightened knowing a wooden cabinet would somehow stand for nine centuries.

Go with my love and upon your return, I look forward to hearing what, other than our next supper, was in the fridge.

All my love, and be strong, as I know you will, Dad xx

Although all at sea with anxious curiosity, for some reason, Rebecca felt remarkably calm. Considering her emotions, she reckoned the combination of her father's letter and knowing Meredith was not too far away was helping.

With the letter tucked in her waistband, she once again dabbed her sodden hanky on the continual sweat running down her face. She then headed for the area where the fridge would, or at least, should be. On the way, she kept wondering how her father's tallboy and the refrigerator had managed to stay intact for nine hundred years even though everything else was in ruins. For some reason, her time with Etienne came into her head. 'I don't want to be here for thirty minutes, let alone thirty years,' she blurted and laughed out loud.

She then wished she hadn't laughed so loud, because not only did it echo, it started one of those horrid squawking birds off again. She shook her head and continued to plough her way through the creepy, dense undergrowth.

Sure enough, in what was left of the kitchen, under more odd-looking vines and fern was the fridge, albeit more than a little tatty. As she cleared her way, she couldn't help laughing, thinking about how her mum kept this fridge so spotless. She pulled at the door, not really expecting it to move. Bizarrely, it opened easily. Apart from a horrid mouldy smell, inside she could see a wooden box, just as her father's letter suggested.

43

The last ten years has been nothing but boxes and keys she thought, as she lifted it out with a bizarre cocktail of curiosity and uncertainty running riot with her consciousness.

This box also opened easily, which oddly left her a little unsettled, wondering how recently it had been placed there. Thinking about it though, she knew with absolutely no sign of human life other than a few leftovers and remnants, it couldn't have been that recent. She shook her head, at a loss what to think. As her father had suggested, she took out an odd feeling, flat, charcoal coloured square object. On closer inspection, it seemed to be made from an extraordinary mix of glass and plastic that had an unusual silky touch. She then made her way out to where the old breakfast patio area would have been, and again into the sunlight. The direct heat from the sun was unbearable, so she moved to an area where she could stand in the shade while holding the object in the sun. Even so, the intensity of the sun was like hot coals on her arm.

Standing there, she thought, now what. Within seconds of it being in the sunlight, the strange material started making a whirring noise causing her to flinch, something that doesn't happen very often. It then lit up and bizarrely began to unfold like a cardboard box, causing her to drop it. Fortunately, its fall was broken by one of the many large toadstools covering the remnants of her backyard. The tablet, if you could call it that was now around half a meter square, bizarrely though it still weighed less than a small coin.

This is all very strange she thought. However, considering she was nigh on a thousand years into the future, she reckoned this was probably the norm. All of a sudden, another hideous flying creature yelped over her head, breaking her focus completely. She stared up, searching the azure blue, cloudless sky for this creature. Unexpectedly a light started shining from the tablet pulling her focus back.

44

Although to begin with, the screen was a little fuzzy, a strangely familiar, but nonetheless almost indistinguishable lady's face appeared, addressing Rebecca directly.

The voice said, 'Twenty-first century Rebecca, your next mission will follow once you place this mainframe next to your own computer processor. It will link automatically. This device is powered by solar and therefore, can be charged by your sunlight, which is unlike the intense sunlight you now find yourself suffering below. All will become clear once the connection has been made. Head back to where your journey started, and you will find your way home. The destiny of humankind is in your hands now, so be safe, be well, be happy, and continue to remain true to your farsightedness. One last thing before you return. If history is correct, you are a girl principled by curiosity. No doubts, you are wondering how your father's cabinet and mother's fridge stood through the centuries. In short, they didn't, they are physical holograms to give you comfort.'

Shaking her head, not knowing what to think, she felt settled by the last few all too familiar words of encouragement. Even though she didn't know who this woman was, Rebecca felt strangely comforted by her peaceful temperament. Scrambling towards the front of the house, now with her jeans and T-shirt ringing wet with perspiration, she made her way back down towards the lake, occasionally stopping to catch her breath.

She arrived by the lake edge, feeling exhausted, concerned, and somewhat out of sorts. To compound the incessant heat draining her consciousness, she had the words' *destiny of humankind* ringing in her ears.

Now standing by the edge of the lake, she looked around, searching for something that might point her in the right direction. Then remembering what the woman had said, she made her way to the area where she'd found the remnants of the spiral staircase. She stood there with a piece of the bannister rail in her hand, her thoughts abruptly flooded by memories of her first time here.

A little unsure of what to do next, as is often the case, she realised her journey, in reality, started when she found the key. Thinking about it for a moment, she knew her chances of finding an oak that fell over a thousand years ago, in an intensely overgrown area, might prove difficult. Nonetheless, with her usual vigour, albeit exhausted, she headed towards the woods.

Wading her way through the endless undergrowth, with barely enough energy to keep moving, let alone think, she pushed on. Eventually, she came to the stream edge that was barely recognisable, excepting a trickle of turquoise water. Now having a reasonable idea where she was, she made her way, as best she could, to where she reckoned the fallen oak might be. After clambering past some head-high ferns, she came into an opening, and although there was no sign of the oak, it just felt like the right place.

With the sun now high in the sky, making her skin feel like it was on fire, she dodged from one shaded area to the next, trying to get her bearings. After a few minutes and utterly wiped out, she stumbled upon a large piece of decaying wood. Instantly, she knew it was her oak. Sitting down on some yellow spongy moss, with her father's letter and the tablet firmly gripped in her hand, she leaned back against the remnants of the old tree and closed her eyes, trying to focus her thoughts.

Chapter 6 – I Did Not Expect to See That

She opened her eyes shivering and wondered if she was back home. Oddly though, she was sure she'd only closed her eyes for a few seconds, but in the back of her thoughts knew that didn't count for much. Feeling shattered, she was hoping she was back home and not somewhere else. The thing was, her common sense was saying it was way too cold for home. With all she'd been through over the years, she should have gotten used to these ludicrous changes in direction, but this was beyond all reason. As she sat there trying to work out where she might be, her body gradually adjusted to the cold. As she delicately got to her feet, she had a realisation anywhere would feel cold compared to the horrid heat she'd suffered for the last couple of hours. Feeling a tad unsteady, she turned around looking for something to lean on and was delighted when her eyes settled on the old oak tree, just as she knew it. She made her way over, hitched herself up, and breathed a little more easily, knowing she was at least close to her time and reality.

The longer she sat there, she could sense something wasn't right, and again, as she had so many times in the past, looked around for something that would ease her slightly edgy emotions. Still perched on the tree trunk, her mind briefly flickered to the time she'd found the key. As these thoughts rumbled through her head, she leaned back a little and disturbed something, knocking whatever it was down the back of the tree.

Curious, and reckoning she'd disturbed something more than just a twig, she peered behind her. There, lying on the ground among the long grass was the old drawing pad she'd used the day she first found the key to the summerhouse. *This is just plain madness*, she thought, knowing she hadn't seen that pad for a good few years. With an unusual mixture of hesitation and uncertainty, she leaned over and picked it up. The second she did, this strange somewhat comforting feeling came over her as if someone was behind her.

Although she was on her last legs, this sensation took her curiosity up another level. She turned, wondering who this could be, but her wildest dreams could never have prepared her for what she was about to see. She sat there motionless, watching a younger version of herself potter about, mumbling to herself, just as she had all those years earlier. Although seeing her younger self brought a smile to her face, something started niggling at the back of her thoughts.

This little niggling notion suddenly turned to alarm bells in her head as an idea jumped into her thoughts. Her common sense had suddenly taken over and was now telling her knocking the pad from the tree may change the past. With the pad in her hand, she grimaced and carefully placed it back in its original position. She then stood up and moved to one side, all the time keeping her eyes on the young Rebecca.

She watched as her youthful self walked over, sat on the tree, and started sketching. This memory, albeit many years before, was so fresh, it was as if it had happened the day before. Unable to resist, and certain this girl was totally oblivious to her presence, Rebecca crept around the back to see what she was drawing. It was an odd feeling watching her, even though every detail of this girl's actions and movement were exactly as she recalled, even to the point where she knew what she was going to sketch next. As she stood there, she sensed the pattern had changed, but for the life of her, couldn't put her finger on what was different. Peering at the sketch, she suddenly realised she'd never gotten this far, and her pencil had fallen to the ground some moments earlier. She knew only too well that her dropping the pencil ultimately led to her finding the key. The problem was that moment had passed, and instead, the young Rebecca still had the pencil in her hand.

48

With her senses spiralling, she took a deep breath knowing she's probably changed her original path. This concept confused her, because if she had changed things too dramatically, she wouldn't be here now. For all that, though, her young self was still sketching, and the key was still hiding under the tree. Just to add to her jangling emotions, a voice behind her whispered, 'This is how it will always be from this day forward.'

It was her beloved Meredith, someone she believed she'd seen the last of. To compound that emotion, this woman was now standing right behind her. Rebecca was both relieved and delighted, but nonetheless curious. Hesitantly, she turned with open arms, albeit a little unsure what to expect.

'My beloved Rebecca, alas I am unable to cuddle you, even though it is something we would both benefit from. In your time, my spirit has settled. Therefore, what you see now is an apparition of myself. I am here in spirit form, purely to observe your younger self discover the key. Although you also are here in the past, you are in a different dimension to me and your younger self.' In true Meredith style, she then appeared to consider her next words carefully. 'I too am finding this difficult to comprehend and am unsure why I know these things. For all that, I am assured, as is always the case, you have a mission. It is indeed a mission, which is unravelling in my thoughts as we speak. I am sure as with all of today's events it will all become clear shortly.' Meredith glanced down, appearing deep in thought.

Although Rebecca understood to some extent and was confident Meredith would have the answers, she was still a little perplexed. Seeing that Meredith was still deep in thought, she wasn't sure what to say, if anything at all. Just then, Meredith looked up and smiled.

'Many thoughts are occupying my head, although they now appear to be in place.' She nodded with poise. 'I feel confident today's sequence will play forever. In time, you will truly understand the importance of your journeys and how they can have a positive impact on mankind, and as we know, finding the key was the first step.' She smiled in a way that always invigorated Rebecca. 'You now have to dislodge the pencil and then hide it. Although you have always believed it was your fairies, or indeed pixies who moved your pencil, this time it was your future self, in essence, you. You know the sequence, so follow your intuition. I must depart now, although you should be sure that I will always be with you in spirit. Know that Ethernal and I will always be there to catch you.' In a breath, she was gone.

Although Rebecca's mind was dancing around an emotional maypole, she knew she had to focus. Intently watching her younger self's every movement, she stood back, awaiting the right time to intervene. After a few moments, which seemed to take forever, the young Rebecca put her pad down, laid her pencil carefully on top, and then stood up. This was her opportunity, and using as much stealth as she could, sneaked over, and picked up the pencil. She then laughed at herself for tiptoeing around, knowing full well, she could shout at the top of her voice, and still wouldn't be heard, only perhaps by the nearby pixies. She then stood back and watched the young Rebecca look around with a quizzical appearance. The youthful Rebecca then bent down and started scrabbling around under the tree. Remembering the sequence of events, once her younger self had the key in her hand, Rebecca placed the pencil back on the pad.

Seconds later, she heard her youthful self mumble, 'Oh, come along now.' Moments later the young Rebecca was sitting, staring at the key, talking to it in a delightfully familiar way. With this bizarre twist of nostalgia playing havoc with Rebecca's emotions, she sighed, hopeful her job was once again done. She stood for a moment and watched the young Rebecca twiddle the key in her hand. Seconds later, just as she had all those years ago, her youthful self, found the pencil. Young Rebecca shook her head, mumbled about the pixies hiding her pencil, and then headed off in the direction of the stream. As she watched her disappear into the woods, Rebecca wondered why she was still here.

Within seconds, she heard a scream, quickly followed by Ethernal's voice. 'Do not be concerned, the young Rebecca has tripped on a log and other than a scratch on her knee, is just fine. Your apparently insignificant delay in the proceedings resulted in a branch falling in front of her, whereas when you were here, it fell behind you. She has now dropped the key and will not find it without your help. It is under a dock leaf six feet in front of her. Just place it in her line of sight. This is why Meredith and I will always be here to watch over proceedings. One slight change could well jeopardise future events.'

Rebecca considered Ethernal's words for a moment, realising how significant a tiny change can be. She then headed down a familiar route towards the stream. As she turned the corner, she could see her younger self scrabbling around on the floor with an anxious look on her face. This time, as bold as brass, Rebecca walked past her and spotting a huge dock leaf, headed in that direction. Sure enough, the key was precisely where Ethernal had said it would be. She picked the key up and placed it beside the young Rebecca, who immediately mumbled, 'Oh, there you are, hiding.'

Once again, she stood and watched the young Rebecca head off into the trees. Within a few seconds, she heard a voice calling her. She hadn't noticed a change in her surroundings but was certain it was her mum's voice. As she headed towards the voice, which was now calling loudly, she knew for sure it was her mum, and she was once more home. That's odd, she thought as she made her way back towards the summerhouse, wondering why her mum was home so early. As she came out from the woods, it oddly felt like late afternoon, but with the dense cloud cover, it made it impossible to be sure.

It got her thinking, and even though she'd been through a lot during the last few journeys, no matter how long she'd apparently been gone, it was only ever a brief moment in her own time. Just as she spotted her mum at the edge of the woods, she realised she'd left the tablet-type object down by the fallen oak.

'Hello, Mum, I thought you were out all day,' she uttered, still unsure what time it was.

'Rebecca dear, whatever has happened to you? You look like you've been playing rugby, rather than footie with Tom.'

'Boy, do I have a story to tell, Mum. Forget all the jumping back into the past. My last two journeys make my other experiences colourless by comparison. I must go back to the tree quickly as I have left something there.'

Shaking her head, pulling at Rebecca's torn sleeve, her mother asked, 'where on Earth have you been, and what may I ask is so important back at the tree that can't wait until you get cleaned up. And, we need to throw these clothes away. It is one thing blackberry juice on white jeans, but this...'

As she led her mum back to the old fallen oak, she asked, 'What time is it, Mum?'

'Quarter past four, why do you ask?'

'This is so odd because all my other jaunts have been seconds in our time no matter how long I've stayed elsewhere and that includes all those years with Etienne. This time though, it appears I have in fact been gone for hours in our time. I left home about ten this morning, so that's a good six hours, and boy it feels like six weeks.' She then shook her head. 'Very odd, although thinking about it, I'm now wondering if it is because I have been on two jaunts.'

'Two jaunts, hmm, I can't wait to hear your chronicle of events.'

Just as her mum spoke, the penny dropped, 'I know,' she blurted, 'I fell asleep between my two trips.' She nodded, 'although it seemed like I only shut my eyes briefly, it's clearly not the case. Mind you, I am not surprised I fell asleep. Mum, you wait until you hear about my tale. Essentially, the word chronicle is a good choice. Thinking about it, that's not a word you often use, even though it truly will be a chronicle.' She then narrowed her eyes, 'do you know something, Mum?'

'No, I don't, and am not really sure why I chose that word.' She nodded. 'Maybe once we have found what you're looking for, you can tell your father and I all about your two journeys,' she said and chuckled. 'Whatever next, two journeys in one day. And, I might add, you have come back looking like you've spent a few weeks in the wilderness.'

Chapter 7 – The Tablet

As Rebecca entered the kitchen, her father was sitting at the table with his palm up and a quizzical look on his face. Although all the events of her two previous journeys were clear in her head, Rebecca wasn't really sure what to say or where to start. She glanced at her understanding parents and although both advocates, she faced an uphill challenge getting them to accept this outlandish twist to her already bizarre storyline. The thing that concerned her above all was the significance of her message and then subsequently getting people to act upon her words. It was one thing gaining the buy-in from her parents. It was something altogether different making sure the world listened. She slumped down on the chair at a complete loss where to start.

'From the look of you, it would seem you've done a little more than just meet up with Meredith for afternoon tea. Sit down and tell us all. Crumbs, you look exhausted, Rebecca.' Her father then leaned over and touched her hand gently.

Drinking from her mum's water bottle, Rebecca said, 'Boy I needed that.'

Her mum sat next to James handing Rebecca a fresh bottle of water. She then put her elbows on the table, her chin in her hands and said, 'I've been waiting to hear about your latest journey ever since I found you on the edge of the woods. I am intrigued to know what that plastic thing you went back for is all about.'

Rebecca flicked her eyebrows and half grinned. 'Take your elbows off the table. There's a, Sweetie.' She then chuckled. 'Long time since that one's come up.'

Just as Rebecca started to tell her parents all about her journeys, Duncan walked in. Over supper, bit by bit, she told them all about her two jaunts. Her mum couldn't avert her focus away from Rebecca as she told of seeing her younger self actually finding the key. She often asked the same question, each time using different words. This made Rebecca smile, appreciating just how far her mum had come from the days when every journey was a suggested dream. Her father though, focused totally on her time in the future, clearly appreciating the importance of her message. Meanwhile, Duncan sat there with a somewhat bemused look on his face, clearly not ready for this type of free-flowing conversation about events so bizarre they would twist any brain. However, he did seem to once again take it in his stride.

'What year did you say, Rebecca?' Her father asked, with an ever increasing look of curiosity.

'It was twenty-nine thirty-eight. It sounds barmy to me saying it out loud.' Rebecca shook her head, inwardly unable to believe her own words.

'And you suggested there was no sign of human life,' Duncan asked, with a somewhat understandably perplexed appearance showing on his expression and through his tone.

'Well, it seemed so, although I didn't leave our grounds. Other than a few peculiar looking birds and animals, the likes of which I have never seen before, even on the Internet, there was nothing, excepting a few remnants of our house. Besides, I can't see how humans could exist in that heat unless they lived underground,' she said and shook her head.

'You said remnants,' her father asked, 'what do you mean exactly?'

'Everything was in ruin. All I found around the summerhouse was part of the rail from the spiral staircase, ironically and appropriately,' she said and chuckled while shaking her head in disbelief. 'Our house was just a ruin, and by that, I mean, to the ground. Odd though, your tallboy was still standing, between waist-high peculiar coloured ferns, again the likes of which I've never seen.'

'They don't make stuff like that anymore, all imported rubbish. That is made from a decent bit of English oak.' He then raised his eyebrows. 'So, I guess we best look at this tablet affair you found. Did you say it would automatically connect with a computer from our time?'

'Well, sorry to disappoint you, Dad. The tallboy, as it turns out, was a physical hologram of sorts. It was created to help me deal with my surroundings.' She shook her head, unable to believe what she'd just said. 'So, the tablet, yeah it will connect automatically, and I guess we should have a look,' she said, feeling unexpectedly nervous. 'I really don't know what to expect though, because the whole event was so bizarre, even by my standards.' Part of her brain was intrigued and eager to know more, whereas her consciousness was a little apprehensive with an overriding concern as to what they may learn from the tablet.

Rebecca, Duncan, and James started heading towards the study. Elizabeth held back, suggesting she would join them presently after tidying up.

'That is perfectly okay, Mum. Take your time.'

Now in the hallway, Duncan whispered, 'I am guessing your mum finds the concept difficult, and I get that, to be honest. I am an open-minded individual, as you know, and even I am struggling with the idea of an overheated planet with no humans. It's a bit like some kind of post-apocalyptic film.'

56

Rebecca nodded, and followed her father into the study with Duncan's words still resonating in her thoughts. 'Mum is on the page with us, although she likes to take baby steps, which is fine.' On the one hand, she wanted to tell Duncan of her mother's secret but reckoned this was neither the time nor the place. Besides, she had to respect her mother's point of view, especially as it had taken her so long to tell Rebecca. As they entered the study, she shook her head and refocused on the tablet, signalling towards the computer.

Glancing at Rebecca, James switched on his computer, and the instant he did the tablet started whirring. Seconds later, the computer screen went dark red, and four numbered tabs appeared down the right-hand side, each with a short message next to the number. In an odd way, this startled Rebecca, even though she was expecting something similar to happen.

Her father glanced at Rebecca without saying anything. He then looked back at the screen and sounding unusually edgy, suggested, 'Shall we start with number one, and would you like to press the button, Rebecca?'

'It is okay, go ahead, Dad. My curiosity was already at bursting point as it was, and now reading these headings, I am not sure I could manage to press the mouse properly.'

James nodded, smiled, and squeezed Rebecca's arm gently. He then turned and clicked on the tab numbered one, labelled, *how we got here.*

All three sat silently reading the section that had opened up.

Many years before these anthologies were compiled the obviously apparent warning signs telling of potentially catastrophic global warming were ignored. As early as the 20th century, we knew of the probable outcome. However, we still failed to heed the signs and continued down an apocalyptic road of self-destruction.

By the 22nd century, the core temperature of the atmosphere had increased alarmingly. At that time, no human lived within 200 kilometres of the equator. Nonetheless, we continued to burn our planet's resources and manufacture products that we could not recycle. To compound our damnation further, the now ridiculously over-indulged humankind demanded more, ostensibly oblivious to the well-documented terminal outcome.

By the 25th century, both poles had melted, and much of central Europe, North America, and mid-Asia were under water. All Humans lived in a narrow belt inside the Arctic and Antarctic Circle. Birth control was inhibited by one overriding government, and only one in five-hundred families were allowed to have a single child.

By the year 2813, there were less than one hundred humans huddled together, clinging to life, compiling this work.

Within this document, there is a more detailed account. For now, though, you must act with haste, so read on.

No words passed between the three of them for what seemed like an eternity. Rebecca then shook her head, and said, 'best we read on because clearly, time is not on our side.' She then laughed nervously and instantly regretted doing so. 'I so didn't mean to laugh.'

James smiled, 'it is okay, Rebecca,' he then clicked on the next tab labelled, *what we didn't see.*

This article mostly explained about the warning signs and how they were, firstly, hidden by the various governments around the globe and secondly, ignored by humans in general when splinter groups did manage to highlight the possible outcome. It intimated, in the early years, many groups had stood up and protested. The article also stated that around the beginning of the 22nd century, these groups apparently vanished overnight. It went on to suggest, whole scale conspiracy theories were widespread, although, in the end, no one said a word. It also indicated that by then humans had become so dependent on an overindulged lifestyle that neither man nor woman cared what tomorrow would bring. People had lost their soul, spirit, purpose, and the ability to think for themselves. Decisively, those who still had an opinion were frightened to speak out in case they too vanished.

Again, the three of them looked at each other without the need for words.

Duncan, now noticeably engrossed, surprised Rebecca by leaning over and clicking on the third tab, which was labelled, *consequence.*

This article highlighted the lead up to the apocalypse and countless dreadful events along the way. It told of whole swathes of people disappearing, particularly in the third world. Significantly, it stated by the 23rd century the Internet was banned. It was believed, by those who still had an opinion, this was to stop people from finding out what was happening around the globe. There were now just two continents, known as A and B. B was the Americas, and A was Europe across to China. Travelling more than a few miles was banned.

'My goodness that was hard reading,' Rebecca said, feeling somewhat bewildered and quite tearful. Her common-sense side was asking why she was the recipient of this dreadful information. Importantly, she couldn't get her focus away from what, if anything, she as an unknown individual could do about something that was going to happen several centuries in the future. Meanwhile, somewhere in her subconscious was this flame of hope, she could essentially change mankind's behaviour, and thereby avert their catastrophic demise. She shook her head, and continued, 'whole nations left to their own device, ignored by those who ostensibly had plenty. If this is true, and there is no reason to suggest it isn't so, the civilised societies stood back and did nothing, except make things worse. Then you have the disappearance of, what were the words, "whole swathes of people?" Hardly a conspiracy theory is it?' She shook her head, feeling a mixture of acute sadness and intense anger.

'I think what bothers me most,' said Duncan. 'In the end, some of the areas that suffered a ruinous end, are those areas we would today consider a nice place to visit or live. I think one thing that stuck in my head was the idea of central Europe being fifty degrees in the cooler months. Reading that has upset me and left me feeling panicky, frightened.' He shook his head, 'you know what is starting to bother me, somewhere in my subconscious, I actually feel guilty.'

'Guilty,' Rebecca asked, 'why so?

'I don't know, I think it is because I know how those with plenty are capable of behaving towards those with little.. Yeah, we give to charity, really though, we turn away.'

James appearing noticeably uneasy, said, 'Hell, what are we doing? How are we going to stop this madness?' He shook his head, and gripping Rebecca's hand said, 'This is why Meredith has put so much emphasis on society seeing you as a way forward. Girl, you have a journey in front of you, and one that could lead to mankind's salvation.' He then squinted and said, 'or damnation, if no one listens.' He then turned to Duncan, 'I get what you are saying because I strangely felt the same guilt.'

Rebecca was now feeling oddly focused, albeit, her common sense side was asking questions. 'My thoughts are really all over the place. Part of me wonders what little old me could possibly do, whereas there is something deep in my head suggesting I can make a difference.' She then shook her head, as the days ahead of her started to unfold in her conscious thoughts. 'It is not like I can knock on the prime minister's door and say, hey, I am Rebecca, and I've been to the future. I would be sectioned. Not sure I know how I can be heard and then make a difference without them throwing the key away.' That very word triggered a thought in her head. All of a sudden, she started to consider Meredith's words suggesting mankind would see her as the future. 'She obviously trusts me,' she muttered.

'Who trusts you, Rebecca?' James asked.

She shook her head, 'ignore my ramblings, I just thought about what Meredith said, and I was thinking out loud that she obviously trusts me to make a difference. Anyways, perhaps the last tab will shed some more light.'

James nodded, 'we all trust that you, above anyone, are blessed with the ability to make a difference.' He then nodded and clicked on the fourth tab labelled, *solutions*.

In essence, too much carbon dioxide and greenhouse gases were emitted by humankind into the planet's atmosphere. You, Rebecca, and your generation will know of this in your time. Over many years, this resulted in a catastrophic rise in Earth's atmospheric and core temperature. In addition to this, and a largely ignored problem was our planet continuing to produce plastic material that could not be broken down and wouldn't biodegrade on its own. Again, your generation, Rebecca, was starting to realise this, although it was spoken about, it was on the whole ignored. For sure, people of your time were aghast at footage depicting animals dying as a result of plastic. Still, the "civilised world" did nothing other than turning its back.

Rebecca turned to her father and Duncan. 'It's poignant they refer to the civilised world in inverted commas.'

'Yeah, I got that too,' Duncan said with a groan.

Now staring at the screen, James said, 'this next section is written in green, unlike the red before. 'Hang on a minute; they referred to you by name, Rebecca.'

'I just thought that,' Duncan said, with pouted lips and narrowed eyes.

'Yep, when I first opened the tablet, there was a video message of sorts, and the lady was speaking directly to me. It was odd then, it's odd now and will always be odd,' Rebecca said, nodded her head, and pointed at the computer. All the doubts she'd had were now dissolving as she was beginning to realise, she had to make a difference, one way, or the other. Her brain jumped back to Meredith's aunt, and as if for the first time, she truly understood how she must have felt speaking to largely blinkered, deaf ears. Oddly, this thought increased her resolve. She turned back to the screen and started reading.

When it was too late, the then one global government started investing a substantial amount of money into finding an answer.

Below are listed many solutions to the global problems you currently face. Unfortunately, these were discovered too late in our time. This is why you, Rebecca, were sent to find this journal. When all seems lost, you must continue to strive forward. Trust in yourself, and you will be heard.

The plastic problem was an issue as early as the twentieth century. In the year 2736, a northern European food company that produced crayfish as a sustainable food source discovered a particular crossbreed of lobster and spider crab that could digest all plastic at a fantastic rate. After extensive research, it was learned that the vestiges and remains after the plastic had passed through their body helped reduce ocean acidification.

The most significant problem was the constant discharge of greenhouse gases such as fluorocarbons, halocarbon refrigerants, solvents, and propellant gases. For four hundred years, various governments tentatively tested different theories with little success.

In the year 2810, three short years before the end of mankind, a scientist noticed a small but significant increase in the ozone levels in an area between where France and the United Kingdom had been before global flooding. After extensive research, which took several months, by which time it was too late, we learned of a unique set of wind turbines, which had been set up to produce electricity, had in fact, been set up incorrectly.   Due to this minor fault, these turbines were sucking in bad gasses and producing oxygen atoms, diatomic oxygen, and triatomic oxygen. By the time, we learned of this, the earth was beyond reason and repair. Our only hope is that you, Rebecca, are able to act upon this information.

Via the tabs below, you will find complete detailed documentation for all the above.

Rebecca, if the governments of the world fail to heed your words and act upon this information, humankind will end. The Earth, however, will survive. The last significant corrective process mankind did was to set up thousands of these turbines around the world.

Rebecca, when you visited many years after mankind's demise, these turbines would have started to improve air quality and importantly global temperature. The day I finished compiling this, the outside Celsius was 73, leaving the planet scorched. If our calculations are accurate, you will see Earth on a path to recovery, with external temperatures at 40 Celsius in Northern Europe. The poles would have frozen once again and thereby reducing sea levels towards those that you know in your time. This planet was never ours, Mother Nature is a strong lady, and without us, she will evolve. Disrespect Mother Nature and she will show her hand, as she has done. Who knows what will happen in generations to come? Earth was here before us and will be here after us.

Rebecca turned to her father with her eyes widened. Although she knew the immense task that faced her, she felt strangely calm and focused. In spite of this though, she was at a loss for words. 'I don't know what to say.'

'I think we all feel similar, Rebecca.'

Duncan, both nodding and shaking his head simultaneously, said, 'when you told me of your journeys through time, I never envisaged anything like this.' He then laughed nervously, 'I had visions of *Back to the Future*.'

This seemed to lighten the mood a little, and the three of them sat around chatting until supper was ready. After eating, Rebecca, Duncan, James, and Elizabeth talked some more. Elizabeth seemed somewhat intrigued by her story but suggested she couldn't get her head around Rebecca watching a younger version of herself finding the key. Rebecca knew only too well this was her mother's way of dealing with the enormity of these events.

Suddenly, her mother's tact changed completely. She put both palms down on the table and said, 'As a starting point, I think we need to get Ruth involved. She is now working for the local MP, and that could be a door in for you. At least, he could pass the information to the British parliament.' Elizabeth then leaned her chin in her hand, clearly thinking. 'The thing is, I am not altogether sure how you are going to get anyone to believe your story. For sure, Ruth knows all about your jaunts, but even so.' She then narrowed her eyes. 'With so many green protagonists shouting endlessly about global warming, your account may sound like another ploy to get people to listen. Making them listen we must. Besides, I am convinced Meredith trusts you, and I know for sure we all do.' She then politely thumped her hand on the table. 'We need to start shouting soon. Importantly, you have this fangled computer affair to show and tell.' She then chuckled, but not in her normal way.

Somewhat taken aback, Rebecca nodded to her mother. 'Meeting up with Ruth would be a brilliant, potential way in, Mum. Ever since I started reading the information on the tablet, I have been wondering how I would get anyone to listen. At least, Ruth has a doorway, albeit only just ajar. No time like the present, how about we ring her and see if she is free tomorrow?'

64

With her new profound look, Elizabeth said, 'I will ring her now. Fortunately, the MP she works for, David Wilson, is a bit of an environmentalist, which goes with the territory, living in, and representing an area like the Lake District.' She nodded and picked up her phone. A moment later, she came off the phone and said, 'all set for tomorrow.'

Chapter 8 – Lunch with Ruth

The following morning, Rebecca was already awake when her mum came in with some toast and orange juice.

'Morning, Rebecca. You're awake early, although I am not surprised what with everything going on in your head. I lay in bed last night thinking about all you've been through. I must say, it certainly gives your journeys a different meaning and perspective.'

'I was thinking exactly that. For sure, there was my time with Etienne and one of our subsequent children going on to discover that medicine.' Rebecca took a deep breath as if she had suddenly realised for the first-time what Meredith and Ethernal had meant when they'd said mankind would one day see her kind as the way forward. 'I'm reasonably sure I mentioned this before, Mum. They have forever been saying the world would one day see my type as a way forward. I think for the first time now, I truly understand what they meant.' Appearing a little quizzical, Elizabeth narrowed her eyes in a way Rebecca hadn't seen since she was in her teens. It was a look she knew well and was indicating her mother was hearing her, however. 'Mum, that expression on your face. I've not seen that for a while. What are you thinking?'

She shook her head and smiled. 'You said they, and I'm guessing one is Meredith, so who may I ask is the other person or persons. Is there something, or someone you've not told me about?'

Smiling, Rebecca narrowed her eyes and nodded. 'Well aside from Meredith, there has been another person, if that's the right term. And they've been on the scene for some time now. I never mentioned this to anyone because it sounded daft to me. His name is Ethernal, although I have only ever heard his voice, not actually seen him.' She then raised her eyebrows. 'I know that sounds daft, it does to me. The thing is, since I've seen less of Meredith, other than occasionally being aware of her spirit, or apparition as she called it; he has been there to stop me falling, for want of a better term. To my mind, he's a bit like Meredith. She was my guardian angel, and Ethernal was hers. In fact, he has been there for every girl who has carried this ability to travel. As I understand it, he has been here since before Christ, right back to the original Rebekah, who you can read up on in the Old Testament, where it says she was the wife of Isaac. That Rebekah, evidently, controlled those around her with either her beauty or intelligence. According to Ethernal, she had the same ability as me, whereby she could travel through time. Somewhat like Meredith's aunt, also a Rebecca I might add, who was ridiculed because she shouted too loud about her visions, well... You know how things are in our time. Can you imagine how it would have been in the nineteenth century?' She then nodded. 'Well, I know how it was because she was seen as insane and subsequently banished to an asylum in the Americas.' She shook her head. 'So, as I said, you can only imagine what it would have been like for her, or for me, had I been born during that era. It got me wondering if some of the so-called witches who were burnt at the stake were in fact visionaries like me.'

'I can only imagine, Sweetie.' She then looked down, appearing to consider Rebecca's words. 'I am pleased you have him and Meredith, albeit in spirit around you. I would need more than that if I experienced half the things you have.' She then nodded. 'Just what you've said about, Ethernal is it, and not telling anyone, well?' She paused, clearly thinking. 'I imagine it is going to be one thing getting everyday people to hear your story but trying to make the world governments act upon something they will see as a questionable notion at best is going to be complex, to say the least. However, try we must, and meeting up with Ruth is a great place to start. I briefly mentioned your latest tale to her last night while I was on the phone.'

'Oh right, what did she say?'

'She was actually excited by the challenge ahead of us. She totally bought into your story. In fact, she told me she has been sending off emails all around the world to various governing bodies and has recently joined a proactive cleaner planet group. For all her enthusiasm, she was a tad sceptical about how her boss would take to the idea. Mind you, she also went on to say he was a rather spiritual person, *so the door may open if we push it hard enough.* Those are Ruth's words, not mine.'

'Well, it's a good place to start, and I'm looking forward to meeting up with Ruth.'

'Duncan left early this morning.'

'Yeah, woke me up in the process. He is so noisy,' she said and laughed. 'He has a business meeting in Edinburgh and is stopping overnight. Mum, while I think about it, we need to sort the heating out in the summerhouse. It's about time Duncan and I moved in properly. I know it's getting somewhat warmer now, but it is still a little chilly in the mornings and running half a bath at a time and then topping it up with several kettles, well...'

'I will speak to your father. I don't think either of us realised it was that bad. I will leave you to get ready and go phone James now.'

After her mum left, Rebecca decided to have her breakfast outside on the balcony. It was a beautiful, crisp spring morning, although Rebecca's thoughts were dominated by all that had happened the day before. As she looked down towards the lake, all she could see were yesterday's memories. The

68

stark difference between the scenes she experienced and the calm tranquillity of today emphasised how vital her mission would be. Sitting there, mulling over her mother's words, she felt a tad perplexed and somewhat burdened, wondering how she would get the appropriate world bodies to listen. Considering her possible approach, she suddenly realised she only needed one person of significance to believe her, and the rest would not be such an uphill battle. *After all*, she thought, *I have this futuristic tablet affair to show those who matter.* 'That's it,' she mumbled, 'that's the ace up my sleeve.'

She finished off her orange juice, had a quick shower, and headed downstairs to the kitchen.

'Oh, I am glad you're down sharp, just had a call from Ruth. Amanda is going to meet up with us too.'

Although Rebecca was delighted by the idea of meeting Amanda, she was on a mission. Before she had time to even consider what she was going to say, her mum started talking.

'It's okay. I know that expression, and I thought the same thing. You see, the thing is, we are not the only two who are on a similar wavelength. Our Ruth is plugged in too, and Amanda, albeit a little less so.' She then chuckled in that way Rebecca loves. 'Before I had time to say anything, Ruth said she had all afternoon free. So once Amanda goes and we head back to Ruth's office, we can have some time on our own. I might add, both of us agreed it might be a bridge too far for Amanda, the end of the world is nigh and all that.' Again, she chuckled, this time a little nervously.

'Excellent, you got all the bases covered, again, Mum.'

On the way into town, Rebecca and her mum decided to stop off and book up the spa for the following day.

'I feel like I need a proper detox after what I went through yesterday. It was like being in a microwave. It was so hot I felt like I was cooking from the inside out. The thing is the tablet suggested it would have cooled by the time I was there. Heaven only knows what it must have been like towards the end when it was seventy-odd Celsius. Just crazy and doesn't bear thinking about.'

Around twelve-thirty, they met up with Amanda and headed to some fancy bistro that had just opened up near Ruth's office.

'This is more like it,' Amanda said, swishing her hair back in a way that only Amanda could.

'Every time I see you, you are more like Sophia Loren than her. You just have a film star quality, Amanda,' Elizabeth said.

'Mum, who is Sophia, what's her name?'

'A beautiful film star from the fifties, or sixties. Amanda is so similar.'

The conversation continued down this road for the remainder of lunch. After they had said their goodbyes to Amanda, they headed back to Ruth's office.

On the way, Ruth added, 'I knew we wouldn't get our serious chat meeting up with Amanda, but I wouldn't have her any other way. I get so much energy from her, and she absolutely has film star qualities, in abundance.'

Chapter 9 – Ruth's door is ajar, just

They sat in Ruth's office sipping more coffee, chatting about lunch, and wondering how Amanda hadn't ended up on the big screen. Rebecca, for some reason, wasn't quite ready to talk about what she'd come for, and instead was happy catching up on the past couple of months. Around three pm, Ruth's boss popped his head in.

'I am off now, Ruth, and there's nothing needs doing, so you can lock up and shoot off when you want.' He then smiled, acknowledging Elizabeth and Rebecca.

'Oh, before you go, let me introduce you. These are my two friends I briefly mentioned yesterday, Elizabeth and Rebecca,' she said and indicated in their direction.

'It's a delight to meet you both. I have heard so many good and intriguing things about you. Next time you are in town, perhaps we can have a chat.' He then nodded, 'must dash, off down to London for a meeting in the House of Commons.'

No sooner he'd closed the door, Ruth said, 'for a moment, I thought he was going to stop and chat, then I'd never find out why you came in.' She chuckled. 'Okay, Rebecca, what is your story? I could tell it was something important just by your mother's tone when she phoned me. Besides which, I have noticed this afternoon you often drifting into Rebecca land, for want of a better term.'

Over the next hour or so, Rebecca explained all about her journey into the future. Even though she was graphic in her description, she could see Ruth was intrigued, but at the same time a tad uncertain. This came as a bit of a surprise to

Rebecca, knowing Ruth was already an advocate for her time-travel. If she'd had any doubts, she knew for sure just how difficult it was going to be to get anyone to see her tale as anything other than a fanciful, made-up story.

Rebecca glanced at her mum, and then at Ruth. 'Mum, I think I need to show Ruth the tablet. The one I brought back with me from the future.'

'Tablet,' Ruth exclaimed. 'Tell me more, some kind of medicine?' she asked, appearing vague.

Laughing, while taking the folded tablet from her backpack, Rebecca said, 'Tablet, as in a computer if you can call it that.' She then pointed towards Ruth's desktop computer. 'Is that connected to the Internet? I ask because although I have no doubts it is safely protected, I wouldn't want anyone finding what I am about to show you.'

With a quizzical look on her face, Ruth nodded and said, 'It is totally secure, being an MP's office and all, it has to be.' She then shook her head and narrowed her eyes. 'Now you have me intrigued.'

'Well, I brought this back with me from the year twenty-nine thirty-eight. I can assure you it sounds daft to me every time I say it. Nonetheless...' She shook her head. 'There is some incredible information on here, and I have no doubt it will alarm you. It is truly frightening how horrid, blinkered, and damn right selfish mankind can be. Or should I say, will be?'

'Crumbs, if it is that serious, perhaps we shouldn't...' She stopped. 'I am guessing you're going to link it to my computer.'

Hesitantly and somewhat unsure, Rebecca nodded, having picked up on Ruth's understandable caution.

'Going to a cupboard in the corner, Ruth said, 'I have here a back-up laptop, which has never been used and hasn't been

72

connected to the Internet. Perhaps that's the best way forward,' she said, glancing at Rebecca.

Feeling much more comfortable, Rebecca nodded. 'Yeah, that makes me feel a whole lot easier.'

Over the next thirty minutes, Rebecca took Ruth through everything on the tablet, having had to kick-start it by opening the window to let the sunshine on it briefly.

'Goodness,' Ruth exclaimed, wiping a tear from her cheek. 'That is horribly scary and beyond belief. I am not sure what bothers me most, either our planet being apparently doomed, or the way mankind behaved. Boy oh boy, you have a long tricky road in front of you, one that will be full of pitfalls and bigoted, narrow-minded opinions.' She then shook her head. 'I understand now why you were looking at me in the way you did when you first told me your chronicle, and a chronicle it was, is. My word, I really don't know what to say.'

'I feel a little lost and do not know which way to turn. Mum suggested as you work for a member of parliament that might prove to be a way of getting my story heard. I need to be strong and pushy on this one and tell the world. One way or another, the world needs to listen.' Rebecca shook her head and glanced at Ruth, knowing she knew all about Meredith. 'I feel concerned by the task in front of me, I can tell you that. Although, I trust Meredith will open the doors for me, or at least guide me in the right direction, nonetheless.'

Ruth glanced at Elizabeth, who nodded. She then narrowed her eyes. 'You are referring to Meredith from the eighteen-hundreds?'

'Yeah,' Rebecca said, nodding. 'She is and has always been a kind of guardian angel for me. Although I now have a lot more control over my movements through time, there are still occasions when I feel lost and alone. Somehow, though, I forever manage to find solace, knowing Meredith will be there to catch me. And she always does.' She then opened her eyes wide. 'She doesn't tell me where to go or anything like that. She just reassures me when I need it most. I am here and reflecting on where I've been lately, with a seemingly clear vision. Well, I can tell you there were times when I felt wholly lost and confused. Then she would appear with words of comfort, telling me to trust my intuition. There have been times when all I have needed was the idea that if I took a wrong turn, she would be there to catch me. I hope that makes sense.'

'Perfect sense,' Ruth said and nodded. 'I have often wondered how you felt heading off the way you do. It is nice to know,' she said and glanced towards Elizabeth, 'that you have Meredith there to protect you.'

'It helps me too, especially when Rebecca was younger, knowing she had this guiding light.' She then looked down, clearly deep in thought. 'Right, I have something to tell you Ruth, something that may come as a shock. I told Rebecca just recently of a couple of incidents when I was younger, incidents I kept to myself, and perhaps shouldn't have on reflection.' Elizabeth then appeared distant, clearly thinking.

With obvious curiosity etched on her face, Ruth lifted her palms.

'Sorry, Ruth, I was just considering how to tell you.' She then told the story of her time with Meredith, and the subsequent issues she faced after.

'Oh, Liz, what a sad tale you have, and I fully understand why you've kept this to yourself, considering your father's reaction, and, well... I have to say, although I never imagined for one moment that Rebecca got her genes from you, I also wasn't sure she got them from James either.'

The three sat around discussing Elizabeth's story, before turning their attention back to Rebecca's chronicle. They then spent most of their time trying to think of a way to get the story out there.

'I think we need to start with my boss. David is a good person, an advocate for environmental issues, and not afraid to speak out. I will arrange something as soon as he is back and try to ply him with snippets to test his reaction.'

Nodding, Rebecca said, 'that's a good idea, Ruth. Feed him snippets, almost preparing him, so my story doesn't come as a total shock.'

'I am not sure how I am going to do it without sounding like I've lost the plot though.'

Rebecca was deep in thought, trying to come up with a way Ruth could prime David, when her mum spoke, breaking her attention.

'I have an idea. How about you mention the original Rebekah to David. You know, the one in the bible, just drop her in a conversation in passing. I've been reading up on her, and there are very tentative suggestions she was able to see beyond the obvious. You could take that to mean anything so we could use it for our purposes. You could then lead that onto the many so-called witches from the fifteenth century who was burned simply because they too could see beyond the obvious. You could then offer up what if they could see into the past or future. Just in passing mind and see how he responds.'

'What a brilliant idea, Ruth.'

'Yeah, Mum, more than a pretty face, but hey, I've always known that.'

Chapter 10 – The MP

The following week, Ruth arranged for Rebecca, and Elizabeth, to meet up with David Wilson, her boss. As Rebecca sat there going through her story, she tried to relay the concept as an idea for a novel. A number of times though, she slipped and spoke in the first person, which raised David's eyebrows a few times. Throughout, although politely interested, he didn't really add anything to the conversation.

Ruth smiled. 'I suspect hearing Rebecca's tale is intriguing for you David. However, you need to try and look at this with an open, unprejudiced mind.'

Both shaking his head and somehow nodding at the same time, he said, 'I am not altogether sure what to say. I do now get why you've been plying me with stories of the Rebekah from the bible and witches from the past, however...' He then kind of smiled and frowned simultaneously towards Ruth and then Rebecca.

Ruth nodded. 'I get that, and that's how I was when Rebecca first told me of her most recent journey. I must add, importantly, I have been aware of her ability to travel through time for many years, and I still found this story difficult to comprehend.' She then glanced at Rebecca. 'I have seen proof of her time in the past, and also recently, her time in the future. As difficult as this is, for me, you, and crucially, anyone else, someone has to listen.' She then shook her head. 'And yes, that is why I mentioned the original Rebekah. Overall, you must recognise and understand how complex and fraught with scepticism this journey is and will be for Rebecca.'

Elizabeth then held her hand up just the way you would at school, which made everyone grin, including Elizabeth. She shook her head and raised her eyes. 'For years, I wasn't sure what to think about Rebecca's ability to jump back and forth seemingly at will. It took me a long time to open up and accept she was telling the truth, and I am her mother,' she said with an unusually profound tone, the likes of which Rebecca had only heard on the rarest of occasions.

While Elizabeth was talking, Rebecca decided it was time to show David the tablet. 'I think I need to show you some evidence, of sorts.' She then produced the tablet from her bag and after a few seconds of sunlight, she watched David's expression as it opened in front of him.

With his mouth slightly open and his eyes wide, he just stared without saying anything. He then shook his head. 'Is this some new-fangled computer from China?'

From that comment alone, Rebecca knew this road wasn't going to work too well, if at all. Over the next hour or so, she showed David the contents of the tablet. Although he was clearly intrigued, he was nonetheless, a little distant.

'Looks like it would make some kind of film. You are not trying to use me as a way forward for this story you have concocted, are you?' David then put his chin in his hand and glanced around the table.

Ruth, appearing angered by this question, stood up. 'David, I have worked for you only for a short while, but you have known me for many years. You should know me better. I appreciate you have only just met Rebecca and Elizabeth, but that was bad mannered and discourteous. You will be looking for a new PA if you continue. I do not expect for one minute you are going to accept this tale, but we have nowhere else to go with it. We need your support and ideas.'

He glanced at Rebecca and Elizabeth and then nodded. 'I am sorry, that was rude of me.' He seemed to think for a moment. 'I am sure you realise how this must come across to a stranger. Time travel is a thing for film studios. It is going to take me some time to get my head around this. Besides, initially you offered this story up as just that, an idea for a novel perhaps. Now, you are telling me it isn't fiction, it's fact.' He then nodded, clearly considering his standpoint.

Rebecca was prepared for this reaction and in fact empathised with David. 'I know only too well how this must come across. For sure, it would make a great film. Indeed, I have been working on what I have called a fictional novel, albeit telling of my times in the past. That, however, will need to be shelved now. If I write a fantasy novel about my journeys, no one will listen when it is something as profound as this. It is easy for me because I know the truth, although I struggle to say the year twenty-nine thirty-eight. For years, all those around me thought my stories were dreams at best. There were even times when I annoyingly considered that option. Then one day my parents and I obtained unquestionable proof.'

'Proof?' David asked, 'tell me more.'

Rebecca then explained about stepping into the future and being aware their home boiler had blown up, which subsequently caused her mother serious injury. She went on to explain how she went back in time and wrote a letter warning of the impending problem. Then she told of discreetly hiding the letter in her father's two-hundred-year-old bureau.

'Then what happened,' he asked, clearly a little more focused.

'Well, eventually, and not without debate, my Father accepted and acted upon my letter. He had the boiler fixed that very night. Interestingly, the engineer suggested it wasn't far from blowing up.'

'Yeah, but you could have dreamt it all, knowing the boiler was on the blink. I don't understand how a letter from you in your father's bureau would convince him.'

Rebecca then explained all about the bureau having not been opened for many years. She emphasised, in reality, it had a thick varnish covering over the drawer fittings and clearly had been that way for a long time, certainly before her birth.

Once again, David seemed to have drifted a little and Rebecca knew it was perhaps right to give him some thinking time, for now at least. She glanced at Ruth, who responded by blinking her eyes, acknowledging Rebecca. They did continue to chat for a while longer, and appearing to realise they were not getting anywhere, Ruth stepped in.

'Thank you for your time, David. I appreciate how difficult this must have been for you. Perhaps mull it over for a few days, and if you feel inclined to ask anything, please feel free. Okay, we are meeting up with James, Rebecca's father, shortly for supper.'

'I am sorry I haven't been able to buy into your fabulous, although sadly depressing tale. Possibly, in time, I may open my mind sufficiently to become an advocate. For now, I must consider where I stand on this matter and decide if I have seen enough to believe your story.' He then paused for a moment. 'Then potentially put my career on the line when I become a supporter for your story. The most important campaigner for your tale is the western world, and we already know we have problems ahead.' He then narrowed his eyes. 'Interestingly, my own words have helped me focus a little. Give me time to think.'

'I do understand, David, and I thank you for your time,' Rebecca said, feeling frustrated even though she expected this kind of reaction.

'Before you go, I was going to suggest you chat with a friend of mine who works for the Daily Telegraph. However, I think although they will delight in your tale, they may see it as just that, a tale. On that subject, if your story is true, and you carry it forward, be ready for the nonsense that will come your way.' He then nodded. 'Perhaps that is something I can help you with once the story hits the fan.'

Ruth, now standing, still appearing a tad cross, said, 'Just consider for a moment this tale is true. What should your response be?'

David nodded. 'That is exactly where I am at.'

Chapter 11 – Next Step

After they'd said their goodbyes, Rebecca and Elizabeth met up with James and Duncan for supper. When they were in the restaurant, Duncan spotted a business colleague sitting at an adjacent table.

'Rebecca, that guy once reported for the local newspaper. Perhaps he could help get your story out there.'

'Ruth's boss suggested something similar, although his friend works for a national paper. I wasn't altogether sure how I felt about the idea,' Rebecca said, somewhat dubious about talking to a stranger concerning something she'd hidden from the world for the last ten years.

'I am kinda with Rebecca on this one,' Elizabeth said, glancing at Rebecca, clearly picking up on her uncertainty.

'I completely understand that,' Duncan replied, 'although I do think it may help to chat to him and hear his point of view on the subject. If nothing else, he could shed some light on how he thinks people may react.'

Nodding, Rebecca said, 'that's a good point, Duncan.'

After supper, they met with Duncan's friend, Malcolm, at the bar. Duncan, along with Rebecca, tentatively explained the scenario, without indicating it really happened. They asked what the likely response would be if someone came to you with a story like this, enquiring how he or the paper would react.

'Crumbs, that's an interesting one. Are you writing a book, perhaps?' He then narrowed his eyes in a way Rebecca considered an inquisitive reporter kind of way.

'I am writing a story that is similar, but not the same. It was just while writing I got to wondering how a newspaper would react to such a tale. Certainly, if someone suggested it was real.'

'I can't say I have come across anything remotely similar. The best I can think of is a story that ran in the nineteen-forties about a couple of girls who photographed two fairies at the bottom of their garden, which was subsequently proved to have been faked. Then, of course, there was the infamous story publicised on the radio about an alien invasion, which subsequently sent the public into a frantic meltdown.'

'I remember that,' Elizabeth added, 'I seem to recall the photos were proved to have been faked and the two girls, who had grown into women, were scorned, even though they were naïve children at the time. The radio story I thought was just that, a story of what could happen. I never, in fact, realised it was put forward as a tale of true events.'

Nodding, Malcolm said, 'Yep, that's pretty much it. It would be okay if your stories were put across as fiction, but woe betides the backlash for someone who claimed your kind of story was a fact. The nuclear fallout would be...' With narrowed eyes, he then nodded at Rebecca in a way that suggested he thought she was going to claim her story really happened. 'I will do some research on such tales, and I suggest you do the same, Rebecca. See what the response was. I have no doubts that there will be many who will engage and run with your tale. Ecological and save the planet groups would dash around the block for a story like this. They don't have to live with the fallout though.'

James, squeezing Rebecca's arm gently said, 'I think madam has a lot to consider before she decides on her next step.'

Again, with eyes narrowed, inquisitively, Malcolm looked directly at Rebecca. 'From your father's comment, I can only assume that you folks believe this story to be true. In normal circumstances, I would dismiss it as a made-up child-like notion. However...' He then looked around the room, clearly considering his next words. 'If I did not know Duncan as well as I do, and know of your father's impeccable business reputation, I would be dismissing this tale out of hand. The thing is, I do know you, and I must therefore take this seriously. Well, as much as I can for now.'

Rebecca looked directly at Malcolm. 'I sincerely hope you keep this to yourself, for now at least. As you say, my father and my husband have a reputation to consider. At some point, I will go public on this, for now though, I am considering my best option. So, please in your mind, keep it as just a story that may become a book.'

'I totally respect and understand your point of view. I am intrigued to learn more. From my years as a reporter, you get a vibe for the truth. I get that from all of you.' He took a deep breath. 'My goodness, what a tale you have, and as you say, it needs to be put out there. I will do some serious thinking. It may take me a while to get my head around such a fascinating concept. I am sure you can appreciate that. However, I am intrigued, to say the least.'

Rebecca chuckled. 'It took me a long time, and my parents even longer to accept what was happening. Then to believe and act upon my messages from the past was complex, to say the least. Now though, for me, for my parents, husband, and most importantly the world, this is another level.' She then closed her eyes for a moment and could sense an unusual feeling. She hadn't felt this kind of emotion for a long time. It was as if Meredith had just entered the room. Clearly, she hadn't, although it didn't stop Rebecca opening her eyes and glancing around.

On the way home, all Rebecca could think about was the sensation she'd felt in the restaurant.

'You okay, Sweetie?' her mum asked.

'Yeah, I'm just tired, thanks for asking. I truly find it draining talking and thinking about my stories with complete strangers. I want to think of another word for story, but I can't find the right one.'

'Chronicle,' James said, with a reassuring nod.

'Yeah, I think you're about right. Mum used the word chronicle the other day.' She looked at her mum who was sitting next to her in the back of the car. 'Mum, I felt Meredith walk into the restaurant, as daft as that sounds,' she whispered.

'Crumbs that must have come as a jolt to your senses. Did you see her?'

'No, Mum, I just felt as if she was there looking over proceedings. It was as if I could feel her breath on my neck. I think her spirit was there to reassure me some way.'

'That's a nice way to think about it and it must have helped, especially considering the mountain you are about to climb.'

'Yeah, it does in an odd way. I can't really put it into words, and certainly couldn't express my feeling publically. That would be met with similar derision and scorn. Can you imagine? Oh, by the way, a woman named Meredith from eighteen-fifty-three just walked into the room, albeit it is only I who knows she is here, and you can't actually see her. They would lock me away, even nowadays.'

Chapter 12 – Another Newspaper

The following morning, Elizabeth received a call from Ruth who had been speaking to her boss. David had arranged a meeting that afternoon with his friend who worked for the Daily Telegraph if Rebecca felt up for that. Once off the phone, Elizabeth explained the situation to Rebecca.

'Not sure I feel up to it. Nonetheless, I know I need to at least give it a chance.' In the back of her mind, it was the last thing she fancied, although she knew there were going to be many days and numerous meetings just like this and she couldn't afford to turn her back.

A few minutes later, Duncan called to say he had spoken with Malcolm. He explained that Malcolm had done some digging and found a couple of articles that were similar. One dated back to the early part of the twentieth century, just before the outbreak of World War 1, and was from a woman who claimed she had travelled to the nineteen-forties and seen the world at war. She received so much disparagement and disapproval she was never heard of again. The same newspaper tried to find her after the outbreak of World War 1 and Two. Interestingly, the paper was the Daily Telegraph. The next was from back in the eighteen-twenties when a story was reported by a woman coincidently named Rebekah. She claimed to have travelled a thousand years into the future where she'd witnessed Earth devoid of humankind.

The moment he said eighteen-twenties, Rebecca got goosebumps, then when he named the woman as Rebekah, she knew it was Meredith's aunt. This caused a reaction like nothing she'd ever felt before, and the only thing she could liken it to in her thoughts was the way she felt when she found Millicent's suicide note. Considering this, she realised the only reason she saw cohesion between the two was because both vindicated her journeys as real events. 'Duncan,' she asked, her emotions fuelled with a tad of scepticism amid a whole load of excitement, 'did they say what happened to this woman?'

'It did evidently state that she was mocked, called names, and banished to the Americas, considered a madwoman or worse still a witch. Indeed, history is littered anecdotally with many women who have claimed they could see the future and were considered witches or mad. Rebecca, Malcolm alluded to this exact point of view. In his words, you'll need to find a strength that will help you deal with and bat away whatever comes your way and that includes being labelled a crazy woman.'

Unable to believe what she was hearing both stimulated and confounded Rebecca. On the one hand, she now felt steadfast and adamant she was ready to get her story out there and take all that came her way. Her sentiment fuelled, knowing the conflict Meredith's aunt faced in her short life. However, the rational side of her was asking if society was ready to hear her story and if she was prepared for what would follow. She came off the phone and just sat there staring into the garden.

'Whatever is the matter, Rebecca?' Her mum asked, putting her hand on Rebecca's shoulder.

She then explained all that Duncan had told her. In particular, she focused on the story of Meredith's aunt. She emphasised that although she knew how Rebekah was treated, hearing it from a third party just energized her own determination.

'Crumbs, Rebecca, how did that make you feel?'

'Importantly, Mum, I am all the more determined to get out there and shout about this, irrespective of what may come my

86

way. What's the worst that could happen? They burn me at some stake somewhere.' She shook her head. 'What Meredith's Rebekah went through, and all the others who have told their tale and faced in some cases, nightmarish condemnation, well they deserve me to carry their gauntlet. I am not just doing this for humanity. I am doing this for all those messengers who have gone before. Woman of my making, I might add.'

Appearing tentative, Elizabeth asked, 'So, Duncan suggested that Malcolm had referred to Meredith's aunt directly?'

'Yeah, not as Meredith's aunt,' she said, and shook her head, 'but by her name Rebekah. Even to the point where he'd read, she was sent to the America's. That caused an odd reaction inside me, you know.' She then nodded and with her eyes wide, said, 'you know what, damn the ridicule, she deserves to be heard, and so do I.'

'Perhaps that is why Meredith was in the restaurant, looking over your shoulder, Rebecca.'

'Ooh, I have gone all goosy, never thought of that.'

They chatted a little longer and feeling in need of some thinking time, Rebecca said, 'Right, I am going to have a long shower and decide what's next.'

'You do that, Sweetie. Shall I ring Ruth back and say we will be there?'

Rebecca stared out of the window, and feeling adamant, turned to her mother. 'Yes, for sure, especially as the paper has previous articles along these lines.' She then headed upstairs, and after a thoughtful shower, got her best work clothes on and headed down to the kitchen. 'Right, let's get this done.'

Just before lunchtime, they arrived at Ruth's office, and as they entered the building, Ruth was waiting in reception.

'Hello, Ladies. The guy from the Telegraph, his name is Martin Foreshore, by the way, rang a few minutes ago to say... Oh look, here he is now, she said and pointed towards the door.'

'Good afternoon, Ladies.'

'Hello Martin, this is Elizabeth and Rebecca.'

'I must say, I am looking forward to this chat. David briefly covered the background to your tale, Rebecca.' He then smiled in what Rebecca considered an agreeable way.

'David said he will catch up with us in a bit. He has some essential governmental business to attend to, as per usual. So, it's just us four for lunch, shall we?' Ruth said, indicating towards the front door.

In a way, Rebecca was oddly pleased David wouldn't be there. She didn't know why, just how she felt. On the way to the restaurant, her story wasn't mentioned, and she was happy about this. Listening to Martin chat about meeting up with a spiritualist made her wonder if he was telling this story to make her feel comfortable. She'd always reckoned she was a good judge of character and this guy seemed okay to her.

As they entered the restaurant, David went around the table, starting with Elizabeth, helping each to their chair. This again made a positive impact on Rebecca, and she was now in fact looking forward to telling him all about her time in the past and future.

'Shall we order some lunch and then get down to business?' he said glancing around the table, making a point of smiling towards Rebecca with an unmistakable air of thoughtfulness.

No sooner they'd ordered their food, Rebecca asked with a smile, 'how much did David tell you exactly?'

'Only the brief outlines. The way I understand it, you have this ability to see the past and future. I must say right here and now, I have done some research and history is littered with ladies who have a similar story. Apparently, no men at all share this unique ability, and I am not sure how I feel about that.' He then nodded, 'what I found so profound, was that I unearthed four such stories, two of which go back hundreds of years and one two hundred years. Here's the thing, their name was a variant of Rebecca.' He then shook his head. 'Not altogether sure how I felt about that at the time. That said the more I have thought about it since the more I think...' He then seemed to search his own thoughts for a moment. 'I guess it has opened my eyes to a possible link. Not sure.' He then glanced towards Rebecca and narrowed his eyes in a questioning, perhaps uncertain way.

Nodding, Rebecca said, 'When we were introduced, I got a feeling that you wouldn't be the dismissive type.' She then glanced at her mother. 'This is going to be difficult for me because I have kept my story from the world and only shared it with folks I trust. I am a realist and understand how most people would react to my experiences. So, you need to bear with me, because I am apprehensive, and I don't know why.' She then thought about her emotions briefly. She nodded. 'The thing is, my story has to be heard and believed by everyone, and I think that is perhaps the grounds for my anxiety, maybe. The Rebecca's you spoke of, I know of at least one of them, possibly two. For their sake, my story must be told, listened to, and acted upon, or...' She again glanced at her mother, and then towards Ruth.

'You said or,' Ruth said, 'please go on.'

Not ready to mention the impending disaster, she braved a smile and said, 'I will come to that all in good time. Sorry, it has to be baby steps for me right now.'

'It is okay, Sweetie, you take as long as you need,' her mum said and squeezed Rebecca thigh under the table.

Rebecca immediately felt reassured by this gesture, which made her feel a whole lot more at ease. Over lunch, bit by bit, Rebecca explained the outline of her journey over the last ten years. Occasionally her mum and Ruth added relevant points almost as if they were trying to convince Martin.

'I get the feeling we are heading towards something more significant?' Martin said. 'Before you go any further, I will not print a word of this unless you give me express permission. I know us journalists have a bad rep and our promises are hollow. However, I sense your sincerity, Rebecca, along with Ruth and Elizabeth's genuineness. I must tell you that there will be fallout from this, and I can say that before hearing the story you want me to tell.'

'I know, Martin,' Rebecca said, still a tad unsure if she wanted her story heard just yet. 'Is there a way the story could be told without all the background, as in Meredith and co?'

Martin shook his head ever so slightly, clearly thinking. 'Right now, I am not sure. Part of me is suggesting we sell you and your background and then tell your story. On the other hand, I don't know what you are going to tell me, so it is difficult to give you an answer. I get that it's important, although England ladies playing in the football world cup is also important. Sorry if that sounds churlish, I am just trying to emphasise that I can't give you a straight answer until I know more, and I am not digging.'

'By that, I suspect David didn't allude to my actual story from the future. I am sorry, I just assumed you knew.'

Shaking his head, appearing increasingly inquisitive, he said, 'I didn't know you had ventured forward in time. That now puts a whole different spin on matters.'

'Well, best I get on with it then,' Rebecca said, suddenly feeling a little more at ease. Over the next thirty minutes, she explained every detail to Martin. Although he seemed

90

intrigued, she noticed a slight change in his persona. For some reason, as soon as she mentioned global warming, he appeared to close down a little.

'Okay,' Rebecca said, 'I get the feeling you are a little uncomfortable with the story so far.'

'I wouldn't say uncomfortable, just unsure how we are going to get this out there without a mountain of contempt coming your way. Sadly, many people are, to some degree, tired of hearing about global warming. Trust me; it is one thing publishing a story about a girl who sees the past, especially within the pages of an internationally read newspaper. However, a forewarning of a global meltdown, and doing it as a factual story may be a bridge too far.' He then paused for a moment. 'The problem is that this story of potential global doom and gloom has been done to death by activists, scientists, and outspoken individuals. I am not sure how, firstly, my boss would see this, and then secondly, how the world would see you.'

'I understand that, Martin, and thank you for your straightforwardness. I knew right from the get-go, what an uphill task I had. For all that, I must be heard. I guess it is easy for me because I know what I saw and well, this is the main reason for my anxiety. It is not caused by me being nervous about telling my tale and the aftershock, it is people not responding to it that frightens me mostly. You see, I've seen what this planet looks like devoid of human life. Do you remember the film Planet of the Apes when he walked on the beach and saw the statue of liberty with just her head and hand above the sand? Well, times that by ten.'

'I get how you both feel,' Ruth added. 'I think we all need some thinking time. Perhaps you should chat with your boss, in a roundabout way, and see what he says. And, Rebecca, the statue of liberty, I do recall that film and that image stayed with me for a long time, forever in fact.'

'I think I agree with Ruth,' Elizabeth said. 'I can see how difficult this is for you, Martin. Importantly, I can see how draining it is for Rebecca. I have always watched Rebecca, both from a distance and close up over the last few years. The hardest and most frustrating aspect of her journeys has always been getting people to listen and take her stories seriously. I too have been guilty of thinking her stories were dreams,' she said and squeezed Rebecca's arm. 'I am in a unique position too, whereby I had a similar time-lapse experience when I was young.'

Ruth, with her mouth open, said, 'Liz, you tell Rebecca then me after however many years of keeping it secret, and now you want to tell a national newspaper.'

Nodding and a little teary-eyed, Elizabeth said, 'I have only recently told Rebecca and you of my tale.' She then glanced towards Martin. 'For years, I suggested to Rebecca that her tales may have been dreams. Although that sounds a bit harsh, the reality is, I thought my jaunts into the past were dreams. I should have known better.' She then nodded. 'Had you seen the state of her when she came back from her most recent escapade, you would have known she hadn't simply been playing football with Tommy?'

'That's an important point to consider, with your son being in the public eye so prominently he will also get a backlash from this.'

With her eyes wide, Rebecca said, 'oh my goodness, that thought hadn't even occurred to me.'

'Ruth shook her head. 'Why does anyone need to know Rebecca and Tommy are related?'

'Trust me, someone somewhere will find out. Maybe not at the get-go, they will though. I must say, Rebecca, I agree with Ruth. I too recall that image, and your words have changed my point of view to some degree.'

They sat around chatting for a while longer, without really delving any more. After, they thanked Martin for his time, with Rebecca emphasising she didn't want anything printed yet. On the way back to Ruth's office, Elizabeth explained to Ruth she felt the need to mention her time in the past to back up Rebecca.

Ruth acknowledged her point of view. 'I am curious why you kept it a secret from everyone, and especially Rebecca.

'I guess what with me being so young and that it frightened me, I have hidden it away. No excuse, I know. I am now truly disappointed in myself for keeping it quiet for so long.'

'Mum, it is okay. I of all people understand. I reckon if I had only ever had the two very brief incidents with Meredith, I too may have not mentioned it and assumed it was a dream.'

'Bless you, Rebecca,' Elizabeth said and squeezed Rebecca's hand. 'I just kept convincing myself you had somehow inherited a similar dream-like state from me.' She shook her head.

'Matter not, Mother. We know now, and it's just dandy.'

At supper that evening, the subject was the heating in the summerhouse, and that finally it was up and running correctly. Emotionally exhausted, Rebecca was pleased her story was off the table, for a while at least. Having no appetite, she pushed her food around her plate in the usual way. Suddenly she was aware her mother was watching her. 'Sorry, Mum, I am just not hungry.'

'Why don't you have an early night, Rebecca? You look beat. When is Duncan back?'

'He is home on Friday, so I have a couple more days on my own. I think I will have an early one if you two are okay with that.'

'Yes, Sweetie. I could see how demanding today was for you.'

'Bless you, Rebecca. Good job you are having an early night, you'll need all your get-up-and-go once you and Duncan actually move into the Summerhouse. Then Liz and I will finally get some peace and quiet,' he said and chuckled. 'Besides, you'll need your energy, if you are going to make us Grandparents.'

'James,' Elizabeth said. 'For heaven's sake, what sort of thing is that to say?'

Laughing, Rebecca stood from the table and said, 'It is okay, Mum. I know Dad is only joking.' She then glanced at her father and opened her eyes wide. Turning back to her mother, she asked, 'do you want me to help to clear away supper?'

'No, you go get some rest, and no silly comments please James.'

Chapter 13 – Didn't See That Coming

The following morning, Rebecca was up early, even though she hadn't slept well. The meeting with Martin had left an imprint on Rebecca's thoughts and she'd woken up several times mulling over everything that had been said. After breakfast with her mum, she decided to go and sit by the lake for a while and recharge her batteries. She also wanted to have a look inside the summerhouse, especially now the heating was working, and she was due to move in soon with Duncan.

'Mum, I am going to have a wander down to the summerhouse.'

'Okay, Sweetie. No jumping around though. I am not sure I am ready to know what life will be like in ten thousand years or what we're having for supper next week,' she said, causing them both to laugh out loud.

As she made her way towards the summerhouse, she couldn't fail to notice how long the grass was. *That's odd,* she thought, knowing it had been cut only a week or so ago. The lawn between the house and the lake always grew quickly, and she had forever believed it was because it was once farmed land and as such, fertile. This rapid growth, though, was bizarre at best. From the carefully manicured lawn of a week ago, she was now wading through straw-like knee-high grass. Sensing something was obviously amiss, she paused and looked back in the direction of the main house. Everything seemed just so, apart from the inexplicable appearance of this wild field she now found herself standing in.

In a slightly spooky, but at the same time comforting way, it oddly rekindled memories of the first time she'd walked down to the lake soon after moving in. That was ten years ago, and the grass hadn't been this long since those early days. She refocused her thoughts and headed towards the summerhouse, certain there'd be a rational explanation, not that there ever was in her world. As she grew closer, she caught sight of the jetty and shook her head, unable to believe what she was looking at. In place of the new one her father commissioned just over a year ago, was the old rickety, original one. As memories of those early months flooded her thoughts, she suddenly became aware of the state of the summerhouse. If there were any doubts in her consciousness, standing looking at the tumbledown wreck of a summerhouse, she knew that somewhere between the main house and here, she was once again somewhere other than her own time.

Over the years, especially of late, she'd kind of gotten used to jumping from one era to another, as much as one could. This, though, was somewhat confusing because the main house seemed just as it should be. That was if, in fact, she'd really gone anywhere, not that she could come up with any other ideas. All the spine-jangling emotions she'd experienced that first time she wandered down this way were back and confounding her ability to think straight. She stood there for a few seconds again looking back towards the main house. She didn't really know what she was searching for, just something stable perhaps. After a few seconds, she realised once more she was trying to apply some kind of rational thinking, and that was something that had no place on any of her journeys. Annoyed with herself, she shook her head and thought, just go with it.

Refocused, she made her way along the shoreline, heading towards the summerhouse. She stared at a dilapidated veranda, unable to believe she'd tried to convince her mother it was as safe as houses, and then actually walked on it herself with total disregard. This thought made her wonder if her newly found

96

hesitancy was an age thing, which again brought the annoying rational thinking into play. She shrugged her shoulders and meaningfully, with a tad of adult caution, placed one foot up onto the wooden decking. Now standing on it with both feet, she thought, *it essentially feels okay.*

Just as she was feeling a little more composed, something made her look down. *This is plain ludicrous* she thought, staring at the self-same clothes she was wearing the day she'd met Meredith for the first time. With rational thinking out of the window and her emotions on a merry-go-round, she took a deep breath and tried to regain some level-headedness. Muttering to herself, with her thoughts all over the place, she reckoned she had to be back where it all began. *If that was the case, why,* she thought? Suddenly feeling the need to undo the top button on her old white jeans broke her attention. She laughed out loud and muttered, 'Boy, I was skinny in those days.'

In a flash though, her attention was back on the here and now. In need of some answers, she reckoned the best place to start was inside the summerhouse. She stepped forward, and as she grabbed the door handle, all the sensations of her first visit flooded her thoughts, and with that came her youthful intrepid, carefree attitude. Gone was her annoying logical thinking. Instead, she was feeling unruffled, with a somewhat excited notion to push on regardless of what may lay ahead. She turned the handle, and as the door opened, there was a familiar smell of almonds whooshing past and filling her nostrils with that oh so familiar scent of Christmas. To her, just as it had all those years before, felt and sounded like the old building was whispering to her. 'Hello, old summerhouse,' she whispered.

With her blood pumping hard, the hairs on her neck jangling, nonetheless rebelliously determined, she made her way toward the little green door at the end of the corridor. She paused momentarily to glance in the rooms either side of the hall. In a surprising, yet calming way, the rooms appeared exactly as they had the first time, she saw them. Although she was momentarily tempted to have a quick look at the old bureau inside the right-hand room, the thought of what may lay beyond the green door had a tight grip on her emotions and even if she wanted, was unable to deviate.

She headed down the hallway, stood by the door for a moment, took a deep breath and then turned the handle. It was stuck fast just as it was the first time, she tried to open this door. 'Come on Meredith, you've brought me this far, let me in.'

No sooner the last word left her lips, she felt the handle move once again on its own, and even though this approach had worked for her so often, it still always came as a surprise. While she kind of expected to see the old spiral staircase behind the door, it still oddly came as a jolt to her consciousness spotting it across the dingy, dust-filled room. She took another deep breath, trying to calm her sudden unusual level of hesitancy. 'Come on, woman. You've been here before. What's the matter with you?' she mumbled to herself.

Making her way carefully across the room, she stood at the bottom of the stairwell and peered up into the darkness. Although she reckoned, she knew what was up there, there was still a pulse-racing air of anticipation taking control of her nerves.

While she'd been here before, this was strangely different and not knowing what to expect, she climbed the stairs. She hesitated by the first door, remembering it being dark, but not so dark she couldn't see her hand in front of her face. Memory served her well though, as she leaned forward and placed her hand directly on the door handle. With her heart pumping, she turned the handle until she heard it click. That sound in itself, so clear in her memory, triggered all the emotions she had felt years earlier. Reassuring herself and regaining a little composure, she stepped into the pitch-black room. Just as it did that first time, the door pulled from her grip and once more sent her emotions spiralling. Although she'd been through this all before, the door pulling from her hand still took her right back to day one, complete with her pulse racing, her nerves jangling, and her eyes closed tightly. She kept her eyes closed for a moment, trying to recall what happened next. She didn't have to wait long.

'Rebecca is that you up there?' said a comforting and oh so familiar voice.

She opened her eyes, and everything, complete with the dandy green dress she so fondly remembered, folded neatly on the bed, and the sun blazing through the open window, was just as she remembered. The memories of her first journey that had trickled through her thoughts so often over the years, and had all become a little vague, were real once again.

'Meredith, I am up here, but I don't know what is going on,' she called out.

Seconds later, Meredith appeared at the door. 'What may I enquire, Madam, are you doing back here so soon?'

'Well, umm err...' she uttered, overexcited to see her beloved Meredith once more. Although Meredith asking what she was doing back so soon, did create a mixture of emotions. Her comment would suggest from Meredith's perspective it was just a few days since her last visit, even though that was years before.

'I see ten years on, and you are still umming and erring.'

'So, you know, but you said, so soon. I'm confused,' she said, at a loss what to think. On one hand, Meredith intimated it was soon after her last visit, yet clearly, she knew it was years earlier.

Meredith smiled. 'In my time, you were here just a day since. In your time, it has been many years. I do not know why I know this and am unclear why I suddenly have so many

99

thoughts cascading through my mind.' She shook her head in a way Rebecca hadn't seen before. 'I am not altogether certain what I am about to say to you will make any sense at all. However, I am not the apparition you saw recently, albeit that was in my future,' she said and narrowed her eyes, appearing unusually hesitant. 'However, you are with me in the here and now.' She shook her head again. 'It is of no difference, and I have no doubts there will be an echoing reason for your return.'

Although Meredith's words should have scrambled her brain even further, Rebecca felt relaxed and at ease. 'Does that mean I can have a cuddle, Meredith?'

'I would be disappointed if we were not to undertake that delight,' she said and held her arms out towards Rebecca.

As Rebecca embraced Meredith, many questions were pouring through her head. *Why am I back here*, she wondered, *why is Meredith so unusually puzzled, and how does she know it's her spirit I've seen of late even though it is years ahead of her time?*

Again, as if she'd read Rebecca's mind, Meredith said, 'your thoughts, like mine, are bemused, yet it is of no matter. All these questions you have, I have too. We are here back at the beginning, and I am certain there is an insightful and justifiable reason. Let us sit downstairs and talk,' she said, heading for the narrow stairs at the far side of the room. 'My head is suddenly full of information relating to your most recent journeys, which filled my thoughts the moment I heard your voice.' Again, her appearance and tone, although assured, seemed unusually perplexed.

As Rebecca crossed the room, she leaned over and gently touched the green dress as she passed. Delighted to be back with Meredith, she knew there was bound to be a significant reason for her return. She made her way down the stairs and wondered if perhaps she was purely here for some kind of reassurance relating to the task in front of her. Also nagging in

100

her thoughts was an odd idea that Meredith may somehow hold a key that will help her get her story out there.

She sat at the rickety kitchen table, just as she had years earlier, and considered her thoughts.

'You appear unusually deep in thought my dear, Rebecca. What may I ask is occupying your attention, as if I don't know?' She then leaned across and touched Rebecca's hand. 'I am sorry that I do not have any stale bread and mouldy cheese for you. Fortunately, and thanks to your intervention yesterday, or should I say ten years ago, we now have good food. I might add that it is food that we eat in the main house.'

'I am not altogether sure where to start,' she said, both frowning and smiling. 'I am glad the food rationing has come to an end.' Again, Rebecca smiled.

'Well, my dear, I suggest you start at the beginning. Oddly, though, I know much of that which relates to your conundrum, which is peculiar. Why I know this is beyond me, however, I do.' She then appeared to go deep into thought. This in itself wasn't too unusual, although this time, it seemed to Rebecca as if Meredith's consciousness had left the room. She sat and watched as Meredith's eyes flitted around the room in the most unfamiliar way, clearly without focussing on anything. 'Okay, so the most bizarre thought has just entered my awareness. My grandson thrice will be a prominent parliamentarian in your time. Why this thought has entered my head, creates many questions. Importantly, how I could possibly know of this person is beyond reasonable thinking. These, I am sure will be answered once I know your full story.'

Trying to take on board all that Meredith had just said, alongside being back where it all started, left Rebecca feeling a tad confounded. Knowing she had to focus her thoughts, she started at the beginning of her most recent journey into the future. Over the next hour or so, she explained everything in detail, taking time to clarify some of her modern-day terminologies.

'So, in essence, mankind will burn the planet, using phosphorus fuels I know nothing of. Is that the right word?' she said, once again narrowing her eyes. 'Although much of that which you said is at best gobbledygook, I do understand the pretext.'

'I am sorry if I have confused you, Meredith. That is the right word, incidentally.'

'Matter not, my dear. I do now though understand why I know of my grandson thrice. Clearly, the world needs to understand, and more importantly hear, then consequently act upon your message.'

'Hmm, grandson thrice, what does that even mean?'

'It means my great, great, great, grandson.' She said and chuckled. 'If my math is correct, he, and why I know his name is beyond me, however, David Wilson, will be, or should I say, is alive in your time.'

Unable to believe that Meredith had just mentioned David Wilson, Rebecca sat there with her mouth open. 'Umm, err,' she uttered in her usual way.

'Oh, how delightful to hear your umming and erring again. So, my dear Rebecca, we need to concoct a plan.'

Nodding, Rebecca's focus returned to some degree, but she couldn't get past the name. 'Err, correct me if I am wrong, but did you just say, David Wilson? I ask because I know of a David Wilson in my time and he is indeed a parliamentarian.' She then narrowed her eyes and with her focus now totally on the job in hand, she said, 'I know exactly what we need to do. I have done it before, and it worked.'

'I did indeed say, David Wilson,' she said and shook her head. 'In the most peculiar way, I now understand why I know his name and comprehend the importance.' She then appeared to go deep into thought again, as if she were considering her own words. 'So, back to our mission, I suggest. You said you know exactly what to do and have done it before. Would you please enlighten me further? Unlike earlier, I know nothing of this, which is odd as my mind is full of information I did not possess before your arrival here this day.' She then shook her head, again as if she were considering her own words. 'Today has been, shall we say, adventurously new for me. Not I suspect, as daringly audacious as it has and will continue to be for you, my beloved Rebecca.'

Rebecca smiled and nodded, although once again, the urgency of what lay ahead was now dictating her every thought. 'Well, in nineteen-eleven, I had to write, and then hide a note for my father. I should explain that it was a note that needed to stay in place, untouched until my time. Then, I could retrieve it from its hiding place and hand it to my father. After a lot of careful planning, I chose to hide it in the old bureau, the one in the study. The reason I chose it was because it was there in nineteen-eleven and would still be there in my era.' She then explained all about the incident with the boiler and had it not been fixed, could have resulted in her mother's death. Then a thought popped into her head that the tallboy may not be there in Meredith's time, even though it was ancient.

Nodding, Meredith exclaimed, 'the bureau you refer to in the corner of the study was only delivered a week since. That is if indeed we are referring to the same cabinet. A tall oak affair around twenty inches square with several small drawers.'

The two of them spent a few moments establishing they were talking about the same piece of furniture.

'As delightful as it is to know that the cabinet is still there in your time and that it served you so well with yours and your mother's horrid potential dilemma, I fail to see how it could help us this day.'

'Well, here's the thing, your grandson thrice,' she said and grinned, 'works with my mother's oldest friend and bizarrely...' She shook her head. 'I spoke with him a few days ago about my story, in fact, yesterday.'

'I suspect that was not received too well. I know this and perhaps should have told you earlier, albeit it was not previously significant. My beloved Aunt Rebekah told the same tragic tale regarding the plight of our planet many years before we met. This was the catalyst for her final condemnation and subsequent banishment to The Americas.' She bowed her head slightly. 'Poor soul, she was right about all she uttered, she was. Mores the pity, no one could see what she could see. I must admit that even I, although I was a child, raised my eyes to her suggestion that by way of substances that had yet to be invented or used, mankind would destroy our home.'

'I am sorry, Meredith,' she said and squeezed her hand gently, able to feel this woman's anguish. 'I am struggling to get my head around the fact that I met your future ancestor. And, spoke to him about that same subject your aunt spoke to you about previously. Two hundred years prior to me, I might add. That is, and will I suspect, continue to be bizarre.' She shook her head again.

'Somehow we need to leave a letter that will be read in your time by David Wilson. The letter writing will be the easy part. I will just explain that you will visit him on a certain day with news of future events that he must take seriously.' She then nodded. 'Now, how and where can we leave it in a place whereby it will remain unopened and intact? Moreover, David will take it seriously and act upon your words.'

'Perhaps your husband, George, can leave it in a vault at the bank with express conditions that it should only be opened by

David Wilson on a certain day. Plus, the bank has specific instructions to inform David that he has to attend the bank on the said date of our choosing. That's a plan, I think,' she said and chuckled nervously.

'It does indeed sound like a complete plan. We now need to work out which bank from my time will be there in your time.'

Shaking her head, Rebecca said, 'perhaps the Bank of England?'

'We have the Bank of England, and coincidently, George's brother works in the City of London at the Bank of England.' She then shook her head. 'Although I should be astounded by this uncanny coincidence, and how seamlessly this is all joining together, for some reason I am not.'

Over the next twenty minutes or so, and after considerable word changing, they put together a letter for David. Meredith then assured Rebecca that she would make sure the letter would be in place, at the bank, in readiness for her time. They then set a date for the letter to be opened on the 15th May 2013, which will be the day after tomorrow in Rebecca's time. This would importantly allow Rebecca time to get back and then make arrangements.

'I am just thinking aloud here, Meredith. I am trying to work out how I can bridge the subject of the letter with David. Although thinking about it, I do not need to because if this letter works, as it should, he will be contacting me. Well, you would hope so, especially as he already knows of my story.'

'All we can do is to try our best. Besides, if it does not work, I have no doubts you will be back.'

The two chatted for a little while longer, then cuddled, and said their goodbyes. Just as Rebecca was about to head off, alarm bells started ringing, knowing what was about to happen to Millicent in a few days. For a moment, she wondered if telling Meredith that Millicent was about to commit suicide and

Meredith would subsequently be charged with her murder would somehow interfere with history. Mulling this over for a few seconds, she could see Meredith staring at her.

'Meredith, there is something essential I need to tell you.'

Meredith narrowed her eyes in an oddly, yet obviously insightful way. 'For some reason, on this day, I have been able to know much of which you are thinking. This time though, my subconscious is drawing a blank, other than I should not know what you are about to impart to me. Therefore, I would suggest there is a reason, and I believe this means I should not know.' She then appeared to think deeply. 'I suspect whatever it is you are about to tell me may change our destiny, and perhaps our paths may not cross as a result. Therefore, I suggest you allow whatever it is to play out the way it has always played out.'

'But,' she uttered, knowing how much turmoil Millicent's death would cause. Then suddenly the penny dropped. 'Perhaps you are right,' she said, realising that if Millicent didn't follow the path she did, Meredith's spirit would not have been in limbo. Therefore, there would be no reason for her to travel back to Meredith's time to help settle her soul. She nodded, 'you are right, as you always are, Meredith.'

The two bid their farewells and cuddled again. Rebecca took one last look and then headed back upstairs and across the bedroom where it all started. She stood at the door leading to the spiral stairs, gripping the handle. She shook her head, realising she hadn't ventured home this way often and when she had, it was always complicated. In the past, many of her journeys back, irrespective of her route, invariably had a twist of sorts, whereas this was unusually seamless. With that thought now resonating with her, she tentatively opened the door and made her way downstairs, feeling a little unsure, not knowing what to expect next. At the bottom of the stairs, now in total darkness, she stood by the door leading out. After a few seconds and one more glance up the stairs, she took a deep breath and fumbled the handle. Click, it opened. Although this should have settled her nerves, it, in reality, put her on edge a little more, wondering if she would be back home, or somewhere else. 'Too easy,' she muttered.

She stepped outside onto the veranda and glanced up at the window. For some bizarre reason, she was expecting to see Meredith. For a brief second she thought she saw the curtain move, then as quickly dismissed it, knowing in Meredith's time, this window wasn't actually there.

She shook her head and made her way along the shoreline and back towards the main house. For some peculiar reason, although in no doubt she was home, something wasn't quite right. She stopped by the jetty, which was once again new and glanced back at the summerhouse. Again, it was back to its sparkling self. She stood there for a moment trying to make her mind up if she preferred it new, or the ramshackle wreck she'd found all those years ago. She shook her head and made her way towards the main house. All the way up the hill, everything looked and felt right, although there was still something nagging at the back of her mind. This train of thought continued all the way up to the front door.

'My word, that was quick, Rebecca,' her mum called out.

'It might have been for you, Mum. I have been back to Meredith and where it all started. Madness, but I was there ten years ago, even to the point where...' she then looked down at her clothes and although pleased, was nonetheless a little surprised to see she was back in the outfit she had on when she'd left home earlier.

'To which point, Rebecca?' her mother asked, standing by the kitchen door, lowering her glasses, with a familiar look of suspicion.

'Well, I walked down to the summerhouse, and when I got there, it was back to being ramshackle. So, I went in, opened the little green door, met Meredith in eighteen-fifty-three, and unbelievably, I was dressed in the clothes I was in the first time I met her,' she said and took a deep breath. 'I might add, my white jeans were a little tight,' she chuckled.

Smiling her mum said, 'It's a long time since I've heard you talk at a hundred miles per hour. So, tell me more, once you've got your breath back.'

Over the next few minutes, Rebecca explained every detail. Often, she hesitated as her mother's eyes narrowed, wondering what she was thinking. Briefly, she found herself half expecting the annoying daydream suggestion, but dismissed that quickly, knowing her mother had left that a long way back. When she paused for a moment to consider this, she realised her thoughts were perhaps contaminated by her expectancy of what may lay ahead. She knew full well she was likely to face some kind of condemnation, with suggestions that she probably dreamt the whole thing. Just then she realised her mum was speaking. 'Sorry, Mother, what did you say?'

'I knew you weren't listening,' she said and chuckled. 'Well, let's hope the letter works. I really can't believe we have to wait two flipping days to find out.' She then blinked her eyes a couple of times. 'I am truly excited now and ready to bat away any stupid dream suggestions that any narrow-minded individual even considers offering up.' She then pointed at herself and shook her head.

Rebecca smiled, annoyed for even considering her mum may think anything along those lines, certainly, since she'd opened up and told of her own time in the past.

Rebecca went to bed that evening thinking about her mum's story and how hard it must have been for her to hold on to her tale for all these years. Feeling tearful, considering what her mother had gone through as a result of telling her father and the suffering she experienced as a result made her appreciate just how lucky she was to have the understanding of her parents.

108

Chapter 14 – Next Steps

The next two days dragged by for Rebecca. It was now Thursday, the day she hoped to hear from David Wilson. With a mixture of excitement and trepidation, she was up early and sitting downstairs in the kitchen waiting for a phone call from Ruth or perhaps David himself. Moments later, her mum walked in.

'Hello, Sweetie, you're up early, not that I am surprised. I have to say, it was the last thing I thought about as I went to sleep and the first thing that came to mind this morning.'

'Mum, it is the fifteenth of May, isn't it?'

'Check your phone, Rebecca.'

'Damnations,' Rebecca blurted.

'Whatever is the matter? And no swearing please, or it is carbolic soap for you, Missy, twenty-four or not.'

Rebecca shook her head. 'I knew something was wrong when I came back.'

'Out with it, cat, curiosity, and all that,' her mum said with her eyes wide open.

'I left my phone on Meredith's table.'

'What, in eighteen whenever it was?'

'Yep, in a nutshell,' she said, nodding. 'You know, it never occurred to me, even when Meredith kept looking at it in a funny way. It was off, so she may have just thought it was...' Then out of the blue, a bizarre idea occurred to her. She jumped up and headed out of the kitchen. 'Two ticks,' she called out from the study door, only to turn and see her mother right behind her.

'Where are we going, Rebecca? I don't want to miss this.'

Rebecca walked into the study and over to her father's Tallboy, 'I told Meredith this was still here in our time. I have an idea,' she said as she opened the little draw. She screamed, 'my phone, she is a girl, that Meredith. My phone, which I took with me for the first time ever, left it there and well, here it is.' She shook her head. 'This is just mental, it is still on thirty-eight percent too, and that's exactly what it was two days ago. How can that be?'

'Well, maybe you left it at home, and Dad put it in here.'

'Please do not dare go down the rational excuses' road, Mum. Besides, even if I had left it at home, why would Dad put it in this drawer? Anyways, it would not still be on thirty-eight blinking percent.' She scratched the side of her forehead. 'And that just makes it even more ludicrous. In two days, it would have lost its charge, let alone over one hundred and sixty years.' She then put both hands over her cheek and exaggerated blinking her eyes as she shook her head. 'I've seen some things over the last few years. Never will I get used to these mad, absurdly outlandish twists. It is no wonder everyone struggles with my stories, especially when they even shock me.'

'I must admit, even by your standards, this is a little too far to the left.' She shook her head. 'So, is it the fifteenth?'

Nodding, Rebecca said, 'missed a call too, from an unknown phone number. I wonder if that was David.' Staring at her mum, she rang the number back, and seconds later huffed. 'Some stupid sales call, I hate them. We'd be better off without these nuisance calls, and that's a fact.' She shook her head again. 'I am going to give Ruth a call. See if she knows anything.' After a brief chat with Ruth, she came off the phone.

'So, curious cat again,' her mum said, with her palms raised.

'He is in Brussels and won't be back for two days. That's a bloody nuisance. I am not sure I can wait that long.' She then followed her mum into the kitchen and after a chat, some toast and coffee, she said, 'I am going for a walk, Mum.'

'Down to see Meredith, perhaps? Hey, maybe you could travel forward two days into the future and speak to David. By the way, Madam, I am serious about the swearing. It does not suit you, and besides, you're far too intelligent and need not resort to those words, frustrated or not.'

'Well, you never know,' she said and chuckled, 'Na, just down by the lake, and maybe have a walk in the woods. I will see you in a while. And I know you're right about swearing, Mum, just so frustrating.'

'Be careful, her mum said and kissed Rebecca on the cheek.

'I will, Mum, see you in a while.'

Chapter 15 – Where This Time

As Rebecca wandered down towards the lake, everything seemed just so. *No jaunts today*, she thought. She sat for a while by the summerhouse, thinking about finally moving in with Duncan. Looking across the lake, all thoughts of David's expected call evaporated as memories of her time with Matilda flooded her head. After a while, she started thinking about where she'd found the key all those years ago. With a bright blue spring sky, and the sun becoming increasingly hot, she decided to go and have a look at the old fallen oak and get some shade under the beautiful tree canopy.

Heading through the woods, thoughts of her first time here brought a smile to her face. Moments after she'd entered the clearing where the old oak was, she heard an oddly familiar voice singing. Although she suspected she had gone somewhere in time, she was a little edgy having previously thought nothing was afoot today. Strangely, everything seemed just so, and besides, she hadn't gotten any of the usual warning signs, or vibes that proceeded a jump through time. She stood there listening, confident she knew the voice but at the same time was drawing a blank on who it was.

Listening carefully, the voice seemed to be getting closer. She peered through the trees, trying to get a glimpse of whoever it was, when she heard another voice. This time, she knew exactly who it was, albeit the voice sounded very young. 'Meredith,' she called out. There was an eerie silence, which kind of increased her uneasiness. She called again, 'Meredith, is that you?'

'I am here,' said a voice from behind her.

Rebecca shook her head sure the singing voice was coming from the other side of the coppice. She turned to be greeted by a very young-looking Meredith, standing beside her Aunt Rebekah.

'Hello,' the little girl said, holding out her hand. 'Have you come to visit with my aunt and me again?'

Rebecca squeezed the little girl's hand. 'Hello Meredith, hello Rebekah,' she said and smiled. In the back of her thoughts, she was wondering why she was here. Then it came to her, recalling that Meredith told her that her aunt also foretold of mankind's demise. Feeling oddly comfortable, but at the same time curious, and a tad edgy, she leant her back against the fallen tree. 'I met with your older...' she said and hesitated. Her rational side was suggesting it might not be that simple to explain yesterday's visit to this child's older self. She reckoned Meredith was no more than six or seven and may not know what lies ahead or be able to comprehend that they will meet in the future.

Meredith held her hand up, 'I understand that you met with my older self. I do not know why I know this, I do though.' She then chuckled, and although Rebecca could see the older woman in her, and in spite of her obvious understanding of what was going on, still felt she had to be mindful of her choice of words.

Rebekah smiled. 'I too know, although I know everything, as do you.' She glanced around the clearing. 'I am only surprised Ethernel is not here with us. Today is a significant day for us. In a few days, I am going to the Americas.' She shook her head. 'You, my dear future friend will be my solace, and I will take today's events with me, in my thoughts and heart, knowing my work is done.' She then again glanced around the clearing, as if she was looking beyond the trees. 'If what I know is right, he should be here today.'

A little taken aback by Rebekah's words, but at the same time oddly reassured, Rebecca considered her emotions. In an odd way, she also felt today carried an important and significant meaning, not that she knew why, she just did. What she knew for sure was that she wasn't here just to chat with Meredith and Rebekah. 'Rebekah, you say you think something significant is going to happen today. Do you know what?'

Shaking her head, without making eye contact and still staring into the trees, or beyond, as was her way, she said, 'No. I just know it will be something that will give meaning to my life's vision, and it will happen today.' She then turned and made direct eye contact. 'Most would not comprehend or understand this. You, my dear Rebecca do, as does my niece, in spite of her youth. That is and will forever be enough for me. Aside from my beloved niece, Meredith, and of course Ethernel, you are the only person who truly knows and appreciates the journey I have travelled. In your time, Rebecca, I know it is a little easier for you to tell of your visions. I do also appreciate that you too have faced adverse reactions. This may continue for you for a while longer. I suspect that, although it is not clear, today's events will shape and help pave the way forward for you. We must tell mankind of the horrors that lay ahead for them unless they act soon.'

Hearing Rebekah speak so clearly and unaffected by her future, something she suspected this woman knew only too well, helped her feel better about Rebekah's sad plight and came as a relief. She glanced at Meredith, comforted by the fact that young or not, she seemed to be taking everything in her stride. For some odd reason though, she felt a little concerned whatever was about to happen, may be a bridge too far for one so young. She didn't know what was causing her

114

trepidation though, and this in itself, created a touch of apprehension.

'I am going to say something to you now, Rebecca, although I do not know why I feel the need to say this,' Rebekah said.

Meredith nodded. 'I too am duty-bound to say something, and I also do not know why.'

'Meredith, you tell me first,' Rebecca said and again squeezed the young girl's hand.

'I must hurry to see my mother shortly, so must leave you alone and that is all I need to say.'

Nodding, Rebekah said, 'How very peculiar, because I too was about to suggest Meredith needs to visit with her mother shortly. Although I am bamboozled why I feel the need to say this, I am also certain that this will unfold as part of the planned events that lay ahead for us this day.'

'I have noticed during our recent meetings together that you,' she said making eye contact with Meredith, 'have been able to read my thoughts and see that which is about to happen.' She shook her head. 'I suspect, like you both, that this bizarre journey we follow will forever amaze and confound us.' Suddenly, a thought occurred to Rebecca that they were now in or around 1823 and that the tree was still standing in that time. With shivers running the length of her body, she turned around. 'What,' she blurted.

'Whatever is the matter, Rebecca?'

Pointing at the oak tree, which was somehow standing, even though she had only a moment before rested against its fallen trunk, she uttered, 'I just do not understand this.' Seeing the inquisitive look on both Meredith's and Rebekah's faces, she nodded. 'I best explain,' she said, unable to believe what she was about to say. 'This tree,' she said, touching its trunk, 'had fallen when I got here and indeed, I leant back against its trunk only a moment ago when we first spoke.' She shook her head.

'You in fact leant against the bench,' Meredith said, appearing unusually confused while pointing at the bench.

'Now that is just plain daft. I was certain when I got here the tree was fallen and then I heard you singing, Rebekah.' Nodding, as it all fell into place, she said, 'I get it. When I got here and saw the fallen tree, I was still in my time. Then I heard you singing, you came over, and I leant back thinking I was leaning against the tree when in reality...' she nodded. 'That's the only explanation, and I think I am going to run with that.'

The three chatted for a little while longer. In particular, they talked about Rebekah's vision of the future. In a comforting way, this assured Rebecca that they had both witnessed the identical scenario. Then, from the direction of the summerhouse, there was a voice calling Meredith.

'That is my mother,' Meredith said. 'I am late and best hurry.' She then cuddled Rebekah, before turning to Rebecca. 'Can I cuddle you also?'

Holding her arms out, Rebecca said, 'I would be disappointed if we did not have a hug.'

'I will see you again, of that I am certain.' She then kissed both on the cheek and hurried in the direction of the calling voice. Just as she reached the edge of the clearing, she turned and blew a kiss.

Both Rebecca and Rebekah went to speak simultaneously.

'You first,' Rebekah said.

'I can feel the mood, or vibe has suddenly changed since Meredith left. It really is quite odd and rather unnerving.'

116

Rebecca narrowed her eyes and glanced around not really knowing what she was looking for.

'I too feel similar to you.' She also glanced around with a somewhat vague appearance. 'This is most peculiar, the likes of which I have never felt before. I knew something was afoot today, and it was something significant. This though is most bizarre and out of the ordinary.'

'It is weird that's for sure. Do you feel hot?' Rebecca asked, feeling uncomfortably warm. At once, it reminded her of her time in the future, although that was a damp, sweaty heat, whereas this was a dry, arid heat.

Nodding, Rebekah said, 'for sure, I too feel flushed. It is as if the sun is blazing upon us. Clearly, it is not,' she said, glancing up at the tree canopy shading them.

Chapter 16 – Really

The two sat there chatting for a moment about the sudden change in temperature, which most bizarrely seemed to be on the increase. In the back of Rebecca's mind, she was wondering if the two of them had travelled together and if so, what may lie ahead. Suddenly, the grass she was standing on felt unusually soft underfoot. She glanced down, and everything appeared just so, even though it clearly wasn't. She banged her foot on the ground a couple of times, and instantly her shoes covered in a cloud of yellowy dust. *That's odd*, she thought, knowing this area was damp even in the middle of summer. Besides, they'd had the most awful winter, with it raining virtually every day during January and February. Only a few days earlier, she'd sat on the grass nearby and got a soggy backside. She knelt down to examine the ground, and as she did, could feel Rebekah looking at her.

She glanced up. 'Sorry, Rebekah. This ground feels odd.' Then a thought occurred to her, realising it didn't matter what sort of winter she'd had in her own time, she was in 1823 or thereabout. 'What kind of winter have you had?'

'Incessant rain, which makes this...' She knelt down next to Rebecca. 'This ground is bone dry, how can that be?' She then grasped a clump of grass and pulled it out easily. Frowning, she examined its roots. 'This soil is sandy. Normally, it is peat-like and too damp to kneel on. Besides, where is the moss?' she asked, looking around.

'This is just daft. I suspect like me, you've had some bizarre experiences on this road we share. Nonetheless, I am never surprised by how often I am taken aback by sudden changes. I am sure, from what you've said, you also travelled into the future when the Earth was so intensely hot. This is a different heat, almost desert-like.' It suddenly occurred to Rebecca that she was chatting with this woman as if she'd known her all her life. 'It is uncanny you know, the way we've talked openly, right from the first moment we met, it's as if we were lifelong friends, which we are of course.' She then squeezed Rebekah's hand.

'It is a different heat, and oddly you are right, it is desert-like, although I have only read about deserts.' She then looked deeply into Rebecca's eyes as if she was looking into her soul. 'I too feel I am with a lifelong friend and confidante. For sure, I have young Meredith by my side. However, your appearance in my world has given my essence a meaning, purpose, and direction that I never had before. For that, I thank you with all of me.'

'Thank you for those beautiful words and thoughts. I too have gained strength from our coming together today.' She glanced down and considered how today's events will be with her forever. She then looked up and smiled. 'So, I went to Oman sometime back, and this reminds me of the way plants were somehow clinging to life, unless they were near a river or such like. The heat is similar too, arid to the point where it tastes dry.' With her focus back on where they were, she shook her head. Her confused thoughts were going in circles wondering where this sudden climate change was taking them. 'So, tell me again, Rebekah, how did you feel when you travelled to the future?' As she sat down, she said, 'The grass is almost changing before our eyes, very odd. It appears almost straw-like now.' She shook her head, aware the environment seemed to be changing gradually. Whenever she'd jumped anywhere, it had been relatively instant, even when she found herself a thousand years into the future. This was different

119

from anything she'd ever known, and she reckoned it was probably the same for Rebekah. 'This is most odd, because it is as if the world is changing around us, slowly. Have you ever experienced a change like this before, Rebekah?'

'I was thinking the identical thoughts, although we should not be surprised by this, being of the same body, mind and spirit. In answer to your question, I have not experienced anything like this before. In the past, if I moved from winter to summer, the change was instant. This is most irregular.'

The two then sat on what was left of the now straw-like grass, comparing their experiences in the future. It was clear to both they had gotten the same message, with the one difference being Rebecca had found the tablet in the remnants of her home, something that would serve no purpose to someone living in the 1820s.

'I believe it reasonable to assume we are on a journey together, seemingly to a time or place neither of us have seen before. The odd thing though, this is unlike any other trip I've been on previously. Normally, I get a very distinct, familiar vibe in the back of my thoughts. This time, there was nothing other than this ludicrously mad change in the environment.' She then noticed Rebekah was looking down, appearing a little tearful. 'Whatever is the matter?' she asked, touching Rebekah on the back of her hand.

With tears in her eyes, but somehow forcing a smile, she looked up. 'My uncle, the one who has arranged for my departure to The Americas used that exact term when describing me.' She then looked away again. 'He referred to me as ludicrously mad.'

'Oh my gosh, I am so sorry, Rebekah. I don't know what to say.' She shook her head several times, acutely aware how difficult life was for this poor soul. 'I really should have been more considerate, especially as I know your sad tale of condemnation. To think, I get cross or upset when someone refers to my visions as imaginative make-believe or worse still, dreams.'

Nodding, she smiled again, this time appearing less troubled. 'I know what you mean. I too am subconsciously forewarned when I am about to journey. This is most dissimilar, and I am suspecting it may be because of the gradual change in the surroundings,' she said and giggled in an almost childlike way. 'Like you, I always get this peculiar, yet familiar sensation each time I am going somewhere. However, this is most strange. In the past, I have jumped instantly from one era to the next, although I have always known something was afoot. Today, I knew nothing of the approaching change until you appeared. Most strange, our movement appears to be happening gradually. As you said earlier, it is indeed changing before our eyes. This grass now appears lifeless.' She shook her head, and without looking up from the grass, said, 'in the past, I have only ever travelled alone. You by my side is creating the most bizarre emotion for me.'

'Oddly, my common sense is suggesting we believe we are going somewhere because of the change in the soil and grass. Especially as neither of us felt the usual emotions. My gut and less rational side though, in spite of the missing vibe, sensation, whatever we call it, is telling me something is most definitely on the horizon, if it hasn't already happened. The question is what?' Her thoughts were now going from Rebekah's life of turmoil, the change in the soil, and wondering where this gradual transformation would take them. 'I am not sure how I feel at the moment. For some odd reason, it is leaving me a tad on edge. Perhaps wherever we are going, there is a good reason for the steady change. I really do not know what to think or make of it all. I feel uncomfortably comfortable if that even makes sense.' Rebecca then looked down, trying to get to grips with what might be happening.

'You appear deep in contemplation, Rebecca. What, may I ask, are your thoughts?'

'I am just speculating,' she responded, and then from the corner of her eye, something jolted her consciousness. She turned and gasped. Pointing in the direction of the oak, she uttered, 'Where's the oak? It is one thing that it had fallen when I got here, and then was standing seconds later, but now...'

'Oh my, I've gone all goosy ganders,' Rebekah said, standing up. 'There is no sign of it.' She then rubbed her arms, exactly the way Rebecca does during this kind of bizarre scenario.

Rebecca stood beside her. 'What is going on? How can a tree that is the best part of five hundred years old, or more, just vanish? Hang on a minute,' she said peering beyond the area where the tree was originally standing. To get a closer look, she stepped over a fallen branch, catching it with her foot. Instead of moving or tripping her, it disintegrated as if made from dust. She turned and glanced at Rebekah who was looking equally confused. She beckoned her with her eyes and headed towards a large peculiar looking plant a little way off. She took a few steps forward and again trampled on a branch, which again crumbled underfoot. She paused for a moment trying to focus on whatever it was that had caught her initial attention. For a second, she was sure she had seen it move, whatever it was. She turned to Rebekah. 'I am not sure if I am seeing things, but that odd-looking plant just moved.'

Nodding, she said, 'It did move, and I am now considering it may not be a plant at all.' She then turned to look back and gasped a child-like cry. With her mouth open, she grabbed Rebecca's arm and pointed.

'What,' Rebecca said, looking back towards the clearing. In place of the green lush tree-lined area was sand as far as the eye could see. With her nerves rattling, she glanced at Rebekah and as she did, noticed several palm-like trees to her left. With her mouth open, she turned Rebekah around and indicated with her hand. As she did, she again spotted the plant, which she'd initially seen, and it was definitely moving. With her brain now on overload, she stood there for a moment trying to regain a little perspective, if that was at all possible. She then shook her head, realising what she was looking at was in fact, a camel overloaded with straw-like pampas. Unable to speak, she again pulled at Rebekah's arm.

Shaking her head, appearing both confused and excited, she mumbled, 'whatever is that creature?'

Jumbling the words in her head, realising she may not know of a camel, Rebecca was unsure what to say. 'Err, umm, it is something called a camel, and we normally associate them with desert areas in North Africa and the Middle East. Countries such as Oman, Yemen, Egypt, Syria and Jordon, are the places you would expect to see such creatures.' She could see Rebekah appeared a little confused. 'So, these animals are used like horses and are for carrying people and goods from one area to another. The countries I mentioned are mostly covered in desert-like terrain, which are intensely hot, and have an arid environment. Just like...' She shook her head, scarcely able to believe her own thoughts. '...the area we are clearly in now.' It was one thing changing time zones, but never had she left the grounds of her parent's home, other than with Queen Matilda, and that was on foot. This though was a completely new level and to say her consciousness was scrambled would barely cover her emotions.

Nodding, she said, 'I understand, although I have not heard of a couple of the countries you mentioned. Matter not. I know the area that you refer to as the cradle of civilisation and the birthplace of the Bible. I was reading an encyclopaedia recently, and if we are referring to the same area, it is where mankind first started to read, write, and make laws.' She then narrowed her eyes. 'I believe it was once called Mesopotamia. Interestingly, many a strong woman lived in this world, with men being advocates for their abilities and their place at the top of society. This is unlike the world in which I live,' Rebekah said and then lowered her head.

123

'I know of this too and was reading an extract from the bible all about this area. It is interesting because I decided to do some research when I discovered you spell your name differently to me.' She nodded, 'It refers to Rebekah as being the wife of Isaac who was in turn the son of Abraham and Sarah. Incidentally, in my time woman are major players in the world and have a voice, a loud one at that.' She shook her head as the most bizarre thought entered her head.

'Whatever has occurred to you?

'I am not altogether sure.'

As if she was aware Rebecca was a little uneasy, she touched her gently on the arm. 'I too was reading the same pages of the Bible, for the same reason.' She then narrowed her eyes, just the way Meredith often did. 'Do you think...?' She then shook her head. 'Now that is a mad thought,' she said and chuckled nervously.

Guessing Rebekah was on the same page as her, she said, 'I thought the same thing. However, in the past, I have never left home ground when on my jaunts, other than on foot. For sure, I or should I say we, jumped a thousand years into the future when hereabouts looked like another planet, let alone another country. The idea of us somehow jumping not just back four thousand years, but to another continent is indeed outlandish.' Unable to believe what she just said, she shook her head. She then noticed Rebekah was beaming a radiant smile. She looked at her in a questioning manner.

'How very exciting though if we have indeed jumped back to not only the birthplace of the Bible but to have a chance to meet the people that have been written and read about for thousands of years.' She then looked around, once more superficially staring at nothing. 'I am feeling an odd sensation as if something is afoot. Oddly though, I feel it is for me, not you.' She narrowed her eyes. 'I feel compelled to tell you that

124

our meeting today has given my life a tangible meaning and for that, I will forever be grateful.'

'That must be a strange sensation and there really is no need to thank me, because meeting you has also given my life providence.' Rebecca then rubbed the hairs on her arm, which were standing up as if she'd had an electric shock. She then looked up. 'Rebekah, where are you?' she called, looking around. With no sign of her anywhere, she again called out. There was no response. With her eyes scanning all around, and absolutely no sign of Rebekah, she suddenly felt a tinge of sadness mixed with real concern. If indeed, they had travelled back to the birthplace of mankind, she was sad that her newly found confidante was not here to share this journey. She considered this for a moment or two and as she had so often in the past, both hoped and reckoned it was part of a bigger plan. Suddenly, she heard a woman's voice, which although it sounded like Rebekah, clearly wasn't. Then the voice came again, and she knew for sure it wasn't Rebekah.

'Marhabaan kayf halik.'

Rebecca turned and standing right in front of her was the most startlingly beautiful woman. She was barely able to take her eyes off this woman's face. Her jet-black hair and pale olive skin enhanced her almost translucent, crystal-like caramel eyes. When she did glance down, she was invigorated by this woman's full-length wrap-around turquoise shawl. Her eyes flitted back and forth between the woman's face and her clothing. She briefly became preoccupied with her short dark blue jacket, which was adorned with multicoloured sequins and the most intricate lace embroidery. Both jacket and shawl had a wonderful shimmery, almost satin effect. Rebecca stared, as both jacket and shawl seemed to change colour as this woman moved. Aware she was acting impolite, she looked directly at the woman and smiled.

The woman now with a slight grin, bowed her head slightly and said, 'Marhabaan kayf halik.'

125

For some bizarre reason, Rebecca knew this meant, hello, how are you. As pieces started to knit together, she reckoned she had perhaps somehow transported to the Middle East. In fact, she was certain she had. She had learnt a few Arabic words at university and was beginning to think they might now come in handy. Stretching her memory, she offered up, 'ana ribika, saeid limuqabalatik,' which she believed said, "Hello, I am Rebecca, pleased to meet you."

Again, the woman bowed her head slightly. 'Bishakl ghyr mutawaqae, 'ana 'aerif kayf 'atahadath lughtik.'

Rebecca shook her head. This was a bridge too far for her limited understanding of Arabic. With her brain going in circles, still with thoughts of Rebekah, and where she had vanished to, she offered up, 'ana murtabik,' which her friend had told her to say if she gets stuck.

The woman smiled and leant forward touching Rebecca gently on the cheek. Her touch left her feeling as if she had been caressed by someone otherworldly. To compound her emotions, in the most bizarre way, she experienced a tangible innocence resonating from this princess of a woman. With her mouth open, Rebecca uttered, 'umm, err,' and was instantly annoyed for doing so.

'Matter not my treasure from a life beyond mine. I knew that one day you would visit my world. For an inexplicable reason, I am able to speak in your tongue. This is most curious. To my thoughts, I hear my chosen words, yet I also hear your most unusual language resonating from my mouth.' Appearing a tad bemused, although still with the grace she was clearly born with, she nodded. 'I am Rebekah from Mesopotamia, an area you would perhaps know as Middle Asia. However, I have suspicions you already know this. You can speak freely as it seems I will comprehend your chosen words, although I know not why or how.'

126

Still enamoured by this woman's elegance and radiant sophistication, Rebecca shook her head inwardly, knowing she was perhaps appearing rude and really needed to focus. 'You seem to know of me and know that I am from a time beyond yours.'

'I have waited many eons for your appearance in my world. I have known since I was a child you would one day come to me from four millennia, burdened with a heavy tale. I also know we are of the same creation, whereby we see beyond the observable. We see, perceive, and can examine the past and future. I have many questions for you, as I am sure you have for me. We can take some refreshment and while we do, I suggest we lay a plan, moreover, diagram your next steps. Once we have a map for your forward movement, we can share each of our lives narrative.'

Chapter 17 - Mesopotamia

The woman beckoned Rebecca towards a round building that had light brown sides and appeared to be roofed with some kind of bamboo and straw. As Rebecca followed the woman inside, she touched the sandy like walls and was astonished how cool they were. She then noticed the woman indicating for her to sit on a lavish tapestry-like carpet, woven in every variant of red, green, and orange. As she approached the woman, Rebecca's eyes flitted along some bronze-like shelving, lined with wonderfully flamboyant ornaments, the likes of which, she'd only seen in a museum. Another woman then appeared, apparently oblivious to Rebecca's clothes and general appearance. She nodded politely to both of them and then poured a hot liquid from an elaborate, pear-shaped glass affair into tiny delicate glasses. The woman then nodded again, somewhat subserviently and left without uttering a word.

'She is my first aide and a close confidante. I have told her of your coming and hence her unsuspecting acceptance of you. I offer for your understanding, she is a trusted advocate who knows of my vision, alongside my husband, Isaac. Not even my progeny, Jacob and Esau know of my images of the past and future. As I am certain in your life, our breed is not viewed with an open schema. Hence, this is why I have a limited confidential and trusted audience. It is a true delight to sit with an activist who truly understands my world.'

'In my time, you are written about as a visionary, a woman of beauty, guile, verve and a superior intellect.' She nodded and aware this woman was indicating for her to drink, so sipped from the glass. A little startled by the odd taste, which seemed to be a mixture of tea and coffee, with the aroma of frankincense, she blinked a couple of times.

Smiling, Rebekah said, 'the drink is made from herbs carried here from a country you know as Oman. It is best drunk warm, so please enjoy.' She then sipped her drink. 'Thank you for your kind words. Although it was unanticipated you would know of me in your time, my inner thoughts suggested otherwise. You see, to me, I am just a mortal woman from Paddan Aram, who has a unique ability to see beyond the next hill.'

'In my world, your life is chronicled in a book read worldwide. We refer to the book as the Bible and those around you and this area is known as the cradle of civilisation.'

'I know of the book in the future and all those it references, although I was unaware my namesake was mentioned.' She sipped her drink, while her eyes danced around the room as if she were considering her next words. 'It is an enchantment having you by my side, someone who understands my journey, a believer I can share a familiar perspective with. I know there will be many who will follow in my footsteps and carry the same bodily foundation, as do you? We share a vision and path to all that has occurred before and all that will transpire after our existences. My heart is heavy, knowing of our mortal plight millennia beyond yours. I have seen the day humankind ends primarily because they ignored the many chances they were given.' She then hung her head.

'I too have seen our world beyond humankind, and it too saddens me, that as you say, in spite of our many chances, we carried on our damnation road, regardless. I suspect, as I am sure you do, we are here to concoct a plan, a way forward. I now believe that I am perhaps humankind's last chance. That is the message I've been given by others of our making. Between you, my other advocates through time and me, I am

129

hopeful we can change our supposedly predestined, hopeless road to ruin.'

Over the next hour or so, the two continued to chat about their own lives and how similar, yet diverse they were, especially to those looking in from outside.

All at once, an idea occurred to Rebecca. 'I think I have a plan. In your time, your people build tall buildings that in my time we call pyramids.' Stretching her memory, she said, 'I believe you refer to them as Ziggurats.'

Nodding eagerly, although still maintaining her elegance, Rebekah smiled. 'I assume from your words, perhaps incorrectly, our Ziggurats, temples are still there in your time, being four millennia from this day.' She then shook her head somewhat disbelievingly.

'In essence yes, albeit many were buried by sand and were found by adventurers who explored this land. Although, as I understand it, most were not uncovered until a century before I was born.' She then nodded, 'I estimate by your tone and expression, you know what I am about to suggest.'

Again, nodding eagerly, she said, 'I leave an inscription within the temple walls. One that is well hidden, and only you and I know of this. You can then, in your world, uncover this evidence to show of humankind's plight.'

Thinking, Rebecca said, 'the problem is how I will know where to find your temple. I am sure you do not have map coordinates.'

Smiling, Rebekah said, 'the Sun, Moon, and stars are in the same place for always. We use these as our maps to guide us. I have a star map that will show the exact location of our chosen temple and importantly, I can show you where my scrolls are hidden.' She then narrowed her eyes. 'A plan has just occurred to me. Mostly, our inscriptions are in Arabic or with the use of hieroglyphics. We believe the use of illustrated monograms will stand the test of time. Thereby, people of any era would be able to interpret our messages. This is just a thought that may have a significant impact in your time. I suggest I compile my scripts using your language.'

Shaking her head, Rebecca said, 'I know nothing about stars.' Then the stupid penny dropped, and she uttered, 'but there are plenty in my time that can use your star map as guidance. Importantly, a script written in what we call English, one of the most widely used tongues, will indeed have an impact.' She then shook her head, realising just how significant this would be in her time.

'We are constructing a Ziggurat now. It is a one-day ride from here. I suggest we sleep soon, and by the dawn, we can travel. I can then show you exactly where I will locate my scroll. I would suggest we hide it in an unsuspecting, yet easily accessible place. I would hope our temple will be one that will stand through time and therefore be easily accessed in your period.' She then touched Rebecca on the arm.

Again, Rebecca felt a surge go through her body, the likes of which she'd rarely experienced before. 'You certainly live up to your billing, intelligent, beautiful, and graceful. There is more about you though.'

'I thank you, my equally gracious, handsome friend from the future. We are kith and kin, and they are the words. Now, let us eat well, and you can grace my life partner, Isaac and our offspring, Jacob and Esau.'

Rebecca then followed this woman to another building. As she entered, she was a little taken aback by the number of people and the din of laughter and conversation. Rebekah introduced her to Isaac, something that had a profound effect on Rebecca, knowing of his place in the Old Testament. As she sat next to Rebekah, she was aware of many eyes following her every move. As if she was aware of this, Rebekah picked up a shawl and laid it over Rebecca's shoulders. She then looked around the room with one finger placed over her lips. For a moment, the silence was deafening, then everyone looked away, and within seconds, the din of laughter and chat was once more joyously loud. She sat mostly chatting with Rebekah, occasionally plucking up the courage to speak with Isaac. After a few drinks, and aware they were alcohol-infused, she began to relax and feel comfortable in her surroundings. Initially, she became preoccupied with Jacob and Esau, who were perhaps around eight or nine years old.

Isaac touched Rebecca gently on the shoulder and said, 'your spirit is strong, your soul excellent, and there is an effervescence that resonates from you, the likes of which I have only ever experienced from my life partner, Rebekah. You are kindred, and will live in my life's memories, however short our encounter.'

This had a profound effect on Rebecca's consciousness. It was one thing that Rebekah knew of her ability. However, to have someone who perhaps wasn't of the same making as her being so accepting of her ideas was thought provoking. After the evening had drawn to a close and she lay in her bed, her mind was preoccupied with thoughts of meeting people who had engraved their presence within the history of mankind.

Chapter 18 – Ziggurat

The following morning, Rebecca woke to the sound of an unrecognisable animal making a peculiar coughing sound. The combination of that sound, a dry mouth, and the arid heat made her realise, she definitely hadn't been dreaming. Not that she went to sleep with any doubts, but this journey was so far removed from anything she'd experienced before, at times it had felt like a dream world. Sitting up and looking around trying to get her bearings, she rubbed the side of her head, aware she'd perhaps drunk a little too much of the peculiar tasting alcohol the night before. As if she needed one, this served as another indication that she was on a jaunt like no other.

A moment later, Rebekah's aid entered the room. She walked towards Rebecca, laid a tray of biscuit-like cakes plus a glass of clear green liquid next to the bed, and smiled engagingly.

Without thinking, Rebecca, enchanted by this girl's loveliness, smiled, and held her hand out.

Appearing a little startled, the girl smiled and touched Rebecca's hand, albeit with an air of obvious hesitancy. She then nodded and pointed to the drink.

This girl hadn't said a word since Rebecca first saw her. Curious as to why, although aware there was a language difference, Rebecca felt a need to try to speak with her, even if it was only a few exchanged words. She smiled again and beckoned the girl to sit next to her on the bed.

With slightly narrowed eyes, and still showing obvious signs of hesitancy, the girl sat down and lifted the tray for Rebecca.

Rebecca smiled, held her hand on her chest, and said as best she could, 'ana ribika, wayasrani muqabilatak,' which she believed translated, as, I am Rebecca; I am pleased to meet you.

Clearly a little startled, the girl smiled and holding her chest, quietly said, 'ana eadilat, wayasrini muqabilatak.'

Recognising the girl's response, she reckoned she'd said the "pleased to meet you" right. Unsure, about the name, she held her hand to her chest again, and said, 'Rebecca.'

The girl smiled again, and said, 'Adela,' in a tone that was oddly delicate, yet smooth and refined.

Seconds later Rebekah came in and said, 'you two seem to be getting along just fine, in spite of your language differences.' Again, she smiled and then spoke to Adela in her own tongue. Her tone was smooth, yet at the same time a little forward, almost as if she were giving Adela instructions.

The girl smiled at Rebecca and left the room, returning a few seconds later with some clothing. She then neatly laid it on the end of the bed before leaving again.

'We have a long day ahead of us, and you need to be dressed accordingly. This morning, I compiled a script somehow in your language. How I was able to do this is far from my understanding.' She then handed Rebecca the scroll. 'It is one thing that I am able to speak in a language that is both ahead of my era and not previously within my knowledge. However, to have within my consciousness the ability to compile this script using your words, and to then understand what I have written is beyond all reason.

134

Rebecca took the scroll and read the two pages, occasionally shaking her head. 'This is perfect in every way. Your choice of words, and the way it is laid out. Essentially, the message is clear and perfectly represents what I need to say in my time.' Considering the unbelievable and profound impact uncovering something like this in her time may have, she said, 'Your scripted words and the clear unquestionable message they carry will make a significant difference in my time. I feel confident that without a doubt this will make the people of my time listen and effectively act upon our collective message.'

'We must make humankind respond. It has occurred to me, of our kind, you are the one who is in a position, whereby you are in a situation to halt the destruction of our lands. From our conversation this last day, I believe you have many advocates who will listen. In addition, your world has the capacity through its futuristic knowledge to change events.'

These words alone came as a jolt to Rebecca, not that she was in any doubt about her responsibility. What had just occurred to her though was Rebekah's reference to our lands. This made her realise that this woman perhaps didn't know of any land beyond that which could be reached by camel. To the point where she perhaps had no idea how vast and diverse the Earth was. The thought that this woman may believe the world was one huge desert, or conceivably flat, brought a smile to her face.

'You smile, may I enquire why?'

'Something occurred to me,' she said and hesitated, suddenly realising she could change history if she said too much.

As if this woman had once more read her thoughts, she smiled and said, 'I know how vast land is beyond my own, primarily because of my journeys through time. I also understand that in time, all men will learn how vast land stretches. I respect that it is not for me to change our natural destiny. We share a life beyond the imagination of most commoners.' Until your time, for generations, our kindred type was aware that those around them were powerless to see past that which was in front of them and understood they had to wait for humanity to discover other lands in their own time.' She nodded. 'You see, I know of those beyond my time who share our name. By example, I know of the Rebekah closest to you and the distressed life she lived only for speaking of her visions.'

Sipping her tea, she considered Rebekah's words. 'Oddly, I am neither surprised nor shocked that you know of my Rebekah, even though I should be. Do you know of our guardian angel?'

'I know of Ethernel, our sentinel, although I suspect like me, you have never seen him. I believe this is whom you speak of and if so, he has been here since our kind emerged.'

Now that got Rebecca's goosebumps going. 'You say since our kind emerged. That would suggest you weren't the first. Also, I meant the guardian angel to Rebekah and myself.' She then nodded, realising she perhaps wasn't making sense. 'Let me explain myself.'

Holding her hand up, Rebekah said, 'I understand. In answer to your question, I was not the first, although I have yet to meet or hear from my predecessors. Ethernel told me of their existence.'

'For some reason, I am neither shocked nor surprised, although I would love to know how far back our kind goes. I guess to the beginning of mankind.' She then nodded profoundly as something in Rebekah's words really hit home. 'One thing this conversation has made me truly understand, perhaps for the first time, is something that both Ethernal and my own muse, Meredith told me. They said that in time humankind would see our type as the way forward and that acceptance would essentially start with me. I am the one, with your help, along with Meredith and my Rebekah, who will change the way our kind are seen and vitally acknowledge us as messengers and not witches, wizards or fools.'

Nodding with an obvious air of certainty, Rebekah said, 'I have always known you would be the one who has the capacity to change everything. I have therefore waited excitedly for your appearance in my time. Hopefully, our meeting these days will help you in some way.' She then nodded again. 'I am sure you would like to refresh before our long journey. There is a cool water spray for your comfort,' she said, pointing towards an arched door in the corner of the room. 'After, and please do not hurry, I will see you at the front where I will oversee our carriage.' She then smiled. 'Today, our transportation...' again she smiled, 'will be by camel. I would conjecture this might be the first time you have ridden such a beast. I assure you it is undemanding.' She then gripped Rebecca's hand tightly. 'I have always known you, my princess from beyond these walls, will be the one who changes the world's view of our kind.' She then smiled again and left.

After a slightly cool, but refreshing shower, Rebecca got dressed in the clothes laid out for her. Standing in front of the mirror, adjusting a pale blue sari affair - which seemed to be a mixture of lace and silk-like material - she stood back and looked herself up and down. 'Don't look half bad,' she muttered. One more glance and she headed outside, her mind full of what today may bring, aside from riding a camel.

Immediately outside, she was greeted by Adela, who led Rebecca towards a white camel. Adela then spent a moment or two showing her how to climb upon the animal. After a couple of failed attempts and a lot of giggling, Rebecca was up, holding the reins, and eager to get going. Although it felt strange sitting upon such a beast, she was surprised how comfortable she felt. Moments later, she was joined by Rebekah, who was followed by an entourage of meaningful looking men, dressed in red and yellow knee-length smock affairs. Heavily armoured, each bore a blue sash cross with the

137

emblem that seemed to be half-man, half-bird. For some bizarre reason, Rebecca recognised this symbol from something she'd studied at university and was sure it represented the God Ashur. A little taken aback by their appearance, she wondered why there was a need for such cavalry, certain he was a god of war. To compound her emotions further, she wasn't at all sure why she remembered this.

Rebekah sidled alongside her and whispered, 'we have a long day. I hope you are comfortable. Watching you and Adela made me smile. You two have a strong connection, one I am delighted by.' She then smiled and indicated for them to leave.

Rebecca followed alongside Rebekah and Adela, with the soldiers a few yards behind. Once more wondering what may lie ahead, she asked, 'The men with us appear prepared for battle. Should I be concerned?'

Shaking her head, Rebekah smiled. 'Worry not my friend. Their armoury is part of their attire and no more. My family is sacrosanct in these valleys, hills and beyond. It is a showing of feathers for want of a term that you may understand more clearly.'

Feeling a little more comfortable with this explanation, she said, 'I understand that concept.'

They continued along their journey weaving a path between high sand hills that seemed to be devoid of life. After about three hours and now feeling a tad uncomfortable, Rebecca glanced around to see if anyone else was showing signs of fatigue.

As if she was aware of this, Rebekah pointed way off into the distance. 'We approach an oasis sanctuary and soon we shall haven from the Sol while it is at its highest. From there we can see the hills that are adjacent to the life-giving river

138

Euphrates. Close to those hills is our journeys end. We will make a good head and be there afore Sol down.'

Weary and with her intrigue, and anticipation fading a little, Rebecca tried to focus on her surroundings and the important significance of this journey. Several times since arriving, she had shaken her consciousness, reminding herself of what she was doing, whom she was with, and crucially what they were trying to achieve.

'Are you satisfactory, Rebecca?' This graceful woman asked, again clearly aware of her weariness.

Although Rebecca realised this woman was probably reading her state of mind from her frown, as opposed to reading her thoughts, she replied, 'I am struggling to take this in my stride, so to speak. Consequently, I find myself needing reminders.' Seeing the woman's expression, she knew further explanation was needed. 'I best explain. Through every single journey I have undertaken, I am always a little shocked by what happens. However, I do very quickly settle into my new environment, almost as if it were meant to be. This passage though is beyond my wildest imagination. As a result, I have to keep telling myself I am in the cradle of civilisation, with biblical persons I have only ever read about in the Bible. Conclusively, I must keep reassuring myself our mission is to ultimately avoid humankind's demise.' Those words alone triggered her awareness to a completely new level. 'Here we are at the beginning of time, trying to avert the ending of humanity.' She shook her head, unable to believe her own words. 'This is bizarre, because within my consciousness I feel out of the ordinary, almost as if I were dreaming, yet inside I feel I belong here.'

'I understand my friend and you do belong here. I too have the same emotions often. I have voyaged to times beyond my awareness and as you do, soon adapt emotionally, and feel peaceful in each environment. Even though I am aware I should be unsettled, I am not.' She then looked ahead. 'I can only imagine how you must feel, although your chosen explanation highlights your emotions well.' She then nodded agreeably. 'A few minutes and we will rest and talk some more. I will say if we were troubled and powerless to respond to our new environment, we would not have the right to this gift of seeing the unknown.'

Nodding, Rebekah's words resonated wholly with her. 'That is a significant point, one I had not thought of.' I recall vividly when I was just fifteen years old and inexplicably travelled back one-hundred and seventy years before my time. Although I took several deep breaths and had to calm myself, I very soon accepted what was happening and felt at ease in my new, bizarre environment.' She shook her head. 'It is strange now looking back because I should have been alarmed and beside myself with grief, but I wasn't. I think with today, it is more a case of having to remind myself why I am here and the importance of our time together.'

'That is exactly what I suspect is causing your trepidation. It is not being here with me, although I understand that will impact on you, it is more your journey ahead, most of which will be in your own time.'

'That, Rebekah, is exactly what it is. In my time, we have a saying, which says it is good to talk. Right here, right now, that represents my feeling perfectly.'

Chapter 19 – Oasis

With the sun high in the sky, and Rebecca feeling as if her skin was burning through her clothes, riding under a canopy of enormous palm trees came at exactly the right time. The astonishing coolness of the air and instant relief was both startling and delightfully refreshing. Now bizarrely shivering, Rebecca felt as if she'd just opened the door to a fridge and got inside. She turned to look at Rebekah, who was grinning.

'I recall the first time I visited this extraordinary place. To step into this cool air is a wonder of the gods. Some believe a certain God looks across this land. Others deem it is the rivers from the Euphrates, which run under this blessed place and naturally create this environment. Either way, it is a wonder. We will rest here for some nourishment. Our journey has been expeditious today and therefore time is on our side.'

'Earlier, you said Sol, I am guessing you meant the sun,' she said, pointing to the sky.

'Sit here beside me, while Adela prepares some refreshment. Yes,' Rebekah said, pointing upwards. 'Sol, yes Sun, my forefathers recognised its consistent movement and therefore we now understand the length of each day. In my era, we are only beginning to comprehend what you refer to as time, and how it works.'

That came as a jolt to Rebecca. She hadn't really considered how an item such as a clock could potentially have a significant impact upon this world. This, in turn, got her to thinking about the words she might use without realising they may not be understood. She then watched Adela who was clearly tired and in spite of this, went about her business without blinking. 'May I ask, and please hush me if it is none of my concern. Adela must be equally exhausted, yet she has to serve us first.'

'She delights in being my aide, even though her family has its own wealth. This, therefore, is her chosen direction. I admire that you show concern and recognise that in your life, all are equal. I must say, when Adela and I are alone, we are as friends. Out here though, with eyes abundant, we must act as expected. If we were on our own, I, and I suspect you, would be helping Adela.'

Moments later, Adela came to them with a dish that reminded Rebecca of something she'd had in a Moroccan restaurant in Liverpool. She then returned with another elaborate bottle of liquid and poured the drink before returning to sit with the soldiers.

'Please help yourself to the food and drink. I had previously suggested to Adela that we use fewer spices, so I hope you will find the food to your tasting. The drink also is calm and will not give you a dumb head,' she said and chuckled delightfully.

Thirsty, Rebecca sipped the drink gently. With her eyes wide, she said, 'Oh my, this is delightful. It is a mixture of almond and orange to my mind.' She then finished the drink in one.

Smiling, Rebekah said, 'drink as much as you need, and it is indeed almond and orange, although there is mint from the river valley.' She then drank her own before pouring more. 'So, my, 'Amira, you suggested that within your conscious thoughts you felt as if you were dreaming, yet your gut feeling was that you belong. Have you always had these emotions after you have travelled, or has it just occurred today? I know you talked briefly; however, I would like to know more.'

142

Rebecca knew Amira was Arabic for a Princess. Picking up on this, she decided to respond with what she believed was Arabic for queen. 'Malika,' she said and smiled, which in turn caused Rebekah to smile back. 'This is the only time I have had these emotions to this extent. Although speaking with you now, I think I understand why.' She then narrowed her eyes and tilted her head slightly. 'In my time, you and your people are sacred, historical, legendary, and to some degree, mythical. I think for me it is like being on a film set. That notion alongside the importance of my time with you is causing my emotions to spin.' Instantly she could see Rebekah's expression and realised she would have no idea what a film was. Not having a clue how to explain the notion, she spent the next few minutes trying to illustrate by way of drawing in the sand. All the time, in the back of her thoughts, were these ever-increasing considerations for her choice of language, and escalating awareness of what may be every day to her, has yet to be considered in this era.

'So, like our scrolls, except they move and have people in the message?'

'Err, umm, yeah, kind of.' Although she wanted to explain more clearly, she reckoned it was best left at that.

'Your Meredith told me that you umm and err in the most delightful way.' She then smiled, almost as if she knew what impact these words would have.

With her mouth open, she stared at Rebekah, unable to think of a single word. Inside, what little was left of her conscious rational thinking was wondering if by some chance she meant her Meredith? She shook her head knowing she could only mean her Meredith.

Rebekah leant forward, tapped Rebecca's chin, and said, 'Close your mouth, Sweetie.'

Not only did this woman just mention her beloved Meredith, she now used the same words her mum used so often with, unbelievably, the same gesture. 'Err,' she shook her head once more at a complete loss what to say. It was one thing, coming to terms with being here in the middle of the Bible, so to speak, and standing by a woman she'd only recently read about, this now though sent her head spinning. This woman was not only referring to a person she held dearly but also mimicking her own beloved mother. Just as she'd gathered her thoughts sufficiently to speak, Rebekah started talking.

'I met your dear Meredith days before her spirit settled and she spoke of you with love. Your Meredith met with your mother. I am sure you know.' She then tapped Rebecca again on the chin, 'and this I believe, is what Meredith did to your Elizabeth. I suspect a lot of human traits are a mixture of nurture and nature.'

'So, my mother got that mannerism from Meredith?' As the words left her mouth, she instantly recalled Meredith doing the self-same thing to her. She nodded. 'I know this well and recall Meredith doing the same thing to me. Although, and I guess understandably, I immediately associated it with my dear mother. She is always doing that.'

'Meredith learnt it from her Aunt Rebekah, who in turn learnt it from Belle, having been passed this mannerism from Queen Matilda. Many of our kind have suggested it started with me. It was, in fact, my mother, because I often sat, mouth open, marvelling at the wonders of our planet. You see, we are in a world where our mouths are continually opened by surprise revelations.'

'So, you also know of Queen Matilda? I liked her a lot. Who though is Belle?'

'And Queen Matilda, my Amira, liked you also. After all, you were the one who became her salvation. Like Meredith, without your intervention, their spirits would be ordained to

144

nowhere. She spoke of your intrepid fearlessness, selflessness, and importantly that you were a tactile spiritual giver of love. These, I suspect were tests for you, and your ultimate goal to save humankind from a horrid damnation. Many of our kind have travelled to the future or the past in an attempt to save the spirit of Meredith and Matilda. However, they did not have the wherewithal or fortitude to see their task through to the end. Their attempts though were not without valour or conviction.'

Delighted by this woman's words, she was still eager to know who Belle was or is, or perhaps will be. 'Umm, you mentioned Belle.'

With her lips pursed, she nodded. 'You may meet Belle, you may not. She is not of this life we live.'

'I am not sure I follow, what do you mean?'

'I am finding it hard to explain.' She nodded. 'She could be standing next to us now, although we would be unaware of her presence. It is as if there is a wall of silence between her world and ours.'

Instantly, Rebecca recalled Meredith saying she was now in a different dimension and all Rebecca was seeing was an apparition. 'So, Belle is like your gods, in that you know they are there, you just cannot see them. The word I would use to describe the scenario is that they are in an alternate dimension.'

'Your explanation is perfect, and I think we are of the same thinking. Although I know not of an alternate dimension, I understand the conception.'

The two sat around chatting for a while longer about their different, yet so similar paths. In the back of her thoughts, Rebecca couldn't stop wondering how many of their kind had there been and, in the end, felt she needed to push the subject a little. 'Just curious, how many of our kind do you believe there has been, leading up to my time? I am guessing you may not know of all beyond your time. It's just my curiosity has the better of me, certainly after you mentioned Belle.'

'To my mind, I reason every generation before my mother gave birth to one female who shared our character. I believe it reasonable to consider this path would continue onwards towards your world.' She then looked away briefly. 'The path of our kind was and will mostly be, as was the case with Meredith's aunt, perilous, and fraught with conflict and condemnation. For many generations, certainly, towards your epoch, many of our kind were burned as evil spirits, fiends, and demons. I suspect several never spoke out beyond their youth, like your blessed mother, for fear of derisory comments, or worst still, scolding. All those I have met in the past or future knew of your coming and hoped, nay, believed you would open the way for our kind to be accepted as customary. Therefore, it is for you now to carry our flame and open humanities eyes to our spirit.'

Just these few words magnified the enormity of her journey and it got her thinking about the scrolls. 'I am considering that it may be better if Meredith leaves a message for my time, indicating the whereabouts of the Ziggurat and scrolls. An idea just occurred to me. Meredith, should, instead of me, place a letter in a bank telling of humankind's impending doom and suggesting I should be listened to. Of interest, I have the exact person in mind. It should be addressed for the attention of this influential person in my time, someone who is respected, will be listened to, and can subsequently make a difference. It would then be up to me to try to explain to this person how the letter came to be, without referring too much to my time in the past. I want them to treat it as a message from his distant relative, which Meredith is. If I then drop on his lap, oh, by the way, there's an undiscovered ancient pyramid, with a similar message. And I do have the coordinates. Well, he may think it is one huge scam and stop listening.' Rebecca considered her idea for a moment. 'I just thought about the British Museum, which is still there in my time, and importantly was well

146

established in Meredith's time. Perhaps she could leave something in a vault in the museum. Attach a letter stating that it should not be opened until such-and-such a time. Importantly, we address the scrolls to this person also. Incidentally, his name is David Wilson, and he is a parliamentarian.' She then shook her head. 'The thing is I will have to try and find my way to Meredith in an era when she can do something. I have never yet forced the issue when it comes to going back and forth. I just take it as it comes.' She shook her head, not sure, how this was going to work itself into a workable scenario.

Nodding, but with narrowed eyes, Rebekah asked, 'May I enquire, what are a bank, a museum and a parliamentarian?' She then smiled, and said, 'I understand, no need to explain. Of interest, you will never have complete control of your movements through time. The way I understand it, if it is right, you will find a way. That, I believe is the nature of our kind and our journeys. We are here on a mission; ultimately, it would seem, to save humankind. Therefore, any movements are part of a plan, all leading to an ultimate resolution.'

'That is how I took this chronicle of jaunts we share. In my inner soul, I have always felt that if I got lost, Meredith would show me the way, and I like that. What you say, suggests there is an overriding power that facilitates our movement, and that includes Meredith always being there when I need her most.'

'Ethernal is our ultimate guardian. To me, as I am sure he is to you, a voice of reassurance and no more. A guiding spirit if you prefer. Either way, he shines the light, while watching over our every step.'

Considering this woman's words, and reassured by them, Rebecca said, 'So you are suggesting I will find my way to Meredith if it is the right way to go?'

'I believe so, and moreover, your path will be seamless.'

147

Suddenly a thought occurred to Rebecca. 'On my journey here, I was with Meredith's aunt, right up to the point when I met with you. Moments before I saw you, she seemed to vanish; perhaps back to her own time. Conceivably that was a way of Ethernal telling me that neither Meredith nor her aunt should be involved in my journey. Not directly, more by way of a concealed message from Ethernal.'

'I suspect that is indeed the state of affairs. It has been delightful sharing our knowledge and reassuring we hold similar opinions.' She then nodded in the most agreeable way. 'Now though, it is time to move forward towards our next step. We should be at the Ziggurat before long.'

This time, Rebecca found it relatively easy to climb up on the camel and was sure this was due to her newfound confidence with such creatures. No sooner, she was on and stable, they were back out under the intense heat of the sun. Just as they were about to head off, Adela came over and showed Rebecca a canopy affair one of the soldiers had fitted to Rebecca's camel during their break. It lifted in a pram like fashion, covering her head and body, acting as a perfect shelter. She also handed her a leather pouch affair containing some flavoured water.

'Drink much,' Adela said and smiled engagingly.

Within a couple of hours, the once distant mountain range stood high above their heads. A gentle mist surrounding the lower levels created a somewhat surreal, mythical appearance. Rebecca assumed this could be caused by the nearby river mentioned earlier. Either way, she wasn't in any mood for rational thinking and moreover, liked the mood created by the low cloud. Pointing she asked, 'the mist that covers the mountain. Is that so the gods who live here about can come and go freely, and watch our movement?'

'Generally, that is indeed the case,' Rebekah said and chuckled in the most engaging way. 'In this instance though, it comes from the river just beyond the sand dunes that we approach. It will serve perfectly to hide our temple. We can soon position our scrolls and know that they will be safe from marauding eyes from the north.' She then raised her eyebrows. 'They will be of no concern to us, however, after we have passed, in centuries to come, they will search out and pillage all that is not hidden. This is written in the future.' Again, she raised her eyes. 'Even with my knowledge, I can do little to prevent this. What I can do is to protect what we have now and make certain it is sufficiently hidden for aeons to come. By example, I know that in three centuries, this temple will be covered entirely by sand. To this end, I had a message sent earlier for the men working here. They would, by now have created a sanctuary for our message, which will serve our purpose and ultimately be our salvation. It will stand the test of time.'

Moments later, as the camels surmounted a small sand dune, Rebecca could see stretching out in front of her the most amazing structure. It was a rectangular affair that she considered to be over one-hundred meters in length and around forty meters tall. As they grew closer, she could see it appeared to be made from huge sandy red slabs, each being over four meters long and two meters high. This vast - what she believed to be a step pyramid - had a flat top and almost vertical sides. Almost as if emphasising its own importance, there was a huge twenty-metre wide stairway leading to the top. It was completely different from the triangular pyramids of Egypt, and she couldn't help wondering why she knew so little about these buildings, other than this blurred recollection lurking somewhere in her subconscious, perhaps a hangover from something she'd done at school. *Pyramids*, she thought, *are depicted in every holiday brochure and encyclopaedia, yet these buildings are pretty much unpublicised.* The more she thought about it, the more she wondered why they were not in every history book, especially considering they were in an area that many generations believe to be the cradle of civilisation. Again, thinking about this, she reckoned in her time this area

149

was mostly stricken by war, so that would answer the holiday brochure thing. But even so, she couldn't stop wondering why there was so little documentation within her history. She shook her head.

Once more, as if this woman had read her thoughts, she said, 'These buildings are constructed to stand strong for millennia. Although, I understand they will be covered in sand and not until your year nineteen-thirty will they once again be uncovered. I know this from my time in the future. I also know this structure will remain covered until you tell of its existence; therefore, it will serve our purposes exactly. I am also conscious this area will be plagued in your generation by warring factions. I also identify that in your exact year, there will be momentary peace, and therefore, our scroll can be excavated.'

Moments later, Rebecca was dismounting her camel and following Rebekah and Adela towards the front of the structure. As they approached, they were joined by a sophisticated looking man, dressed in a dark red, full-length shawl. He bowed, his enormous frame befitting of someone ostensibly in charge of here about. He then handed Rebekah an elaborate bronze box.

From a leather holdall, Rebekah produced the scrolls, placed them inside the box, locked it, and handed Rebecca a palm-size ornate key. 'This is the only key, so guard it well.' She then turned back to the man and handed him back the box. He climbed to the edge of a recess within the lower exterior of the structure and placed the box deep inside. Turning, he beckoned several men, who by use of a wooden cradle affair lifted the slab into the recess, fitting to the point where Rebecca could barely make out the edges.

Rebekah walked towards the structure and beckoning Rebecca to follow her, pointed to a large flamboyant R chiselled into the slab. This came as a bit of a surprise to Rebecca, especially since she couldn't see the mark from six feet away. Bizarrely, up close it was clear. 'This denotes the scrolls' exact location and once the temple is uncovered, you will be able to show those concerned its whereabouts. Pointing towards the bottom right corner, she indicated towards a small square also appearing to be etched into the brick. 'Uncover this by means of removing the sand we will place along the edges. Then press once in the middle, wait five breaths and the slab will free from its position. Do not press it more than once, as it will free itself. Be of enduring mind. It will only work once, but work it will, irrespective of what may happen to this building through the years ahead.'

Rebecca, holding the key tightly, asked, 'All I need to do is push the square and it will open?'

'That is all it requires, however, when this building is first excavated, initially the square will appear invisible. With a blade, you will be able to uncover the position of the square. It is therefore imperative you recollect its exact site.' She then handed Rebecca a star chart and explained the Ziggurats position in relation to the stars. 'Those who study the stars will be comfortable using this chart, so bother you not with its complexities. It will work throughout every period that your era refers to as months.' She then handed Rebecca an outline diagram of the building and marked the exact spot where the scrolls are hidden.

Rebecca took the star chart, diagram, and inserted them into the leather pouch Rebekah had given her. Wondering what was next, she turned to Rebekah. With her mouth open, Rebecca watched as this woman's appearance became increasingly misty, to the point where she could just make out her mouthing. "Goodbye."

Chapter 20 – Back

Looking around, she knew in a flash she was back home on familiar territory. Not only had she travelled thousands of miles, but she had also jumped four thousand years through time, and all in the blink of an eye. Shivering from the sudden drop in temperature and still coming to terms with what she'd just been through, she took several deep breaths, trying to regain a scrap of composure. All the time, nagging in the back of her thoughts, jumbled in amongst this sudden change, were so many questions relating to her next steps. Trying to apply a little rationality and considering the conversation she'd just had with Rebekah, she glanced around wondering if she was back in her own time, or perhaps with Meredith. As the fallen oak caught her attention, she reckoned she must be home, knowing the tree was still standing for the majority of Meredith's era. The more she examined her surroundings, the more she realised there was a slim possibility she could be in Meredith's time after all, just after the tree had fallen. With her emotions now all over the place, her mind started to wander off, thinking about the first time she met Meredith, and how that made her feel. Shaking her head, she knew she had to focus.

With the leather pouch containing both the key, Ziggurat diagram, and star map firmly tucked under her arm, she checked to make sure all were still inside. 'Good,' she muttered, clutching the key close to her chest. 'Keys, keys and more keys,' she mumbled.

'More keys?' a voice from behind her asked.

Knowing it was her mum, the person always there for her after such events, she turned with open arms.

'Oh my, you're all shivery, and what is with the pink cheeks? Actually red, I should say. Where this time, Sweetie?' she said and narrowed her eyes in that delightfully familiar way.

Pleased to see her mother and hear her voice, she cuddled her tightly. 'You never told me Meredith tapped you on the chin when you had your mouth open, Mum.' She instantly thought, *of all the things to say*, and shook her head.

Narrowing her eyes again, Elizabeth asked, 'Okay, now I need to know where you have been.' She then touched Rebecca's cheek gently. 'Somewhere hot, I suspect, maybe into the future again or...' She shook her head, unable to hide her curiosity. 'And, what may I ask is that package under your arm?'

'You are so not going to believe this, Mum. Even I can't comprehend what I've just done, and where I've been, and whom I've been with and well...'

With her curiosity now obvious, Elizabeth said, 'slow down, Sweetie. You've not been this excited since you were fifteen. Okay, start with where you've been.'

'Mesopotamia for starters,' she said, barely able to believe her own words. 'It is an area we refer to as the cradle of civilisation. It's the first place, according to many sources, where complex urban communities were created.'

'I kind of think that I've heard of that. Somewhere past Europe, but not as far as India, I believe. Hmm, so how does Meredith come into it?'

'Err, Meredith, not sure that I know...' Rebecca then realised she'd just mentioned her name. 'Oh, so right. I met the original Rebekah; you can read about her in the bible, in the

153

book of Genesis. So, not only did she know Meredith, she'd met her as well. Rebekah reckons she used to do the chin tapping to Meredith when she was young. Well, I assumed it was when she was young, Meredith that is, not Rebekah. She suspects, actually reckons, you may have gotten the chin tapping from Meredith.'

'Hang on a minute, this biblical individual knew not only of Meredith but knew of me too. When are we talking about?'

Pointing towards the fallen tree, Rebecca said, 'we best sit down for this bit. So, according to history, this woman, beautiful and graceful, I might add, lived two thousand years before Christ.'

Narrowing her eyes to the point where she was squinting clearly mystified by Rebecca's tale, Elizabeth just stared with her mouth open.

'See, you do sit with your mouth open,' she said and gently tapped her mother's chin. 'We all do it. It's the wonders of the world that make us do it and we, mankind, have been doing it since the beginning of time.'

'Wonders of the world, hmm, you just told me that not only you met a woman who lived four thousand years ago, she knew me personally and knew your girl, Meredith.' She shook her head. 'No wonder I have my mouth open. So, what is in the bag?'

Rebecca took the key and both charts from her bag and then spent the next thirty minutes explaining all about her time with Rebekah. Several times, she emphasised the importance of the star map, diagram, and the key. 'So, there you have it, all ties together perfectly. I now have to convince David Wilson, once he's read the letter from his nineteenth-century aunt, to then act upon my star chart.'

'That is not going to be easy. Your father, Duncan, and I will have trouble getting our heads around this. Even you are struggling with the whole concept. Only just a few seconds ago, you said I needed to sit down, and that was from your perspective. How you are going to convince a virtual stranger is, well...' She shook her head and then gently squeezed Rebecca's arm. 'Make him listen, you must though.'

'Well, here's the thing. I reckon Meredith could hide this key and both charts in the British Museum, with instructions that it must only be opened by David.'

'So, how are you going to go about that may I ask, Missy?' she said with her eyes wide. She then looked away, before looking back with her eyes now narrowed. 'Catch a taxi to eighteen-fifty-three? Not like you've ever gone anywhere on command unless you've not told me something.'

'So, here's the thing, I don't know. As you suggest, I have never travelled on demand. I do reckon, or should I say, hope it will happen as these things often do, on its own, simply because it's right. If it's not right, well I will reconsider my options. Either way, what with the letter hidden in the bank and this scroll hidden in a temple for four thousand years, David has got to take notice.'

'That sounds like a long shot, but if it comes together, it could well work. Well, you'd think so. How else would you know about a temple hidden in the sand for four millennia?' She shook her head. 'I am still trying to get my head around some woman, two thousand years before Christ I might add, knowing me personally. I mean, really, I only spent moments with Meredith.' She glanced around, clearly thinking. 'On that subject, I still don't know why it took me so long to tell you of my time with her. Still, at least now you know I accept your stories are legit.'

'Good job I know they are legit too. I mean, really, as you so rightly said. I now have a mission to convince someone who doesn't know me from Adam, that not only have I been a thousand years into the future, I also popped back to the beginning of the civilised world. I mean, really, really.'

'Well, you have me, your father and of course, Duncan. Then you have Ruth as your doorway to David and the man from the Daily Telegraph. Then this letter from Meredith, the star chart, the key to a hidden temple. That is a lot of evidence,' she said and waved the map. 'And to add to it, you have that tablet thingy.' She then waved the temple diagram. 'Most importantly for me is this diagram of the temple. I mean, who could argue with that. Oh, by the way, I've a diagram of this temple in the middle of the desert, the one that no one knows about.' She then shook her head, almost belligerently. 'Debate that if you dare.'

Wide-eyed, Rebecca said, 'Mother, be careful. That is parchment, it's not a photocopy.' She then thought for a moment. 'Your point about the diagram. I knew it was important, even so, your words. As you said, debate that if you dare.'

'Sorry, Sweetie,' she said, carefully handing it back to Rebecca. 'This for me is more than a key, it's a door opener, for want of a better term.'

Rebecca shook her head and grinned. 'Even the chart turns out to be a key. Love your analogy, Mother.'

Over the next couple of hours, the two of them sat and went over the story several times. Each time something new occurred to Rebecca, and the more detail she gave, the more comfortable not only she felt, but her mum as well.

'Well, let's go back and chat with your father and Duncan over supper this evening.'

That evening, Rebecca explained the whole scenario to her father and Duncan. Glancing occasionally towards Duncan, Rebecca could see he periodically looked a little lost, although she appreciated he was trying to keep up. Her father, on the other hand, was totally engaged, and borderline belligerent, often stating, they will listen, or else. Whenever Rebecca asked what the or else was, he laughed it off, but she knew he meant it and was a man of his word. Indeed, the more often he said it, the more focused Duncan became. One thing Rebecca knew for certain about her father was that he had this unique ability to get people to see it his way.

'Well, what's the day today? When is this MP man supposed to be opening the letter?'

'So, here's an annoying situation. He is in London and will not be back until the twenty-seventh of May.'

'No excuse, this is a matter of life and death, literally. Besides, it is only the 18th today.'

'Dad, he is in Parliament, and dragging him out is not going to help things. I need his head unoccupied and open. Besides, I have to try to find my way back to Meredith. In addition, I have a meeting with the guy from the Telegraph on the twenty-first.'

'So, can we order a taxi to take you to eighteen-fifty?'

'That is what I asked,' Elizabeth said, grinning.

'Well, as I said to mum, one thing I now know for sure is if I am meant to find my way to a certain place in time, it happens, almost on its own. More so recently than ever before and certainly since the summerhouse was rebuilt. I just walk down that way, and boom, I am wherever I am meant to be. To my thinking, that means if I should go back to Meredith and get her to leave the star map for David, then it will just all fall into place.'

Clearly showing he was coming to terms with Rebecca scenario, Duncan held his hand up, almost school child-like. 'So, let me get this right. You wander down towards the summerhouse and seamlessly jump to another era and in your most recent situation, to another continent?'

Smiling, Rebecca nodded. 'No need to hold your hand up, Duncan,' she said and chuckled. 'So, in essence, yes that is about it. There I am, minding my own business and seamlessly, as you said, I am wherever, in another dimension or time zone.'

'Excuse me, Sweetie. You never mind your own business. I remember when we moved here, the first words from your mouth were, "that has to be where they locked up the princess." You then went on a mission to find out everything you could about this house and, well...'

Grinning, Rebecca said, 'you know what I mean.'

They continued to chat for a while about what lay ahead for Rebecca. Her mother, father, and Duncan to a lesser degree, all volunteered ideas, and potential solutions to Rebecca's plight.

'I think where I am right now, is to just take it in my stride and try to let it unfold on its own. That has always worked in the past, so I really don't see a need to try to change the formula now.'

'Just a thought, Rebecca,' her father said, narrowing his eyes. 'Won't you need the star chart to show the man from the Telegraph?'

'Good point, Dad. I will take it with me and if I have the need to show him, I will, if not, I will just allow things to unfold on their own as they always do. Besides, I have the Ziggurat diagram I can show and tell.'

Chapter 21 – Meredith or Not

The following morning, having had a restless night with so many ideas running around in her head, Rebecca woke feeling exhausted. After a refreshing shower, she joined her mother downstairs for breakfast. As it was such a lovely warm spring morning, they decided to eat outside for the first time this year.

'I have missed sitting out here with you, Mum, especially on days like this.'

'Me too, Sweetie. So, do you have any plans today? Only, I am meeting up with Ruth and Amanda at the spa if you fancy. A detox might help after all you've been through over the last few weeks.'

Although she was tempted, Rebecca had already decided to head down to the summerhouse and see if she could actually force things. Also nagging away at the back of her head was a belief that every time her mum went to the spa, something significant was usually going to transpire. 'I think I will give it a miss, Mum. I am so tempted, but the first thing I thought of when I woke up was getting back to Meredith. It was like that old sensation I used to get when I was younger. I can't really explain it, just a notion in the back of my thoughts.'

'That's just fine, Sweetie, I know you have a lot on your mind and a list of things to do as long as your arm.'

'I mentioned to Dad last night, I was going to take a few days off work, and he was just fine. I think he knew, without saying as much that I had to try to get back to Meredith.' She then thought for a moment, knowing she'd never truly had this kind of mindset before. These words made her think about

159

Meredith telling her to focus her thoughts and make it happen. *Maybe this is what she meant,* she thought. Aware her mum was looking at her, she said, 'Sorry, Mother, I was miles away. By the way, Roxy is popping over tomorrow and it will be nice for us all to catch up. Hey, maybe you could invite the girls for lunch if they are not busy.'

'What a lovely idea. I will certainly suggest it to Ruth and Amanda. It will be like the old days. Now there's a thought, perhaps a trip to Fairy Glen in Wales wouldn't go amiss.' She then rubbed her hands together in a girl like way. 'I reckon that's a plan. Obviously, you have a lot on your plate, but maybe it would be a good outlet for you.'

'What a fantastic idea, maybe in a couple of weeks after I've spoken to the reporter and the MP guy.'

After breakfast, her mother left to meet up with the girls. Rebecca finished off the last bit of tidying up and headed out the front door. The second she closed the door she felt this peculiar sensation. Reckoning something was almost definitely afoot, she decided to go back inside and consider an odd feeling for a moment. Going on a hunch, she grabbed the star map and left the key in a safe place along with the diagram, even though she wasn't sure why. When she went back outside and again felt the same vibe, just stronger this time, it came as a bit of a jolt to her consciousness, having not had her emotions affected so strongly for a long time. The more she thought about it, the more convinced she was this particular sensation was only ever there when she was about to meet Meredith. 'Hey, maybe that is what Meredith meant when she said I need to focus on where I want to go and it will happen,' she muttered. She shook her head, still feeling a tad sceptical whether she could control her movements with such clarity. She paused for a few seconds. She then decided the only way to find out was to continue down the path and see what was waiting.

Walking towards the lake and glancing around, she smiled, noticing the grass was once more perfectly manicured. *Hmm,*

160

she thought, recalling her most recent jump through time happened long before she got anywhere near the summerhouse. Thinking about this, she also realised when she saw her mum's accident as a future event, she was also a good distance from the summerhouse. She was miles away as she approached the lake and suddenly realised the odd feeling she had when she left the house had gone. Stopping by the water's edge, she turned around and glanced back where she'd come from. Everything seemed just so. Wondering if perhaps something was going on near the main house, as opposed to the summerhouse she considered perhaps heading back to see if the emotion returned. As this thought rumbled around in her head, she heard a somewhat distantly familiar voice. She listened carefully and was reasonably certain the voice was coming from the direction of the main house, which kind of answered her question.

As she was trying to pinpoint the exact location of the voice and hopefully work out whom it was, something off to her right grabbed hold of her consciousness. With chills going up and down her spine, she could see a cart standing in the middle of the field. If she wasn't mistaken, somewhere between home and the summerhouse, she'd jumped back to 1943, the time of Judith and the orphanage. The thing that was confusing her most was there being no sign of the orphans or the working land girls. As she stood there considering what was going on, she suddenly realised the last time she saw the cart was in the middle of a wheat field and right now, to the best of her judgement, that same field was corn or maize. *That's odd*, she thought. A little uneasy, nonetheless curious, she reckoned, as always, the best way to find out what was going on was to wander up in the direction of the voice she heard a moment ago.

As she started heading towards the main house, a newspaper page fluttered up right near her. Putting her foot on it, she thought, *that's out of the ordinary*, reckoning perhaps higher forces were at play here, sending her some kind of message.

161

Although she picked it up with the intention of searching for a date, the heading caught her attention.

<u>We are at peace; God save King George VI; the war is over.</u>

She didn't need a history degree to work out it was September 1945. 'That's why the corn looks ready to crop,' she mumbled and shook her head unable to recall ever jumping into a different season to her own time. She headed in the direction of the main house, and although feeling a tad uneasy, at this point, her curiosity had taken over and her instinct was to go find out. Just as she was wondering if the orphans were still here, Tabitha jumped into her thoughts. Knowing for sure Judith and Christopher had adopted Tabitha brought a cascade of emotions flooding her veins. 'Maybe he still likes to be called the Major,' she said and chuckled to herself.

Just as Rebecca was approaching the horseshoe drive at the front of the house, a large green lorry grumbled across the gravel drive. On the side, in old-fashioned gold lettering, it said, "J Lyons & Co, and underneath was, *caterers to the famous.* Narrowing her eyes, she thought, *I know that name for some odd reason.* Before she had time to think about it, her thought process was interrupted by Judith appearing at the front door.

As Judith headed towards the vehicle, she stopped still in her tracks and turned towards Rebecca. Smiling, she then hurried towards her with open arms. 'Oh, my goodness, I have so much to tell you, future girl.'

Instantly Rebecca's brain went into overdrive. She was certain Judith didn't know anything about her coming from the future, so couldn't understand why she would refer to her this way. However, if nothing else, she'd learnt throughout her time in the past and future that things change. She was also aware occasionally it would be when she least expected it, or as is the case this time, an inexplicable change. Before she had time to consider this thought further, Judith started speaking.

162

'Give me a cuddle and do not look so surprised. Meredith came to see me specifically to inform me all about your imminent journey and task, and you would return when the time was right. And, get this...' she said and squeezed Rebecca's hand, kissing her on the cheek, 'the King is coming tomorrow, so your timing could not be any better.'

With her thoughts going in circles, Rebecca was finding it difficult to take in all this woman had just said. Not knowing which part to respond to first, she uttered, 'err, lovely to see you, Judith, umm,' she said, fumbling through her words.

'Lovely to see you also, Rebecca. I must say, you seem unusually confounded, understandable though, what with me referring to you as a future girl. Although, having learnt from Meredith all you've been through, one would suspect you should be used to out of the ordinary events at the very least.'

Trying to focus her words, Rebecca said, 'so, Meredith came to see you?' She then shook her head still unable to comprehend Meredith had visited Judith. 'I didn't think you knew about me and...' She touched her forehead, trying to centre her thoughts. 'So, from what you say, you presumably know I am from the future? Obviously, you just said it, and you know Meredith is from the eighteen-fifties.' Again, glancing down, she shook her head, with her thoughts still going from one thing to the next. 'And you know about my time in the past and the future. Is that right?'

'I do know both you and Meredith have this unique ability to travel from one era to another. As much as it is a mystery most peculiar, it answers many questions that were scrambling around in the back of my head after your last visit. I remotely suspected the day when you last graced my presence with your strength and character you were not my daughter, Rebecca. Because I didn't have any substantial reason to think otherwise, I pushed that idea to the back of my thoughts and accepted the change was due to the war. However, the day you left Etienne I was certain something had changed even though you were

163

seamlessly replaced with my Rebecca.' She looked away a little tearful. 'My Rebecca didn't have the same compassion as you, although she was equally fearless and intrepid. Again though, I accepted things as they were because I wanted to and had no significant reason to think anything was amiss. I believe, as humans, we have an ability to accept, all which is in front of us simply because it feels okay at best, and because we find it difficult to question the unusual. It is odd and I am struggling to acknowledge that I know of our time together thirty years into the future of my life. I do though recognise this as the truth because I was shown that world by Meredith during her second time with me.' She glanced away briefly almost as if she was truly acknowledging her own thoughts. 'The first time Meredith came to visit me was just after you left while we were still at war and the orphans were living here. She gave me a glance into my future life and told of the importance of your time on this Earth.' She touched Rebecca gently on the shoulder. 'I have had many a day to consider the message Meredith carried during both her visits. I understand your plight and suspect, as a result, you have something important for me. Perhaps I should say you have something important for King George.'

Although initially, Rebecca was wondering why she was here with Judith, her last few words totally focused her thoughts. 'That's it' Rebecca blurted. 'King George is my doorway.'

'Although I know you carry an important message with you, I may need a little more detail before I let you loose on the King, 'she said and chuckled. 'I am open to any suggestion though, especially since having a rough insight into the mission you face, however...'

'Sorry, do you know of the future and what will...' She stopped dead, realising Judith may not know about the end of civilisation, and she needs to pick her words carefully or it may all come as a shock. She glanced at her and seeing her nod, continued. 'So, you are aware humankind will struggle, due to

164

its own greed?' Again, seeing Judith nod, she carried on. 'Well, I have a message for my time that will hopefully change our destiny.' She then spent the next few minutes explaining about the star chart, the hidden message in the Ziggurat and that she had a key to a hidden box. She also went into a little more detail about humanities fate, again choosing her words carefully.

'I understand now. So, you can give the star chart to King George and he can authorise an expedition to that area to uncover the Zig, what name was it? And then in your time, you can take the key and open the hidden box.'

'Yep, in a nutshell, and he, King George doesn't need to know about the future demise of mankind, my time-travel, or anything that might affect his focus. I can just say I found the star chart in the loft or something. I am sure between us we can come up with a plan. I can make out I am your daughter, not as if we can't get away with that,' she said and giggled. 'Incidentally, Christopher, or should I say, the Major, does he know that I am from the future?'

Nodding, she said, 'he does indeed and has been looking forward to seeing you again. He has to thank you for bringing him and me closer and well...' She smiled and squeezed Rebecca's hand. 'The King is here to present Chrisy with a medal of honour. Besides, they are friends from Eton School, which helps. That, my dear, will be the doorway you exclaimed about earlier.' She then again touched Rebecca on the arm and kissed her on the cheek. 'I must say here and now, I thank you for your guidance. Also, I thank you for bringing Christopher and myself back together which essentially brought him out from the cupboard he was hiding in. From that day forward, we have been back to our happy selves. Of interest, one of the little girls you took a particular interest in, Tabitha, well we adopted her as our own. She often speaks of you, almost as if she knows you are different from my real daughter, even though the similarities are impossible to see to anyone other than those who know both hearts. She knows, even though she does not say as much.'

Smiling inwardly, Rebecca said, 'Tabitha lives a long life and indeed she came to see me many years from now, in my real-time I might add. I think Tabitha's daughter struggled with the concept that Tabitha knew me from nineteen-forty-three.' She shook her head, unable to believe how this conversation was unfolding. Although to most it would be a twisted mess of people, incidents, and eras, it all oddly made perfect sense to Rebecca, and all added towards her mission.

Chapter 22 – Judith

Over the next couple of hours, Rebecca helped Judith organise food preparation. Although some of their time was spent in a quiet corner chatting about Meredith, Rebecca's journeys through time and the importance of her message for King George.

'Of interest, my daughter is visiting Etienne's ill mother in Scotland for a few days. Like you, she married him, bizarrely on the same day, and at the same church. So, for all those arriving at our function, we can introduce you as Rebecca, my daughter. The only one of the guests who know that my real daughter is in Scotland is Christopher. No one will suspect anything strange because my daughter and Etienne now live in Vancouver. A new city bursting into life on the west coast of Canada.'

No matter how many out of the ordinary circumstances offer themselves to Rebecca, the news that Judith's daughter actually married Etienne and unbelievably on the same day and at the same church, came as a jolt to her awareness. To compound her sentiments further, Sam Pollard her teacher at University moved to Vancouver, albeit in 2012 when it was an established vibrant city, and one of the best places on the planet to live. This news though did make her mission clearer, as piece by piece, she was ever closer to realising her time both in the past and future as part of her destiny and the reason for her very existence. 'You know, it is odd because when I returned home from my many years with Etienne and having two children, all

I could focus on was one of my children went on to discover a vaccine for a disease that would not become prominent until my time. Although I felt some loss, I was concerned that I somehow had no detachment issues.' She paused for a moment, trying to recollect how she really felt. 'I spoke with both my parents about this, and my father suggested it was because I was living out someone else's life. It has just occurred to me that often my mission, role, or destiny is to stop time taking a different route.' Again, she paused, having noticed Judith's somewhat vacant look. 'By that I mean that had Etienne's and my child not gone on to discover that vaccine, there would have been an epidemic that would cause massive loss of life in the Far-East.' She suddenly realised Judith would have no idea this happened. She glanced at her and smiled openly, trying to engage her to speak.

After a few seconds of Judith clearly thinking, she said, 'so, in essence, your child with Etienne went on, or should I say, will go on, to discover a cure for a virus that will kill many?'

'It would have indiscriminately killed millions, actually. It spread at epidemic proportions across the Far East, and I have no doubt could have spread to Europe. I kind of got an idea then that my time in the past was to prevent time changing direction and not only affecting the people I met in the past but also the people in my time. The biggest wake-up call for me was a plague that came over from Ireland in sixteen-twenty-three and took many lives locally to here. The workers were here working on this very house. Now get this, had I not gone back to stop the workers and subsequently stop the plague, my mother's ancestors would have succumbed to the plague and therefore my mother would never have been born.'

'Oh gosh, that is incredible. How did you work that out, because presumably you went back and stopped the plague?'

'Well, here's the thing, and this was all a bit scary for me if I am honest. I went back and failed to stop the plague on my first attempt. I then bizarrely ended up in Meredith's time, and

168

she showed me my reflection in the stream behind the summerhouse. Get this, I was brunette and looked completely different. Anyways, I found my way back to the sixteen-hundreds and stopped the workers coming over from Ireland, and bingo, moments later I was back in my time and back to being me again, pink freckled cheeks and all.'

'Wow, that is a truly amazing tale, and when you add in your time with Etienne and the task that is now ahead of you. All I can say is humankind is most definitely dependent on you.'

'You know what is really odd, although I've known all along about the importance of my role. However, just a moment ago when you mentioned your daughter marrying Etienne is when the penny truly dropped. I get it now and importantly accept my destiny. Often Meredith would allude to my providence, although I guess I just washed over it, and if I am honest, I found it difficult accepting I was worthy of this position.' She paused for a moment considering the impact of what she'd just said and actually accepting that humankind was going to vanish into oblivion unless she could convince enough people in her time to change their habits of greed. 'It is up to me to do a good job convincing King George tomorrow to act upon my star map.' Rebecca paused for a moment. 'Something has just occurred to me. It was Etienne's and my son who invented the vaccine to stop the virus.' She then hesitated again, and nodding she said, 'Well, it would seem providence has been set, what with your daughter and Etienne marrying at the same church on the same day, so presumably the rest will follow suit, albeit in Canada.' She then nodded, feeling a little more comfortable. 'I am sure if things do not work out, I will be back to set the clock at the right time.' She then laughed, albeit a little nervously. 'My focus now must be mankind's destiny.'

'Well, King George has a close friend whose name is...' Judith paused for a moment, 'I think it is Sir Michael Wooley.'

169

Unable to believe what she just heard, Rebecca said, 'I think it is Sir Leonard Wooley.'

'That's it, how do you know that?'

'I read up by way of the Internet, err sorry, an electronic encyclopaedia that he, Sir Leonard, spent many years in the area known as Mesopotamia uncovering pyramids.' Seeing the vague expression on Judith's face, Rebecca said, 'it is an area in the Middle East that we know as Iraq, Iran, and Syria and so on. The Bible suggests it was the cradle of civilisation, and it is. I know because that is where I met the original Rebekah and she gave me the star map. I mentioned that Rebekah earlier. So many Rebekah's or Rebecca's, it must be confusing for you. I know them all individually, so it's easy for me.' Again, she chuckled.

Shaking her head, Judith said, 'well, let's go and check the guest list because I am certain Sir Leonard is on the list.' She then headed down the hallway towards the kitchen. 'Mary dear,' she said to a woman who had the appearance of some kind of matron, 'where is the guest list?'

'The stern-looking, nonetheless, smiley woman shuffled some papers and handed a fancy looking tan coloured paper schedule. 'Here you are, Madam.'

After a few seconds, Judith turned and handed the schedule back. 'Thank you, Mary.' She then beckoned Rebecca to follow her outside. 'Sir Leonard is the first name under King George and his wife, Elizabeth.'

Rebecca narrowed her eyes. It was one thing hearing the name King George but hearing Judith mention Elizabeth came as a bolt to her senses. Then she realised who Judith was referring too. 'Oh, of course, the Queen's mum was Elizabeth too. Sorry, in nineteen-fifty-two, King George's daughter, Elizabeth becomes Queen, and is still Queen in my time.'

'When is your time, out of interest?'

170

Smiling, she said, 'twenty-thirteen. It sounds like the distant future to me, so heaven only knows how it must sound to you.' She smiled and said, 'I am so looking forward to meeting Leo tomorrow, an extraordinary explorer by all accounts.'

'Leo, oh you mean Sir Leonard. Saves us keep saying Sir Leonard Wooley, I guess,' she said and chuckled in the most delightful way.

The remainder of the evening passed quickly as Judith, now joined by Christopher, chatted endlessly about Rebecca's adventures.

Slightly annoyingly, Rebecca was given Tommy's bedroom, which on reflection nearly made her smile. As she closed the door, she thought, *twit's room* and suddenly realised she hadn't seen him for two months, what with his football and all. 'Must make arrangements to catch up,' she muttered as she lay in her bed.

In what felt like seconds, she was being woken by Judith. As she stirred, she had the weirdest remnants of a dream rumbling around at the back of her head. 'Morning, Judith. Crumbs, I slept well. I was having the most peculiar dream.'

'Morning, my dear Rebecca. I am glad you slept well, and please do tell me more about your dream. I have done a lot of research on dreams. They always intrigue me.'

'Well, I was sitting at a table with a pleasant man who was typing at what we call a laptop in my time. You'd know it better as a typewriter. Anyways, I was telling my story as if it were a chronicle. I told him every detail about my time in the past and future, while he typed it all up as a novel. Well, by the time we had finished, it was closer to three or four novels. The odd thing, unlike some dreams, it was actually my story. You, Meredith, Matilda, my parents and even my twit of a brother were in the story. So odd, it was as if I was standing next to him, by the way, I think his name was Stephen, which oddly in

171

French is Etienne. Anyways, there I was telling my tale. Now here's the uncanny bit, I wasn't talking, I was just thinking, and he was typing away. Every now and then, I had to correct him. Bizarre, it felt real and still does even though I am awake.'

'How very strange. Dreams are rarely that realistic to my mind.'

'Exactly, anyways, we need to get on, got things to do today, like meet the king of Great Britain, oh yeah, and save humankind.'

'I have had a bath run for you, and the maid has laid out some appropriate clothing for today's events. I will see you downstairs in the reception room when you are ready, perhaps not in your dungarees and tee-shirt,' she said and giggled.

After a long soak in the bath, Rebecca picked up the most delightful full-length silk, amber coloured dress that was enhanced with long layers of chiffon hanging down from what she considered to be an empire waist. To match also in silk, were a bolero jacket and a beautiful pair of shoes in a similar colour. She stood there admiring these garments when there was a knock at the door.

'Hello, come in,' Rebecca said, pulling a long towel around her body.

'Hello, Miss. I have come to help you dress and fix your hair. I have also brought you a cup of tea.'

'Oh, how delightful,' she said beckoning the woman in. 'Can I ask your name please as I prefer not to be formal?'

Appearing a tad sheepish, the woman said, glancing down, 'my name is Rhonella and I came to this country from Poland with my father who was a pilot for the British Army during the war.'

172

'Well, it is a delight to meet you, Rhonella. I must first introduce myself. My name is Rebecca and my family, and I thank you and your father for his gallant service towards peace. May I ask of your mother's whereabouts?'

'Sadly, we lost our mother during the early days of the invasion. This though, is why my father joined the British movement, which in turn brought us to this beautiful and great country.' She then glanced away, touched her cheek, and then looked up. 'My mother, although sadly missed by my father and me, would have delighted in our newfound life. So, we will always be thankful to her for her light that guided us here, alongside her motivational mothering ways.'

'That is inspiringly lovely that you are able to find good from such a horrid loss.'

'My mother and father both taught me this way. They showed me a way to look forward and not backward and to search for goodness in the most remote place.' She then smiled, 'although we have two hours, Miss, we need to coiffure your hair. Miss Judith has suggested a chignon braid and here is a photo so you can decide.'

A little excited by this scenario, grinning, Rebecca took the photo and taking one look, said, 'that is perfect, just as I would have imagined for such an occasion. Please do call me Rebecca.'

Smiling the girl - whom Rebecca guessed was no more than sixteen-years-old - took the photo and said, 'please call me Rhonella.' She then chuckled in a way that befitted her petite frame, long wavy brunette hair, and porcelain-like skin.

Having thought she recognised the hairdo, Rebecca suddenly realised it was a style the beloved Princess Diana wore. She was just about to express this when she realised this girl would not know of Diana. Instead, she smiled to herself and sat in an elaborate woven chair facing a grand three-sided

173

mirror. 'Let's go for it, Rhon. I am rather excited to see how this turns out.

'Let us go for it indeed,' the girl said and giggled quietly once more.

'You can push me around, no need to stand on ceremony with me. You have a job to do and I am not made of glass,' Rebecca said, thinking, *I like this girl, a lot.*

The two continued to chat while Rhonella firstly applied make-up to Rebecca and then tied her long blonde hair up in the most beautiful way. Staring in the mirror brought a tear to Rebecca's eyes, amazed by her appearance. In a distantly odd way, she was sure she could feel Meredith's spirit looking on.

'Right, dress now then. I am so glad you are here because I would not have a clue how to put this dress on.'

The girl then handed Rebecca the most amazing silk-like pale yellow underwear and then turned her back. Rebecca took the underwear and having only ever undressed or dressed in front of her mother and Duncan, she was somewhat glad the girl looked away. To her amazement, both pieces of underwear fitted perfectly. 'Okay, shall we get into the dress?'

As with the underwear, the dress, along with the shoes fitted as if they'd been made for her. Shaking her head, she noticed the girl smiling in a somewhat inquisitive way.

'Rebecca, you seem somewhat surprised.'

'I am a little surprised how well this all fits.'

'Well the number of times the dressmaker visited, we would hope that it fits,' she said and smiled.

Those few words came as a realisation to Rebecca that once more she had to be mindful and choose her words and behaviour thoughtfully. 'What time is it now?' she asked and glanced around the room with her subconscious half expecting

174

to see Tommy's Mickey Mouse clock on the wall, which made her smile.

'It is ten minutes after twelve, Rebecca. The King is due to arrive at two this afternoon.'

'Shall we head downstairs then?' Rebecca said, glancing towards the door.

As the two made their way downstairs, with her dress swishing silently over each step, Rebecca's thoughts jumped between her appearance, her wedding with Duncan and Meredith's daughter's wedding. So lost, she didn't notice Judith standing at the bottom of the stairs grinning like the Cheshire Cat. Spotting Judith, Rebecca took a sharp intake of breath. Gone was the scraggy ponytail hair and army clothing that she so fondly remembered, and in its place was a woman fit for any King. She was wearing the most vibrant pink floral dress, similar in shape to Rebecca's dress. Her hair again was similar to the way Rebecca had hers. For some reason, Judith's appearance reminded her of someone she felt she knew fondly. Then, as she greeted Judith at the bottom of the stairs, a flood of emotions filled her head. As a young girl, one of Rebecca's favourite films was The King and I, with Deborah Kerr and Yul Brynner, something she watched incessantly. Judith's appearance reminded Rebecca of Deborah Kerr. This character had had a huge impact on Rebecca, and she learnt so much from her. Seeing Judith now, brought a lump to her throat.

'My goodness, Judith, you look so beautiful, graceful and elegant. Shall we go and cut some wheat?' she suggested and chuckled in a way she hadn't for a long time. Suddenly, the burden of the task in front of her fell into place, gone was the anguish and uncertainty and in its place was a sudden newfound focus and determination to succeed. Seeing all this beauty and being reminded of so many great things, she knew there and then that she had to succeed.

Chapter 23 – The King

Rebecca opened the door to the reception, which was the room opposite where her father's study would be in 68-years. This room was one that Rebecca had only ever been in during her family parties, and this thought made her feel quite odd as she closed the door behind her. Feeling modestly ladylike and not wanting to crease her beautiful dress, she chose to stand rather than sit while she chatted to Judith and Christopher. Over the next hour or so, several stately looking guests arrived, all dressed in the most amazing array of elegant costumes and suits. The nearest Rebecca had ever gotten to such an occasion was watching one of the royal weddings on television, and here she was, part of a similarly grand event. With each new arrival, came a new greeting. Mindful of her modern dialect and a woman's position in the 1940's culture, Rebecca chose her greetings carefully, maintaining a respectful demeanour.

Meeting so many refined individuals, all clearly from the higher echelons of society made her feel a little strange, oddly though she wasn't at all uncomfortable. Feeling increasingly relaxed, she did have to keep reminding herself why she was here and of the job in hand. Having just finished speaking with a senior field marshal and his wife, whose name she knew from somewhere in the recesses of her memory and was trying to recollect why she knew his name, Judith beckoned her over.

'Rebecca, this is Sir Leonard Wooley, and his good lady wife, Constant Wooley. Sir Leonard, Lady Constant this is my daughter, Rebecca.'

176

Knowing Judith knew the importance of this man to her task Rebecca tried her hardest to avoid glancing wide-eyed towards Judith. Instead, Rebecca shook their hands and introduced herself as politely as she could. All the time, her inner thoughts were shouting at her to tell him there and then all about her star map. Meanwhile, the rational aspect of her brain was calming her down, telling her to bide her time, stay focused, and act as normal as possible. It helped that both this man, who she considered being in his late sixties and his delightfully gracious wife had a charmingly engaging manner. Indeed, Rebecca ended up talking with the woman, Lady Constant, for several minutes about her and Leonard's adventures to the Middle East.

Rebecca was actually pleased with herself, being able to relate to this area so well and hold down a good conversation.

'My word, young lady, you know a lot about this mostly undocumented area of the world. I was most pleased to hear you refer to their temples as Ziggurats. Many an educated individual would have annoyingly called them Pyramids,' Leonard said.

'I believe they are occasionally referred to as step pyramids. Although as you say, a pyramid they are not. My understanding is they were often built with the knowledge they would be, over two to three centuries, covered by sand, thereby shrouding their existence.'

'Rebecca is it? That is profound, of that I am certain. Only a small handful of people, with specific knowledge of the Mesopotamian customs, would know this fact.' He shook his head. 'How may I request, are you with such knowledge?'

Almost on time and saving Rebecca from having to answer such a tricky question, for now at least, there was an announcement.

'God save the King,' a strong and dignified voice called from the hallway.

Judith whispered to Rebecca, 'The King's carriage is approaching.

Rebecca nodded and followed everyone outside. Glancing around, although she should have felt madly out of place, she was remarkably comfortable. With barely enough time to look around and admire the forty or so guests, the carriage pulled up. It made her smile as all these dignified people politely jostled for position. Rebecca took a step back and watched as King George and a young Elizabeth, someone she knew simply as the 'Queen's mother,' stepped from the carriage. If seeing such a youthful Queen's mother came as a shock, seconds later the Elizabeth she knew as Queen stepped out, followed by the stunning Princess Margaret. For some reason and out of sequence, the young Elizabeth paused, glanced around and then seemed to make direct eye contact with Rebecca, almost as if she recognised her. Slightly thrown by this and doing the maths in her head, she reckoned this girl she knew as the Queen was around 19 years old. With her emotions all over the place, Rebecca held her hands behind her back, all the time telling herself to act normal. She shook her head and almost as if she was speaking to her rational self, she inwardly muttered, 'how am I supposed to act normal?'

Judith tapped her on the shoulder, and whispered, 'stop mumbling. I know what you must be going through. It is bad enough for me, a little old nurse, opening my home to the Royal Family. Ooops, I nearly swore then,' she chuckled quietly, but not quietly enough because someone in front of them, who clearly didn't know Judith was the host, turned and almost snarled. She then tugged at Rebecca's arm and whispered very quietly, 'He, that twit, clearly doesn't know that I am the host, hmm. Anyways, you must be seeing people, which you know from your time who are aged in their seventies, eighties, or nineties. How weird must that feel?' She again squeezed Rebecca's arm.

'Twit, my favourite term,' Rebecca whispered, again not quietly enough because the same person turned and snarled once more. Turning her nose up and unable to help herself, Rebecca snarled back and raised her eyes.

Fortunately, a second later, King George, eased through the people and said in a loud voice, almost as if he had noticed what was going on, 'Ah, the delightful Judith and the Major, our wonderful host's.' He then bizarrely glanced at the man Judith had referred to as a twit and announced. 'It is a joy to meet up with my old friends. The Major, most of you will know as Christopher, led our armies on a number of successful battles in Africa.' Lifting his glass, he said, 'here is a toast to The Major and his good lady wife, Judith.'

Simultaneously, everyone lifted his or her glasses in the direction of Chris, and then towards the King, and said, 'God save the King.'

King George then turned to Rebecca and said, 'and you must be the intrepid Rebecca. The one I have heard so much about. According to your father, you are a gallant, fearless individual. I must introduce you to Sir Leonard Wooley, a good friend and ally. He and his good lady wife are also gallant adventurers.'

Rebecca, unsure if she should say anything, curtsied the best she could, maintaining eye contact at all times.

'There we go, a girl of spirit, like my Elizabeth and Margaret, keeping your eye on the subject.'

Just then, from the corner of her eye, Rebecca noticed Sir Leonard watching.

'I have already had the pleasure of meeting this widely versed and pragmatic lady, King George,' Leonard said and nodded graciously. 'She has already alluded to an extensive knowledge of a subject that is close to our hearts. When we have the opportunity, we three must speak.' He then narrowed his eyes ever so slightly in the direction of Rebecca, with an obvious look of curiosity etched on his face.

179

Over the next thirty minutes or so, the King greeted each guest individually. It was clear to Rebecca he was considerably more comfortable with some, whereas with others, his facial expression changed, and his renowned stutter took over. Watching this man, along with the Queen Mother and young Princesses Elizabeth and Margaret, generated the most surreal sensation in Rebecca's thoughts, the likes of which she'd never felt before. Although she understood the enormity of this occasion, and how she should feel, also knowing what a fantastic opportunity this was for her plight made her feel surprisingly relaxed. The whole mood of this grand occasion, along with a constant flow of champagne would have been an easy trap for anyone. Rebecca though, now felt totally at ease and focused enough to keep her hanky over her empty glass. She kept telling herself that tomorrow this would be a fabulous memory, but not if she fails to deliver the star map in the right way. Just as this thought resonated once more in her head, Christopher came over to her.

'Rebecca, it seems you have made a significant impression, not only with the King but also his close friend and advocate, Sir Leonard. So much so, that the two have requested your company in the drawing room. This, my girl, is your opportunity to impart your star map and hopefully leave a lasting impression.'

As he finished, Judith came over. 'I have no doubts your Meredith is here about for sure, watching over proceedings. If your mission is successful, I understand you will find yourself back in your own time in a flash, with little or no opportunity for goodbyes. If this proves the scenario, please take with you our blessing and love.'

'We hope you are able to bring a halt to humankind's journey of greed and thereby save our destiny,' Christopher said. 'All the many lost souls on both sides of our recent conflict would have been a waste if mankind then goes on and destroys our home, this planet. All you can do Rebecca is your best. What little I know of you, I have confidence you will

180

succeed, and if at first you do not, you will keep straight until you do. God Speed, dear girl.'

Rebecca acknowledged them both. 'I suspect our paths may cross again. Please love Tabitha, although I know you will and send my love to Etienne,' she chuckled, 'but don't for obvious reasons. Thank you, Christopher, for your kind words. I will resolve this, one way or the other. Today is just another piece in place.' She then leant forward and whispered, 'I travelled four thousand years into the past, and this is the easy bit.' She then chuckled in a slightly ironic way as her own words resonated inwardly. She then took Judith's hand and whispered, 'I have loved every minute we have been together and that includes the thirty years of my last visit. I have learnt to love you and you will always hold a special place in my world.'

Christopher smiled, nodded to Judith, and said, 'shall we join the King and Sir Leonard?'

Rebecca then followed Christopher into the room that would become her father's study.

'Aha, here is the girl of the moment,' King George said. 'First off, as we are amongst friends, I put forward we dispense with dignitaries. I am George, and this is Leo. Shall we call you Rebecca?'

Rebecca glanced at Christopher and he smiled back.

'So, it is George, Leo, Chris or father and Rebecca.' Christopher said and nodded to all, again smiling towards Rebecca.

'Leo, you have a pressing question for Rebecca, I believe,' the Kind said.

'I do indeed. Earlier, you imparted knowledge of an area in the Middle East that is close to my heart. I have spent many years there excavating the Ziggurats. The question I have for

181

you, appreciating that very few people know much of this area, other than through readings of the Old Testament, how do you know so much?'

Although Rebecca was ready for this question, it still came at her like a ludicrously hard exam problem. She glanced at Christopher to give herself some thinking time. He smiled back and nodded. 'So, in the loft of this house, an area I was banned from going to I might add, I found some ancient papers that talked extensively of this area.' She immediately thought I should not have said that. Then as quick, a resolution came to her. 'Sadly, many of the papers were destroyed in a small fire. However, I did manage to save this parchment, which I believe dates back four thousand years.' Both George and Leo were now sitting staring at her with their mouths open a little. Rebecca had already placed the scroll inside its leather pouch safely in the study. At the time, she didn't know why she had done this, it just felt like the right thing to do, and somewhere in the back of her brain, she had convinced herself it was Meredith's idea, so she went with it, as she always does. Pulling the star chart from the pouch, she took a sharp intake of breath. Originally, it had been written in English, although now, unbelievably it was in hieroglyphics. Unsure what to make of this, part of her was reckoning she'd thought it was English, just as she was able to converse with Rebekah who could actually only speak her variant of Arabic and that higher powers were once more involved. In actual reality, the parchment was always going to be written in either Arabic or hieroglyphics. *Hmm*, she thought, *perhaps it's for the best as it would appear faked and out of place.* She placed the map on the table and even though she couldn't read what was on the paper, she was able to recall exactly what each part said or indicated. 'So, this area here as you can perhaps work out is a chart of the stars and from what I can ascertain, relates to the summer months. This aspect here,' she said pointing her finger, 'refers to a buried Ziggurat. It is just west of the Euphrates River where it runs close to Therthar Lake.'

'This is a previously unexplored area, which makes this map potentially of great importance and significance. Indeed, we believed there were no temples built this far north.' Sir Leonard then scratched the side of his head, glanced at King George, and then frowned in a questioning manner towards Christopher. 'Please excuse me asking, you seem to have a great understanding of these hieroglyphics, how so? I ask because it took specialists in this field years to interpret these messages, primarily because they are unique to this area.'

Rebecca hadn't already prepared herself for this potentially difficult question, so decided to wing it. 'It really is a matter of mathematics and understanding how these people, who were just at the beginning of what we now call the civilised world, would attempt written communication.' She could see all three frowning and knew she had to make this count. This was the first and biggest part of her jigsaw. 'With my limited knowledge of hieroglyphics, which I would suggest is a good starting point, I came at the problem with fresh and importantly open eyes.' Seeing Sir Leonard's expression, she knew she was making headway. 'I just thought to myself that these people obviously wanted their message read and so would create something simple. I counted the number of different symbols, which was thirty-six, similar to the Greek alphabet and then applied an undemanding maths process to this uncomplicated riddle. By this I mean, a letter for each symbol. I got lucky, guessing a few that fell into place with relative ease.'

Both King George and Christopher were nodding and smiling. Sir Leonard, appearing intrigued, said, 'that unfussy and clever thinking, Young Lady, is remarkable. It took our so-called experts, as I said earlier, years to solve this, and I use your words here, a simple task. Christopher, you were right, this daughter of yours is truly extraordinary. Please continue, I think I can speak for us all, you have our absolute attention.'

'Thank you, but really I just approached it as a puzzle. Lateral and rational thinking is all I used. So, I am not altogether sure I follow their measurements, but having looked at a map and a star chart, I would suggest... Father, have you a pen and paper, please?'

Her father jumped up and went to the tallboy in the corner, of all things, the same one that is still in place in her time and used by her real father, and handed her a pen and paper, taken from the same draw her father uses for such things.

Grinning inwardly at yet another ironic twist, she drew a map showing the exact location of the Ziggurat in relation to the river and lake. 'So, from what I can work out, and please understand that my calculation is at best approximate, the temple is one mile south of the lake, and between the lake and temple are small rocky hills. This would make sense because...' She stopped dead in her tracks, realising she couldn't possibly know there were marauding tribes from the north. Before she could continue, Sir Leonard spoke.

'This does make sense because these people were at constant war with tribes from the north and well, so far everything you have said makes utter sense. So, going by your beautifully hand-drawn map, it would suggest the Euphrates would be perhaps half a mile away and along with a constant supply of fresh water, it would additionally serve as a moat. Because these people were in constant conflict with marauding clans from north of the Euphrates, we never explored this area. You have uncovered a completely new adventure for the British Empire to investigate. Potentially, Rebecca, you have changed history.'

Hearing those words, Rebecca knew this part of her mission was complete, that was until King George suggested she joined Sir Leonard on their next expedition. She went from expecting to be back home as soon as she walked outside to having her thoughts flooded with memories of the many years with Etienne. Almost as if Christopher had worked out this could pose a problem for Rebecca, he intervened in the conversation.

184

'I am sure Rebecca would be delighted and excited to join you. However, she is due to leave for Canada with her husband within a few days.' He then nodded to Rebecca.

'What a wonderful expedition for you, dear Rebecca. The Canadian Red Devils served us well during the war. Our loss though, as it would have been marvellous to have a clear thinker onboard. Perhaps, if, and when you return, you could join another of our expeditions. I would also be delighted if you would at some point lecture on your lateral understanding of hieroglyphics.'

'That would indeed be a delight and honour. Thank you for indulging me over this last hour,' she said and nodded to all three. Still in the back of her mind was this surreal acknowledgement that here she was chatting with King George and Sir Leonard Wooley as if they were at a normal family party.

They sat around for a few more minutes going over Rebecca's map.

'We really must join the other guests. I believe we have been a little too indulgent with our time. I have so enjoyed making your acquaintance, Rebecca,' King George said, and stood up offering his hand.

'Thank you, King George, it has been a pleasure.' She then shook his hand and turned to Sir Leonard. 'It has also been a pleasure meeting with you, Sir Leonard.'

'Rebecca, next time we meet and meet we will, please refer to us as George and Leo. The ceremonious name tagging should be used during certain occasions, not when chatting about something close to all our hearts and with people owning such an intimate understanding of the subject. That is until we name this Ziggurat after you.'

Bingo, Rebecca thought that would do nicely and help my cause. 'Can I suggest that you name it after the original

Rebekah? She was the mastermind behind the building of this temple, so it should be only right.' She could see Sir Leonard narrowing his eyes. 'I see, Leo, if I may be so bold, a look of curiosity on your face. The star map has one name on it at the bottom and that is the only word written in Arabic.'

He glanced at the map. 'How about we name it Rebekah and say it was discovered by Rebecca Hewison?'

They all agreed and suggested it was time to head back into the reception to join the other guests. Rebecca was looking around the room at the many probing eyes. Just as she was feeling a tad uncomfortable, Christopher whispered for Rebecca to join him outside.

'I suspect your time with us is almost up, my dear girl. I believe this part of your mission is complete. I must say it was so clever of you to request they name the Ziggurat after Rebekah. Make your task years from now all the simpler. I will, of course, speak with my Rebecca upon her return. So, if, and when Sir Leonard requests her company, at least she has an idea of what to expect. Like you, she has a very clear mind and can be equally rational. Shall we join the other guests inside with their probing eyes,' he said, then laughed and shook his head.

Just as he had finished speaking, Judith came over to join them.

'I could see you becoming a little uncomfortable in there, Rebecca. Would you like to go for a walk?'

As she followed Judith down towards the lake, she couldn't help wondering why she was still here, other than she hadn't been on her own for more than a second. This though, made her think of Rhonella. 'Judith, may I ask about the maid who helped me this morning, Rhonella?'

'Yes, of course, you can. What would you like to know?'

'I would suspect you know of her background. She is so very intelligent and although young, could become a key part in the running of this house.'

Judith nodded, 'Both Christopher and I have already earmarked her for greater things. We plan to send her for higher education.'

Just as she was about to speak, her heel stuck fast in the grass causing her shoe to pull from her foot. Rebecca bent over and as her eyes focused on the ground, she could see she was wearing her old white pumps. Instantly she knew she was home in her own time, or at least she thought so.

Chapter 24 – The Key and...

Standing up, and looking around, she was fairly sure her time with Judith had been a success. The thing that was nagging at the back of her thoughts was not being altogether sure if she was actually home. Everything looked just so, there was though, something amiss. It wasn't a tangible, obvious something; just things weren't quite right. The more she thought about it, the more this odd feeling increased. This was most definitely a new sensation for Rebecca. In the past, no matter how far she travelled into the past or future, the emotions she got were similar in very slightly different ways, but the mood was constantly recognisable. *I'll go check the house,* she thought, *that will settle me down.* Strangely, though, the closer she got, the more the mood intensified. Glancing around, there didn't seem to be a sign of life anywhere. Part of her brain kept suggesting she'd jumped to a new time or era, while the other part was telling her this was something altogether different. 'This is just plain daft,' she muttered.

'What is just plain daft?' a familiar and comforting voice behind her enquired.

'Ethernal,' she said without turning, knowing there wouldn't be anyone there, just his voice. 'There isn't a sign of life,' and narrowing her eyes, having just noticed something very odd, she exclaimed, 'no curtains up at the windows, plus there are grasses and weeds growing all over the gravel. What exactly is going on?'

'You see a home that is not.'

'What does that even mean?' she said, shaking her head. She would never get used to his play on words, this though...

'Your home, previously Meredith's and Judith's home, yet no sign of life other than us two. This is what this planet would be like without humankind. It would be a home to no one.'

'Oh, I see, you are showing what it would...' She nodded, 'what it would be like without us, in essence without mankind.' Again, she nodded, and although she half-smiled, his message was another jolt to her consciousness, as if she needed one.

'This point is just to emphasise the importance of your mission. You are humanities last hope. If it has to fall to your kind in the future, it will be too late. So, go back and fetch the key you left under the fallen oak. And, your consciousness clearly needs another jolt.'

Shaking her head, Rebecca exclaimed, 'But I put the key in a safe place.' Suddenly alarm bells were ringing amid her confusion.

'Did you? Are you sure? Can you tell me which safe place?'

Rebecca's brain started retracing her steps. 'I never actually put it anywhere, did I? Did I leave it in my pocket and thought I had put it somewhere?'

'Now, there is a question. Have you considered that Meredith may have slipped it into your pocket when you were not paying attention, or is there another answer?' Rebecca then heard a sharp intake of breath. 'Tut, tut. No, you dropped it when you were changing your clothing with Rhonella. She gave it to Judith who placed it in a white hanky under the oak, on the assumption you would find it there in her time, your time, or Meredith's time. Now go and be less absent-minded. Check everything more than twice.'

Before she had a chance to say anything, she saw her mother's car pulling along the drive. A drive that was now free from grass and weeds. Torn between retrieving the key and greeting her mother, she put mum first, reckoning the key had been there for 68-years, so a few more minutes wouldn't hurt.

Her mum got out of the car and slammed the door so hard that Rebecca was surprised the glass didn't break. She looked at Rebecca and shouted, 'The thief stole my purse, right in front of everyone too.' She then hurried over to Rebecca, cuddled her and started sobbing.

Cuddling her mum, Rebecca decided as important as the key was, she would speak to her mother first and rightly so.

Her mum then pulled back and said, 'the indignity of it too. He was no more than thirteen or fourteen and it was right outside the spa.'

'Oh, Mum, I am so very sorry. Let's go and have a cup of tea.'

Rebecca then spent the next thirty minutes helping her mother phone anybody she hadn't already called regarding credit cards and such like. All the way through between consoling her mum who now seemed okay, Rebecca kept thinking, *I am supposed to save mankind when they are capable of doing things like this.* Her rational side, which she had now become fond of occasionally, was telling her this was a one-off and most people are decent. This then led her to consider the stories she'd heard about how people behaved when the temperature turned up and the food started running out. She shook her head and whispered, 'Best save them before then.'

'Sorry, best save whom before what?'

'Oh, I was just thinking about your purse and it got me wondering if mankind is actually worth saving, especially as we know how things will end. Hey though, that is then, and this is now, and as horrible as today's event was, fortunately, it doesn't happen often.'

'I'm sorry if I upset you, Honey. The second I saw you, all the anguish of the last hour came out.' Just then, her phone rang. 'Hello, yes this is Elizabeth. She proceeded to pace up and down the hallway shaking her head while she took the phone call. She then came off the phone and half smiled at Rebecca. 'They caught the dirt-bag. Stupid fool walked into a petrol station, pulled out my purse to buy a bottle of fizz, and get this, right in front of a uniformed police officer. Anyways, when the police officer asked the kid whose purse it was, he threw the purse down and ran. And the silly fool collided with another officer coming through the door.'

'Oh well, that's good. At least you have your purse back.'

'And my photos of you and Tommy as urchins,' she said and chuckled in that delightfully familiar way. 'Right, when I pulled up, you looked like you were on a mission heading towards the summerhouse. Go now, James will be home soon.'

Rebecca quickly explained all about the key and Ethernal.

'Well, Missy, you best go find it, and next time, don't lose it,' her mum said wide-eyed. 'Do you need me to help?'

'No, I am just fine, Mum. I know precisely where it is, or should be,' she said and raised her eyebrows.

On the way down to the woods, Rebecca's thoughts kept jumping between, meeting King George no less, Ethernal's wise words, her mother's horrid incident, and where she was going to hide the key.

Arriving in the woods, knowing the significance of her time with Judith, and then losing track of the key sent a shiver down her spine. She had never been in any doubts about the importance of her task, although leaving the key in 1945 magnified her intent. She hurried through the woods, and

191

arriving in the clearing, knelt down by the oak. Taking a deep breath, she pushed her outstretched hand in among the decaying leaves under the fallen oak. After removing a few twigs and a horribly decayed toadstool, her fingers settled on something that wasn't a dead leaf. As memories of finding the key, which was the start of her adventure, filled her head, it made her feel a little emotional. She shook her head and took a firm grip on what felt like damp material. Carefully, she pulled it out and as she did, the key fell from the hanky and landed in her lap. She puffed out a sigh of relief and clutched the key tightly in her hand. She opened the hanky out to reveal a note that simply said, *"Rhonella found this and I just knew it must be yours and of its importance. Love Judith."*

Clutching the key, she stood up and took a moment to look around. Although this area held a special place in her heart, she sadly hadn't been here on her own terms for far too long. She leaned back and perched herself on the tree and considered all she'd seen over the last few years. It created a real mixture of emotions as thoughts of the pixies, Meredith and Matilda flooded her thoughts. Suddenly, she felt so close to Meredith's aunt, it was as if she could hear her singing. 'Hang on,' she muttered, 'I can.' Looking over her shoulder, she could see Rebekah wandering towards her, singing with a beautiful smile on her face. She walked around the tree and sat next to Rebecca.

'My, girl, I am so pleased to see you today. In two days, I board a ship for the Americas and well...' She then nodded. 'You have the key, the one I failed to find my way to. My soul is free from torment now and I know you will do what I couldn't. Go with my love and be assured, you have all you need to succeed. I must go now, and this may be the last time our paths cross. Please do not be sad, know you have freed my tormented spirit. She then slowly walked back towards the willows until she had vanished from sight.

With a smile on her face, Rebecca sat there with tears rolling down her cheeks. Her emotions were happy, although the

192

thought of not seeing Rebekah again saddened her, but not as much as it should. She knew this was because of this soul's words. She sat there for a little longer until she decided it was time to go and check on her mother.

Chapter 25 – Summerhouse, again

With her feelings a little mixed, but her concerns for her mother dominating her emotions, Rebecca hurried back to the main house.

By the time she arrived back, she'd come to terms with Rebekah leaving for the Americas and her subsequent sad demise. She decided for her mum's benefit, she would put on a smiley face. 'Mother, I am back, and I found what I was looking for.'

'Well, Missy, give it here and let's put it in your father's safe. Of interest, you are meeting with that reporter chap from the Telegraph in a couple of days. Wednesday, I seem to recall. Anyways, are you going to tell him about the key?'

'No, I don't think so. I intended to play it close to my chest at this stage. You know how reporters can be, even with well-respected papers. I thought I'd just keep it basic with him and see how he responds. Besides, in a week or so, I am meeting up with Ruth's MP, David. He seems more receptive and importantly, his door should be a little more open because by the time we meet he should have seen the letter from his distant Aunt Meredith, my Meredith.' She shook her head. 'I still can't believe the coincidence. Not only does Ruth work for him, but also David's great, great, aunt, whatever she is, is flipping related to him. Well, his aunt would be related to him, but you know what I mean.'

'I must say, rather than a coincidence, it seems it was meant to be.'

'Yeah, all part of this unbelievably well planned out route I've been on for the last eight years.'

'We've been on,' Elizabeth said and chuckled in a way that made it clear to Rebecca that her mum was over having her purse snatched.

Over the next couple of hours, they reminisced about many of Rebecca's adventures. Around 5 p.m., Duncan and James arrived home and suggested a meal out at Liz's favourite Italian.

When they reached the restaurant, Elizabeth and Rebecca were more than a little surprised to see Amanda, Ruth, and Tommy all there waiting.

'Take your elbows off the table, Twit,' Rebecca said and giggled. She then patted Tommy on the head and said, 'no football around the table, there's a good boy.' She then kissed both Amanda and Ruth on the cheek.

They all spent a delightful evening sitting around chatting about Tommy's football exploits, along with Ruth and Amanda's recent shopping expedition to New York. Duncan and James joined in, although they did spend most of the time nodding, and adding the occasional comment. To Rebecca's surprise and relief to some degree, her time jumping wasn't mentioned.

'I would love to go shopping in New York, 'Liz said, glancing at James, and then Duncan.

'And there was me thinking it was about time we went to visit Mickey and company. New York, the banking capital of the world it is,' James said, laughed, and glanced at Duncan from the corner of his eye.

'Sounds like a plan. Any ideas when?' Liz asked, grinning towards Rebecca.

'Well, it would be lovely if we all went, and that includes you delightful ladies,' James said and nodded to Ruth and Amanda. 'Although you've just been, so maybe...' He then turned to Tommy and asked, 'are you up for a trip to the US?'

'Nope, we'd love to get back and then Ruth can get that dress she regrets not buying,' Amanda said and rolled her eyes towards Ruth in an ironic manner.

'What about you, Tommy? Football season must be almost over. Surely, you'd like the chance to walk down the road without having umpteen girls blowing you a kiss,' Rebecca said and again patted him on the head.

He tossed his head and raised his eyebrows. 'Sounds good to me, as long as Dad, Duncan and me, don't 'ave to traipse around girly shops all the time.'

'Tommy,' Elizabeth said, 'it is have, not 'ave, and it's I, not me.' She then glanced at James wide-eyed.

Sniggering, Tommy responded, 'Na, it is me, not you, Muvva.'

With Rebecca and the girls giggling, Elizabeth shook her head, and said, 'How much did we pay for him to get good schooling?'

'Mum, the only maths I need is to work out how many assists I managed in the last game.' He then giggled in a way Rebecca hadn't heard for a number of years. 'Mother, Father. The financial burden you undertook allowing me the opportunity to attend such a respected educational environment, was by no means wasted. It is jus' 'betta for me football mates if I talk proper like.'

'So, Rebecca, you have a lot coming up with your meeting and such like,' James said, clearly aware Tommy hadn't been embroiled in Rebecca's latest escapades. 'When would be a good date for you? I think it is good to grasp the nettle.'

'Dad, I'd suggest...' She then thought about her diary for a moment. 'The middle of July suits me.'

Duncan, nodding said, 'sounds good to me, shall I go ahead, and book it up?' He glanced around the room.

Ruth, having just checked her phone diary, said, 'yep, good for me.'

Amanda held her thumb up, 'good for me too.

'That's a date then,' Rebecca said, smiling at her mother. 'Mum, finally we get to go to the banking capital of the universe, yippee.' She then squeezed her mum's hand and chuckled.

The rest of the evening went wonderfully, without a single mention of Meredith, although Tommy did bring up the subject of Disney a couple of times. They arrived home well after midnight, and having said goodnight to everyone, Duncan and Rebecca headed down for their first night sleeping in the summerhouse.

'On the way out of the door, Rebecca called out, 'Mum, the heating is on, isn't it?'

'Yes, Dear. Sleep well you two.'

Entering the summerhouse to actually sleep caused a peculiar feeling and unique experience for Rebecca, having never been in there for more than a few minutes at most. 'This is so weird, Duncan. I don't mean being here with you, I mean...'

Before she could finish, Duncan clasped her hand and said, 'I thought exactly that on the way down here. It must be so odd for you. Right, ground rules,' he said and laughed in his gentlemanly way. 'No creeping about in the middle of the night, checking doors, stairs, cupboards and anything else. Deal?'

197

'That's a deal,' she said, 'although... No, it's okay, I am pooped and will sleep like a rock.' In the back of her thoughts, she knew only too well that anything could, and probably would happen.

Waking the following morning to a delightful spring day, with the sunshine creeping behind the ill-fitting curtains, brought a surge of nostalgia back to Rebecca. Lying there, she remembered the first time she climbed the stairs, entered the pitch-black room, and the way it suddenly filled with sunlight. She shook her head, recalling the first time she heard Meredith's voice and how she felt. As Duncan was still asleep, no surprise as it was 6 a.m., she decided to go get breakfast ready, knowing he had to be off to work by eight.

Heading down the spiral stairs again brought a flood of emotions cascading through her every vein. Deciding to cook a full Scottish breakfast, including the small haggis her mum had bought in especially, she quietly got everything out and ready. Then as she started cooking, she inwardly looked at herself and smiled. Chopping the mushrooms, she wondered if once her mission was over, she and Duncan would start a family. With four pans on the go, she felt rather mumsy and surprisingly broody. 'We will,' she said just as Duncan joined her.

'Morning, Rebecca,' he said and kissed her on the cheek. 'We will what, may I ask?'

'Start a family, once my job is over.'

'That would be a lovely thing indeed. We will make beautiful, graceful and who knows, perhaps time-travelling children. Importantly, we will know, once your mission is successfully completed, we are bringing them into a world with a future.'

After breakfast with Duncan, Rebecca headed up for a little shopping trip into the local town with her mother. It turned out to be a lovely day, although Rebecca did get a rather peculiar feeling as she walked down the road where the old bookshop had appeared and vanished in the space of a few days. Just being there, as if she needed reminding, reiterated the importance of her task, especially after the conversation with Duncan about bringing children into a world with a future. They arrived home and with just Rebecca and her mum at home, they had a lovely girly catch up.

Chapter 26 – The Reporter

The following morning, Rebecca woke up just before her phone alarm. Seconds later, the pesky thing started buzzing, reminding her she had a meeting with Martin Foreshore. Not that she minded the idea of the meeting; she'd never liked her phone and the noises it made. *Must get myself a proper alarm clock*, she thought.

After a nice shower, and with Duncan away on business, she headed up to the main house. She went through and joined her mother out the back of the kitchen for some orange juice and toast. This was much more to Rebecca's liking, compared to the heavy breakfast she'd prepared Duncan the day before. She sat sipping her juice thinking about the day ahead. 'Interesting day I have, Mother. I am not altogether sure how I feel about baring my soul to some newspaper reporter.'

'I am sure it will be fine. It was the last time you met up with him.'

'Yeah, no doubts. I think what is concerning me most is I no longer need his input. I don't mean that horribly. At the time, I was looking for any avenue to get my story told. Now though, I have a clear plan.'

'The thing is you may need him after. If say, the MP, what's his name, David Wilson, buys in, then the pair of you may need Martin's input to help create a bigger stage, so to speak.'

'That, Mother, is a really excellent point. Thank you. I will feed him enough to get his interest and tell him I am meeting David in a few days. Heavens above, it is a few days time, crumbs, time flies.'

Laughing quietly, Elizabeth said, 'Literally time flies when you're around. Just think, you have enough time for a trip to the moon and back before you meet him. The way I see it, you could go somewhere distant and be back before your toast gets cold.' She then smiled and said, 'don't think about it, just in case.'

'Now there's a thought,' Rebecca said and chuckled. 'Are you sure you're okay giving me a lift into town, Mum?'

'Yes, of course. Besides, I am meeting up with Ruth for a spot of lunch, as we do,' she said and giggled in that delightful way.

On the way into town, Rebecca sat quietly in the car, going over everything in her head.

'You're quiet, Rebecca.'

'I think, Mum, I am just going to play it by ear and see how it all goes.'

'Best way, Honey. You normally do, and you know Meredith will be right behind you,' she said and laughed uneasily, 'along with the rest of humanity.'

'Thanks, Mum, as if I needed reminding,' she said and laughed even though she once again felt a tad of pressure.

Just as Rebecca entered the restaurant, Martin was just checking in, only seconds ahead of her. She reckoned on this being a good omen, which made her feel a little easier.

'Hello, Rebecca. It seems we both like to be punctual. I have a table by the window away from nosey ears.'

On the way to the table, he explained that this meeting was completely off the record and she should look at it as a chat with someone who has a vested interest. 'After all, Rebecca, if your story is true, and I am a believer, for sure, I want the world to listen. In fact, I had a meeting with my old senior editor-in-chief and suggested they run a big campaign about global fuel issues and such like and do so from a countryside and seaside impact scenario. I must add, I didn't mention you, or your story.'

'That's a good idea. Get it into the public's thoughts. Then we can go, boom, here's the truth. Mind you, of late there's been a lot of stuff about global warming and the likely impact.'

'That, Rebecca is exactly what I thought. That is why I have suggested an alternative angle on this subject. Perhaps one that is about dried up riverbeds, ponds, low reservoir levels and so on. For sure, we will not run anything about your story, not until we have your clearance. I know you have a meeting with David Wilson in a couple of days. Perhaps, and only dependent on how that goes, we can get together again soon after and see what temperature the water is at, which will perhaps be another degree higher,' he said and kind of laughed with a concerned appearance indicating he was obviously serious.

Rebecca shook her head and said, 'Forty degrees higher if we don't do something soon.'

Throughout lunch, Rebecca chatted about her story, keeping only to the basic outline without saying definitively that she'd actually been into the past or future. She kept emphasising she wanted to tell this story as if it were a book and he was the reader. The more she talked, the more comfortable she became and felt herself trusting his motives and agenda. 'The thing is, if just supposed I have this key, star map, knowledge of this curious four-thousand-year-old Ziggurat and have met with King George VI sixty-odd years ago. If that were the case, alongside having this knowledge of what is to come a thousand years in the future. Just saying what if, hypothetically speaking? How are we going to get the world to listen and importantly act upon a ludicrous story written by a no one?'

'Well, Rebecca, I am in no doubts. The way you speak with such verve, passion, and belief, it would be hard to question the stories' validity. That is accepting you can travel through time. That is the sticking point. However, if there is a letter hidden in a bank vault, alongside this star map that King George used. Hang on, have you checked to see if this Sir Leonard Wooley ever found your temple?'

Rebecca shook her head in disbelief. 'Do you know what, I haven't? Do you have a laptop with you?'

'Yep,' he said, going to his bag. Seconds later, he booted it up and started searching the Internet. 'What did you say the Ziggurat was called? Oh yeah, named after you, Rebecca.'

'Actually, named after the original Rebekah, the one in the Bible and spelled this way,' she said and wrote it down.

'And you say around nineteen-forty-five, just after the war was over.'

'Yes indeed. Any luck finding anything?' she asked, her curiosity now a little over excited, still unable to believe she hadn't thought of looking herself.

Grinning, Martin said, 'here we are, in July of nineteen-forty-six, Sir Leonard Wooley, on an expedition funded by King George VI, blah, blah, blah, discovered a Ziggurat in a previously unexplored part of central Asia once known as Mesopotamia...' He looked up at Rebecca appearing rather startled and astonished. 'It clearly states that King George had been given a four-thousand-year-old star map found in an old English estate attic, by...' Again, he looked up, 'just as you said, Rebecca Hewison of the Deer Park Family Estate. And as you also said, the temple was named after Rebekah the wife of Isaac on the specific instructions of Rebecca Hewison.' He shook his head, and staring straight at Rebecca, a little tearful, he said, 'that's you, just sixty-odd years ago. Oh, my golly gosh, I have hairs standing up on my arm as if they were called to guard.'

Rebecca, holding her head in her hands with a mixture of excitement, relief, and amazement, said, 'that's how my story goes. I just now need to write the end few chapters.'

'I am in, totally. However, it is your story and I will not utter a word of this until the timing is right. I am going to push hard for as many articles in the paper on the subject of global warming as I can.'

'Thank you, Martin, for being such a good reader and believing in my girl's story. We will prevail,' she said and nodded intently. In the back of her thoughts, although a little edgy about him having so much detail, she also felt he was now an advocate and therefore could be trusted.

'We will prevail. Indeed, we must prevail.'

After lunch and exchanging phone numbers and emails, they agreed to get in touch as soon as a new corner approached.

Chapter 27 – Back to Meredith and...

On the way home in the car, having told her mum all about her meeting, she sat there wondering what she was going to do for the next few days. Not that occupying herself was ever a problem for Rebecca; just this time, she was perhaps hoping she could jump forward and get on with it. This idea made her laugh out loud.

'What is so funny, Sweetie?'

'That meeting went so well, I want to get on and meet up with David Wilson, now ideally. I just thought, where is my time-travelling when I need it,' she said and chuckled. 'A jump forward to my meeting wouldn't go amiss.'

'It will arrive soon enough and besides; I am sure you will find something to occupy your thoughts. Perhaps a trip somewhere and I don't mean New York.' Elizabeth then squeezed Rebecca's hand.

With a lot of traffic, they chatted about Liz's meeting with Ruth, occasionally going back to Rebecca's discussion with Martin.

'When is Roxy going to Asia? I take it she is still going to volunteer out there. Hey, maybe you could look her up if you go back to Rebekah.'

'Mum, really, she is going in our time and its thousands of miles away from Rebekah's homeland.   Geography's never been your strong point, has it?' she then rolled her eyes.

'J for a joke, Miss Serious.'

'I am so sorry, Mother. That would be fun. Hello, Roxy, bet you didn't expect to see me.' She then shook her head and chuckled.   'I will miss her, and I am a little worried, to be honest.'

'Why so, Honey?'

'Well, she is going right into the heart of it, on a refugee camp. No doubts she'll be safe and all, she's a big girl now, even so.'

'She'll be just fine, Rebecca. Oh, look here we are home,' her mum said as she entered the long drive. 'So busy chatting, the car got here on autopilot, I think. You've never explored up this way, have you?'

'Now, there's an idea.'

'Who knows where you might end up?'

'Exactly. Duncan is away for a few days, so I might just have a snoop around tomorrow unless you have anything planned.'

'Going back into town with your father and then we are down to London for a few days.' Narrowing her eyes as she got out of the car, she said, 'I did tell you, didn't I?'

Shaking her head, Rebecca said, 'Yeah, for sure, Mum. It just slipped my mind. I hope you and father have fun.'

After supper, Rebecca decided on an early night knowing her mum and dad were up early and she wanted to see them off. When she woke up the following morning, her phone alarm hadn't gone off. Although she'd plugged it in to charge it up,

206

she hadn't switched the plug on. 'Damn it,' she muttered glancing at the big wall clock and seeing it was gone ten. Rebecca was never one for lying in bed, and if she did, it was never past eight in the morning, so waking up at this time came as a bit of a shock. She then mumbled to herself as she headed for the shower, 'unless I have slept for seven days.' She then laughed at her own joke.

Not feeling hungry, she decided to have coffee and toast before going for a walk, especially as it was such a nice day. As she headed out of the front door, it just felt like a normal sort of day. Deciding to head up towards the entrance gate, she made her way along the shingle drive. She spent most of the afternoon mooching around inspecting the old entrance gate and the surrounding area. Around five, feeling there wasn't much here other than a few old trees, she decided to head back. Over the next two days, mostly due to it raining nonstop, she stayed in sketching and catching up on the book she'd started when she left university.

She woke up the following morning to a clear blue sky and sunlight streaming in through the window. She had become so engrossed in her book she'd fallen asleep on the bed, in her clothes and left the curtains open. Leaning over, she looked at her phone. 'Twenty-fourth,' she mumbled, 'three days.' Then as she stood in front of the mirror looking at the creases in her blouse and the state of her hair, she decided to take a long soak in the bath.

After something to eat and drink, she thought she'd carry on with her book down in the summerhouse. With her laptop under her arm, she headed down towards the lake. On the way, she thought about her walk up towards the entrance gate and how she'd felt. The whole area was soulless, and this left her a tad confused. There were some beautiful trees, rhododendrons, and vast swathes of young elm trees, even so... Just as she was walking along the water's edge, she could feel something unusual. It wasn't like the normal vibe she always got. No, this was something altogether different. There was almost an air of urgency, which was making her feel rather edgy. She shook her head and rubbed her arms against her body.

She didn't feel like she'd gone anywhere or was about to go anywhere. Confused, and with her curiosity now tingling in a kind of jittery way, she opened the door to the summerhouse. 'This is odd,' she mumbled. She could definitely feel something and there was even the smell of almonds or Christmas as her mum preferred to say. She put her laptop down and went for a quick check upstairs, thinking perhaps she'd left a window open, or something. Looking around, she muttered, 'nothing.' Shaking her head, she went back downstairs, sat down, and bent over to plug her laptop in.

'What,' she exclaimed with an unusually high-pitched tone. 'Where's the socket?' She then got up and marched around the room, moving chairs, looking behind the curtains. There was no sign of electricity anywhere. *Now, this is plain daft*, she thought, seeing everything else was just so. She opened the door to the kitchen and besides no sockets in there, everything else was as she'd expect. Heading back into the hallway, she decided to check behind the little door at the end of the corridor where she'd first found the spiral staircase. This room was now a cupboard with no more than a few bits and bobs and the electrical main circuit board. She turned the handle without really thinking it might be locked. Damn it, she muttered, finding the door stuck fast. Pulling what she knew was a silly face she stepped back and suddenly noticed the door was green again. Shaking her head, she reckoned Duncan must have painted it green having heard her go on about the green door so many times.

This was plain daft, what with the odd feeling, the smell of almonds, no electricity and now the door being stuck, even though everything else was just as she'd expect, new. Then a bizarre thought occurred to her that perhaps Meredith was playing a game with her to stop her getting bored.

208

'Right, the game is up, Meredith, open the blinking door and put back my electrics,' she blurted, both laughing and shaking her head at the same time.

There was a click. 'Again,' she mumbled, as all the emotions of the first time she'd called Meredith from this door flooded her thoughts. In good Rebecca style, she closed her eyes, gripped the handle, and turned it. As she felt the door open and a whoosh of almond smelling air fizzing past her ears and nostrils, she opened her eyes. 'What,' she mumbled, 'is going on?'

Instead of the expected cupboard, the old dimly lit spiral staircase was back, in all its glory, covered in dust and cobwebs. *Glad I put a white tee shirt on*, she thought as she eased her way between the stairs and wall, wanting to find out what was going on. As she stood at the bottom of the stairs and looked up into the darkness, Rebecca felt more than a tad prickly. At this point, her emotions were all over the place. With memories of the first time she climbed the stairs, mixed with confusion as to what exactly was going on, was this weird excitement? She stood there for a few seconds certain something significant was about to happen. Through every journey, no matter how bizarre, she'd never experienced a feeling quite like this before. She'd always felt something was afoot whenever she walked this road, never had she felt this urgency.

'Right, let's do it,' she mumbled as she started climbing the stairs. Just as it was all those years ago, the stairs were covered in dust. She reached the first door and paused for a second getting her bearings. She remembered it being dark, but it was so dark that she could barely see the door, let alone the handle. With her emotions jumping from one thought to the next, she took a deep breath and fumbled around for the handle.

Finally clasping the handle, she turned it slowly. Click, it opened, as it did years earlier. Just as the first time she was here, the room was in darkness, barring a tiny shard of light in the far corner. Knowing it was a window, she let go of the door. Bang, it slammed behind her. Although she'd been through this before, it still spooked her a little. Just as she was beginning to place the pieces of the jigsaw together, she reckoned this was perhaps serving as a reminder of where her journey started. As she thought how these few steps were emphasising the importance of her very existence, she heard a delightfully familiar voice.

'Rebecca, thank heavens you found your way back.'

Unlike the first time though, that voice was followed by another familiar voice.

'Marhabaan,' the second voice called.

Hearing both Meredith and Rebekah, she instantly knew something very important was happening.

Bemused to find both of them in the old summerhouse, she called out, 'Hello, Meredith. Marhabaan, Rebekah.' With the room now bursting with sunlight, just as it was the first time she was here, she made her way over to the narrow door on the far side of the room. Rebecca's carefree curiosity was always ready to take over from her conscious rational thoughts. Today though, both were working overtime as she stood at the top of the stairs. 'I so nearly swore then,' she whispered, causing her to laugh.

'Do not swear, just come and join us down here,' Meredith called out.

Shaking her head, she thought, *how did she hear me?* She didn't have to wait long to find out, because as she approached the stairs, Meredith was standing at the bottom peering up, clearly waiting for her. Again, this emphasised her gut feeling that something important was about to transpire.

'I know you my girl and knew that amid this breathless journey today, you would consider swearing as you often do,

210

but never succumb.' She then smiled in that oh so endearing way.

'You know me better than I do,' she said. Reaching the bottom of the stairs, she cuddled Meredith. Then as she entered the kitchen, which bizarrely was just as it was the first time she was here, she turned to Rebekah. 'So, I find both of you, in eighteen-fifty-three.' She knew there had to be a momentous reason why they were both here, and asked, 'What may I ask is going on?' She moved towards Rebekah unsure if she should give her a cuddle.

This gracious woman pulled Rebecca by the shoulder and cuddled her. 'I was not sure if I would see you again. Here you are, though.'

'Here you are indeed,' Meredith said, raising her eyebrows and suddenly appearing serious.

Rebecca knew there was a good reason why they were both here and seeing Meredith's expression emphasised that point. With her need to know at bursting point, she glanced at both women in a questioning way.

Meredith took hold of Rebecca's hand. 'There is a problem in the future that compounds your plight.' She then glanced towards Rebekah.

'I was visited by a woman I know not of. She was of our making and travelled from three-hundred-years ahead of your time, Rebecca. Her message was simple in that the timelines have altered. There was no explanation, and she was with me for only a breath.'

Rebecca, although alarmed, in the back of her thoughts was the idea that she still had three-hundred-years. That was until Meredith spoke.

'The predicament is now complex. You may feel as if you still have time on your side. Your quandary is you need a rapid

211

response from the world's governors. If there is no action within months, it may prove too late for humanity.'

'Months,' Rebecca said, 'how many months exactly?'

'When I asked that exact question, the messenger from the future said, and I quote, "like yesterday." So, a forthright and outspoken approach must now be your approach. We have considered how we can help you further. We feel now all that can be done has been done. You have the message within my temple, you have the letter from Meredith,' Rebekah said and glanced at Meredith. 'In addition, you have something from the future that I do not comprehend, an object you refer to as a tablet I believe is the term.'

'There is no more you should need.'

Rebecca's brain suddenly went up a gear. 'Hang on a minute. If you are able to come to meet with Meredith, why can't you come and meet me in my time? Even better, you both visit me in my time.' She shook her head. 'And bring with you Matilda, Judith and your aunt,' she said and touched Meredith's hand. She then nodded. 'I could arrange for the parliamentarian to visit this summerhouse. He couldn't dispute that then if you were all here, could he?'

'We considered that. However, it may actually weaken your position. If for one moment he thinks we are not who we say we are, his subconscious will close down.' Meredith nodded to both. 'If he believes we are in fancy dress, he may think it is one horribly ludicrous scam, irrespective of his initial engagement.'

'Yeah, you're absolutely right. Damn, I never thought of that.'

'So, do we have a revised date, when exactly are we talking about?' Rebecca asked, unsure how she was feeling.

212

'The last of mankind will take one final breath on December twenty-fifth, in the year twenty-three thirty-eight.' Meredith then again squeezed Rebecca's hand. 'It is the meaning for our existence, our destiny. Why we are here, why our kind is so entwined, interlinked, and can move so freely. We are humanities second chance.'

Rebecca had always been aware that her journeys into the past had a reason and that reason was to stop time taking an alternative direction. A direction that would unfavourably alter the lives of those she met and those people closest to her if she failed to make changes. Of late, she had realised her mission was considerably more and humanity was dependent on her. Never had she considered this was the sole purpose for her ability to move through time, and it was all leading to this. 'So, in essence, we are part of a bigger plan. As you said so eloquently, "we are humanities second chance." It seems that our existence is perhaps a preconceived plan.'

'As difficult as it may be to comprehend to onlookers, we are indeed part of a bigger plan. That plan is to offer humanity a chance for redemption, learning from their mistakes and altering the course of time. It is a course mankind has altered to its detriment purely through its relentless self-indulgent greed. In your time, every man and woman know the consequence of burning the planet's resources and littering the land and sea with indefensible products of gluttony. It falls to you, Rebecca, to reverse this process. This is the reason for your being,' Meredith said, and once more squeezed Rebecca's hand.

With a mixture of emotions, Rebecca wasn't quite sure how she felt. Part of her was a little tearful, while her feisty side was brimming with exhilaration and even more determined to succeed. She'd always been comfortable with her ability to see past the obvious, and to some extent, learnt to accept it for what it was, a ludicrously bizarre ability to jump from one era to the next. Now though, this uniqueness made common sense, an emotion she had shied away from in the past.

213

Without realising, embroiled in her thoughts, she'd wandered over to the window. Coming from her semi-subconscious state, she closed her eyes for a second, certain when she turned back to the others they'd be gone and she would be once more on this journey alone. She took a deep breath, and with a little nod, she turned to an empty room. Over the last few months, she'd begun to realise that Meredith, among others, came and went as they pleased, almost as if they were appearing before her only as reassurance and guidance. Still, she would never get used to them just vanishing. Although finding herself still in Meredith's time alone should have alarmed her, it didn't. She shook her head, made her way over to the stairs, and back up to where it all began, confident she would find her way back to her own time.

Chapter 28 – The MP

With an odd pain on the side of her face, Rebecca opened her eyes to find she had nodded off face down on her laptop. Rubbing her cheek, she wondered what was going on. *One minute I am climbing Meredith's stairs, the next I am here as if it never happened,* she thought. Having briefly considered her time with Rebekah and Meredith was some bizarre dream, she shook her head, and mumbled, 'no, that's plain silly.' The annoying thing, having woken face down on her laptop, part of her brain was suggesting it might have been. A little irritated for even considering it, she got up and walked over to the sparkling new spiral staircase. She stood there for a few seconds, and again mumbled, 'no, plain silly, not a dream, I know what I know.'

Right, she thought, *go back to the main house.* She went to close her laptop down, but it was off. She pressed the on-button half-a-dozen times, but there was no response. Then she remembered she hadn't found a plug socket, and when she was looking for one, had somehow ended up back with Meredith and Rebekah. Miffed and unusually suspicious, she swivelled her chair around and could see plenty of plug sockets. 'Hmmm, this just isn't adding up.' The one thing she knew now was that with her laptop dead, she was as certain as she could be that she hadn't been dreaming.

As she made her way back to the house, she annoyingly found herself again wondering if it had all been a dream, even though she knew it wasn't. Approaching the main house, she tried to focus her attention towards meeting up with David

215

Wilson in two days. As she reached the front door, she noticed water brimming over the top of the water butt. Now she knew for sure her mum had emptied the water on the pot plants the evening before, just prior to her and dad going to London. This wasn't adding up, because it was still the same sunny morning just as it was moments before she went down to the summerhouse. She stood there for a few seconds staring at the full water butt, and while she did, she heard the house phone ringing.

Rushing to open the door, and almost pushing it off its hinges, she grabbed the phone just as it stopped. Checking, she could see it was her mum calling. *Odd*, she thought, dialling her back.

'Hello, Mother. Why did you call me on the house phone?'

'Hello, Sweetie. I've been worried about you. I have been ringing for two days on your mobile and finally this morning it wouldn't connect. Hence why I decided to call on the house phone. I thought maybe you left your phone somewhere, like with Meredith,' she said and laughed.

Two days, Rebecca was thinking as her brain went in circles. 'Two days, Mum, what are you talking about?'

'Honey, it's the twenty-seventh. Did you lose track of time being on your own?'

Shaking her head, at a complete loss what to think, Rebecca didn't know what to say. 'Err, not sure what is going on, Mum.'

'What do you mean, Rebecca?' her mum asked with an obvious tone of concern.

Rebecca then spent the next few minutes explaining to her mother all about her meeting up with Meredith and Rebekah, including her thinking it might have been a dream.

216

'Sweetie, dreams don't last three days,' she said and chuckled. 'As long as you are okay, you best get yourself ready because you have your meeting with the MP today. Call me in a while and let me know how you are getting on.'

'Okay, Mum. I love you and thank you for loving me back so much.'

'I do love you so much. Now go get ready, you'll need some time having slept for three days,' she said and chuckled again.

Rebecca hurried upstairs and after a quick shower put on her interview dress, as she called it. Looking in the mirror, she applied a little lipstick and decided to tie her hair up in her new favourite French style. This was something she'd practised since her meeting with King George. 'Perfect,' she mumbled.

Having already called a cab, the driver was waiting as she opened the front door. She got in the cab and said, 'Lord Street in Liverpool, please. My name is Rebecca,' she said, always wanting to be sociable with the cab drivers.

'Hello, Rebecca. It's lovely of you to introduce yourself. You're looking very important today,' the woman said and smiled in the mirror. 'My name is Meredith.'

Well, it would be, Rebecca thought, shaking her head. All the way into town, Rebecca couldn't get her thoughts away from what had happened to the last two days. The more she thought about it, the further her confusion grew. In the end, she started wondering if it had anything to do with her saying to her mother that she wished she could jump forward to today. The closer she got to town, the more she tried to push it to the back of her thoughts, knowing she had to be strong-minded and focused. Something then occurred to her that made her laugh out loud.

'What is so funny, Rebecca? Not this traffic, of that I am certain.'

217

'Oh, nothing really. Just thinking about a conversation, I had a day or two ago.' In the back of her thoughts, she was thinking, *I dare not tell her it was with someone who lived 4000 years ago, and they were talking about her having 300 years to get the job done.* The idea of how this woman named Meredith may respond made her laugh again.

'I understand your dilemma, although I know of your journey. Did you not consider that my name being Meredith was perhaps more than a coincidence?'

With her mouth open, Rebecca sat staring at this woman. She knew it wasn't her Meredith, so wondered who this woman was and how could she know so much unless she was just chatting and...

'Unless nothing,' she chuckled. 'I was summoned here to drive you today. We had to make sure you arrived safely and on time. You need not bother yourself with who I am, just know I am like you, although I am from another dimension.'

Dimension, Rebecca thought, *that's a new one on me. Another era, time, life, but not dimension. Surely, she means time.* She then recalled some time back hearing the term dimension referred to about someone named Belle. Then suddenly a loud alarm went off in her head, recalling Meredith saying her spirit was in another dimension. She considered this for a brief moment and then her focus returned to this woman who could clearly read her thoughts.

'I mean dimension. You share this planet with others who have reached a higher spiritual understanding and live alongside mankind in an alternative life phase. We have watched for millennia as mankind has continued to find ways to wreak havoc on each other and our blessed planet. You, Rebecca, are ours and mankind's last and only chance. Humanity has been warned before, many times. If you are successful in changing Earth's destiny and altering the greed-clock and the subsequent impact it will have on this world, we

218

will meet again. Of that, you can be assured. We are here now. Be brave, intrepid, fearless, and forceful. You know the truth, the ultimate truth. You trust yourself and others close to you trust you, so why would the distant not trust you as well. You have a unique spirit that resonates from one to the next with all those you encounter. Even non-believers cannot help but change their life's beliefs and engage with your visionary standpoint. Your energy and vigour are strong, surrounds you, and engulfs all. Trust that you capture the minds, thoughts, and hearts of those you meet. Go and triumph over the outwardly impossible. The future is yours.'

Overwhelmed, thrown, and at the same time invigorated, Rebecca sat staring from the window with no words. She watched the people coming and going, all minding their own business. Over the last couple of weeks, the importance of her task had magnified and now watching these strangers, all dependent on her mission, focused her awareness. As the car came to a halt, she looked back to Meredith. Bizarrely, but oddly unsurprisingly to Rebecca, the woman had vanished, and in her place was a smiling Asian gentleman.

'It has been a pleasure talking with you, Rebecca,' he said in a strong Liverpool accent.

Shaking her head, she got out of the car, paid her fare, and headed inside Ruth and David's office building. In an uncanny way, meeting Meredith had settled her nerves, even though she was still coming to terms with there being another dimension. Although this should have come as a complete shock to her rationale, she wasn't at all surprised. In fact, the more she thought about it, the more she wondered if the two Rebekah's, Meredith, Matilda, and Judith all moved in and out of this dimension, as perhaps she did herself and that was how she was able to jump from one era to another. Just as she was thinking her time in the past was her actually moving in and out of their dimension, she heard a woman speaking.

'Can I help you, Miss?' the lady on the reception asked.

219

'Oh, sorry, I was miles away. I have a meeting with David Wilson at ten this morning.'

'May I ask your name please?'

'Sorry, yes, it's Rebecca,' she then paused thinking, does he know my married name? She shook her head, knowing he did. 'Rebecca Ferguson.'

The receptionist then made a brief phone call, before looking up and saying, 'He is expecting you. His office is on the third floor.'

Although the lift door was open, Rebecca decided to take the stairs to give her some thinking time. The sound of her heels echoing around the cold stairwell did little to help, although it did take her mind off what she needed to say. In a strange way, this ended up helping, because as she reached the third floor, her mind was clear, and she knew the best way to approach this was to ad-lib and wait for questions. Her mother taught her at a young age that people are more interested in your story if they are having their questions answered. She'd always been one for talking endlessly and even though she'd often been aware that those around her weren't listening, her enthusiasm carried on regardless.

As she opened the door, Ruth was waiting for her.

'I so knew you'd take the stairs,' Ruth said and kissed Rebecca on the cheek.

'Hello, Ruth. This day has been a long time coming and I am not altogether sure how I feel about what I have to say and so on.' She then narrowed her eyes and shook her head ever so slightly.

'David is actually looking forward to hearing your story in full. He has asked me so many questions about you, and your character. Obviously, I kept it pragmatic and, on a need to know basis. He did ask about your time-travel story, more than once, I can tell you. I did though suggest that this question was owned by you.' She then waved her hand a little and said, 'shall we? Would you like me to sit in with you and David, perhaps takes some notes or something?'

'I would love that. You are an advocate and if things slip down the wrong slope, you can pull us back, perhaps.'

As they entered the room, David was sitting drinking from a cup. He looked up, smiled, and asked, 'Would you like a coffee, Rebecca?'

'That would be nice, thank you.'

'I will get a cup for Rebecca and myself,' Ruth said, 'would you like a top-up, David?'

'I am good thank you. Too many more coffees and I won't sleep for a month. Rebecca, please sit down. I am glad Ruth is with us. She has spoken so highly of you. Not only did she say you were wise beyond your years but super intelligent too. Also, a wiz with spreadsheets I believe.'

A little self-conscious, Rebecca nodded.

'I am so sorry; I did not mean to...'

Rebecca held her hand up, 'It is okay, David. I have never taken praise well.' She then turned to Ruth who had just put the coffee down. 'Thank you, Ruth. Boy, do I need this.'

'Rebecca, we have as long as it takes. If we need all day, that's just fine, we can send out for lunch. In your own time and please feel free to take a break and so on.' He then smiled at Rebecca and Ruth. 'So,' he said raising his eyebrows, 'it appears we have a connection with the same person.' He then lifted up Meredith's letter. As if he could sense Rebecca's uneasiness, he said, 'I am in, Rebecca. I do not need convincing about the truth of your time in the past. I was on board before I got this letter from the bank vault, where it had

221

been locked away for more than a century and a half, I might add. However, receiving within the letter a sepia photo of you at her daughter's wedding in the eighteen-fifties was more surreal than a surprise. Nonetheless, it gave me an unquestionable, indisputable insight into your world.'

Unaware that Meredith had taken a photo of her, let alone placed a copy in the letter came as a bit of a surprise. Unsure what to think or say, Rebecca glanced at Ruth.

'Can I see the photo?' Ruth asked. 'Ooh, get you all dressed up and looking fabulous.'

'Let me see,' Rebecca said, knowing she remained in her own clothes throughout her time at both the failed and successful marital ceremonies. 'This is plain daft,' she said, waving the photo. 'No matter how many times I travel back and forth, I will never get used to curveballs like this.' Seeing both Ruth and David appearing puzzled, she explained that she'd been at this wedding, but unlike meeting up with King George, she never got dressed up. 'Oh, hang on, I didn't for the failed wedding, but I did for the one that went through successfully.' Seeing David's expression, she could see he was bursting to say something.

'So, let me get this right, not only did you go to two wedding ceremonies with Meredith, but you also met King George.' He shook his head, 'which King George may I ask?'

'Queen Elizabeth's father, King George no less.' Rebecca said and chuckled, shaking her head. 'I know, all a bit surreal, even by my standards.'

'You never mentioned that,' Ruth said, shaking her head.

'Well, I must say, if anyone had any doubts about your time travelling adventures, your conviction and the way you chat about it as if it happened yesterday and was the norm would be enough to convince even the most unreceptive individuals.'

Inwardly, Rebecca was relieved David was so unexpectedly onboard. 'It's been a long journey for me, and at times it's been hard for me to accept the reality of something that most would see as a mad dream or a brilliant film at best.' She shook her head. 'The mission I have now though has helped me accept that this is neither a dream nor a film. It is, in fact, the reason for my existence, and is my sole destiny. My job now is complex, not because I have to convince people I can actually travel from one era to another, seamlessly. The battle will come when I have to persuade others to act upon my knowledge of the future. Change and engage the minds of individuals who can make a difference.'

'Well, the letter from Meredith does explain that I must listen to your knowledge of the future and act upon it with verve. It doesn't allude to the details of your message, other than to say that humanity is dependent on you and the actions of those you involve.'

Over the next hour or so, Rebecca explained about her journey into the future and emphasised while she was there the planet was on a road to recovery, just without humankind. She also mentioned about her time with Rebekah 4000 years ago. She then told David about the tablet, and that it contained directions on how to repair the damage humanity has caused, suggesting they can come onto that later.

'So, in essence, you've seen Earth without us? In addition, you gave a star map to King George that pointed to a hidden temple that was built two thousand years BC. And, you have a key that will unlock a secret compartment, one that will tell our generation of your time in the past. To compound this, you have an original diagram of this Ziggurat built four-thousand years ago. Then we have the device that will solve our problems.' He narrowed his eyes. 'We need to establish an order of proceedings.'

Rebecca nodded. 'I have already done that,' she said and handed him a handwritten list.

223

Things to do:

1. Convince David Wilson, explaining Meredith's letter, and then showing him the key and tablet.

2. With David, speak to and convince the Prime Minister.

3. Visit the Ziggurat, open the secret compartment.

4. With a convinced Prime Minister, contact scientists who can follow the information within the tablet.

5. Engage the press with all the above.

6. Show the world and engage the world.

7. Travel into the future to 2338 to see if it all worked.

'Right, sorry, some of that is for me. Well, all of it actually. That includes number seven,' she said and laughed. 'I've been thinking about this for a long time. Actually, my kind has known about this since civilisation got their act together.' She then took the piece of paper and said, 'I need to add a number eight.' She then scribbled under heading 8;

Find out what the other dimension is all about.

Once more with narrowed eyes, David asked, 'so you are telling us there are others like you who have lived through the millennia?'

'In essence, yes. I am part of a sequence all leading towards this day.' Not wanting to confuse matters, she still felt it necessary to tell him about Queen Matilda. 'You know, I also met another member of the royal family in the twelfth century. So, my job was to save her from being killed by King Stephen. Her name was Queen Matilda. So, if history had gotten its way, she would have been slain after a mere six weeks on the throne. She was of my making whereby she could see beyond her years and this resulted in her being labelled as a witch.'

224

'So, you are telling me the Scottish Queen Matilda was saved by you and thereby you changed history.'

Nodding, she said, 'yes, I helped her escape, after she had been injured, our destination was Scone Priory in central Scotland. I might add, bizarrely, my husband Duncan is a descendant of Queen Matilda's equerry.' She then tightened her lips questioningly. 'You know of her it would seem.'

'I do indeed. I have read her many chronicles.' He then got up, went to his bookcase, and carefully removed a huge tan book.

As he brought it back to the table, Rebecca seeing the similarities to the books she'd been shown by the bookkeeper who appeared and vanished in her hometown in the space of a few days, made her think, *here we go again*. She then watched as he painstakingly went through the pages. With her curiosity at bursting point, she was thinking; get on with it, while her university head was telling her to be patient, recognising how old this book probably was.

'Here we go,' he said, turning the book towards Rebecca. 'Now the author of this book, Matilda, former deposed Queen no less, states categorically that this chronicle is a work of fiction. Written in the first person and that first person is her.'

'Interesting, I am writing a novel about my journeys, well trying to, between all this, and I too am doing so from my point of view in the first person.'

'Well, interesting that is indeed. Your type, if I can call you that, obviously feel the need to express your journeys through the written word. So, the last two paragraphs are of particular interest. To the point, I had them translated from Germanic to English to make sure my translation was correct.' He then handed Rebecca a folded piece of paper.

Now Rebecca had worked out Matilda was involved with all of this, but until now, she never considered her a time traveller, just a visionary. That was of course if her assumptions of what she'd just read were correct. She then read through it again. Even though it was no more than a hundred words, she couldn't help keep on glancing at David and wondering if he had interpreted it in the same way. When she'd finished, she glanced around the room, unable to focus on anything.

'Pretty damn amazing if you ask me, even refers to you by name and states that you travelled nine hundred years just to save her life. When I first read it, I didn't know you. Now though, these few words mean so much more.'

Appearing a tad surprised, Ruth held her hand out to Rebecca.

Rebecca handed her the paper, glanced back at David, and once more around the room.

'No need to convince me, Rebecca. I am with you all the way, to the point where I will happily risk my parliamentary position to support your quest. I am meeting with the PM tomorrow and hopefully, I can convince her to meet up with you. I am sure once she sees all the evidence, well.'

'Well indeed, I am away with my parents in a few weeks, although only for four days, mind. Ruth, I think the date we booked was on the fifteenth of July, is that right?'

'I will call you tomorrow and let you know how it goes with the PM. I think the sooner we can get the ball rolling, the better.'

Chapter 29 – London and...

The following day, David called around lunchtime. He explained while in his meeting with the PM, he had tentatively divulged some aspects of the story, and the PM had suggested it was another of his quests to stop the UK from using too much plastic. 'In the end, Rebecca, I had to give her some more details about your story and in so doing had no choice but to tell her about some of the proof you hold.'

'That is just fine. Continue to do whatever is needed. I am beyond questioning eyes. There will be many over the coming months, of that there is no doubt.'

'Well, oddly, just before lunch, the PM said, and I quote, "if this is true, David, I urgently need to meet this young lady." So, she then checked her diary and booked us in for the 29th of May. That's in two days. I will call you tomorrow and arrange for my driver to pick you up. I think it is best if we stay in London overnight, rather than driving down on the day.'

'Thank you so much, David. I cannot tell you how much of a relief this is to me and my quest. To gain the buy-in of someone in her position will undoubtedly make my job easier.'

Rebecca came off the phone and just sat staring out of the kitchen window. Although there were times when she'd comprehended the importance of her task, she'd never really felt burdened by it. That was until now and the sensation of her tangible emotional relief took her thoughts to another level. With Duncan and her parents not due back for a couple of days, she decided to take herself off to the fallen oak and do some work on her story, which was now turning into a chronicle of events. The moment she heard the story of Matilda and how she'd written about her life, Rebecca had decided this was something she had to finish once and for all. In fact, having thought about it a lot since hearing about Matilda yesterday, she'd found herself questioning why she hadn't finished her own story. For some reason, she'd suddenly started considering her life's destiny and where this might take her in the coming years. For sure, her future thoughts were with Duncan, her parents and even the twit. However, since meeting Meredith the cab driver, who was from another dimension, she didn't know what to expect. She did realise though, this idea of perhaps finding her way to another dimension or life was only really because she'd spent so many years with Etienne and then returned, almost as if on reflection, she'd been in an alternate dimension. Importantly, she had returned without any emotional detachment, something that still had occasionally resonated in her deepest thoughts.

She decided to give her mother a quick call to let her know she was meeting up with the Prime Minister. Oddly, after coming off the phone, something her mother said made her again think about this other dimension. Although at the time, when Meredith had suggested Rebecca was just seeing an apparition, she'd not really taken any notice, other than thinking that's where rested spirits go. Now though, she was having different ideas and was wondering if these people moving in this other dimension were living a normal life, just somehow neither paths crossed unless they needed to. She shook her head, feeling a little confused, and then a kind of answer came to her. Remembering the time, she went forward and could see her mother's accident, yet apparently, no one could see her, she wondered if she was perhaps in the other dimension, looking on. *Oh well, that will do*, she thought, not really wanting to think about it any longer.

228

Picking up her laptop, she headed down to the woods thinking, *what will be, will be.* For the first time for many years, she was a little worried about what the future may hold for her. Yeah, for sure she had this mission to save humanity. This emotion though was more about her life and she was now adamant she'd try to get her story down on paper.

On the way down towards the lake, she got to thinking about writing. It was all rather odd the way it worked. It is always so easy to say, I'll do it tomorrow, and tomorrow never comes. The thing is, when she had previously started writing, the words just fell from her, and she only ever stopped when she was getting a headache or sore eyes.

Now adamant she was going to at least make a dent in it, she sat on the veranda and started typing. No sooner, she was off and running, the next three hours was only interrupted by the sun shining on her laptop to the point where she couldn't see. Deciding to head indoors, especially as her arms were feeling the effects of the sun, she got up and opened the door. In the back of her head, she was a little surprised when there was no whoosh of the normal, if you can call it that, almond smelling air. Oh, well, nothing occurring today, she thought, not that she'd had any vibes to suggest there would be.

She sat down at the glass table, opened up her laptop and picked up where she'd left off. Another three hours flew by, and she was now looking at seventy-five thousand words. Making a few notes, she realised this would either end up like War & Peace, or she'd have to write three books, at least. Suddenly her stomach started rumbling and she realised she hadn't eaten all day. The odd thing was, every time she became engrossed in writing up her tale, she always lost track of time and invariably forgot to eat.

She headed back in the main house, having decided she only wanted to eat and sleep in the summerhouse with Duncan. She made her way into the kitchen and feeling lazy, decided on a frozen pizza. After supper, she headed up to her bedroom and again started work on her book.

Next thing she knew she was woken up by the sound of her phone ringing. Bleary-eyed, knowing she'd again forgotten to set her alarm, and a tad panicked, she grabbed the phone.

'Hello, David. Sorry if I sound groggy, I've just woken.' In the back of her thoughts, she reckoned she shouldn't have said that until she noticed it was seven in the morning. She came off the phone and with the car due to pick her up at nine, jumped in the shower.

Feeling a little more refreshed and a tad hungry, she decided to have something to eat before the car arrived.

While eating, unsure if she was travelling alone, she reckoned she'd take her laptop and do some more of her book, especially as it was such a long drive.

Dead on nine, the car pulled up with David sitting in the back.

'Morning, Rebecca. I hope you're feeling a little better.'

'Morning, David, yeah all good to go, thank you. How are you?'

'Excited, even more so now I have something that might just interest you.'

With curiosity rearing its head, Rebecca said, 'Oh, do tell me more.'

'Well, after I came off the phone with you yesterday, I had a phone call from the British Museum. So, like the letter in the bank, they too have a letter for me in the vaults that they were supposed to deliver three days ago.'

Immediately Rebecca's thoughts started to go in circles. She knew she had considered and may have even mentioned to

Meredith about leaving another letter for David in the museum, one that told of the Ziggurat. She was though, sure she'd decided against it. 'Do we know who it is from and what it is about, David?'

'Well, how very strange is this. It is from Queen Matilda, no less. Written in the twelfth century and addressed to me in person.' He shook his head appearing more than a little perplexed. 'So, we can go to visit the museum once we are in London. Fortunately, and perhaps not surprisingly, I booked at the hotel opposite. I can't tell you why though. Normally Ruth books such things, however, I decided to book it myself and when I did a search on the Internet, it was the first one to come up.' Again, he shook his head. 'Now get this, because I was feeling a little unsure, although I can't tell you why, I went back on my computer. The thing is, when I did another search for hotels, the one I'd booked didn't come up, well not until I'd scrolled through hundreds of others.'

'That'll be Meredith intervening, for sure. That is exactly what she does,' Rebecca said, still wondering what on earth Matilda's part in all this could be. 'I am curious what she has written to you about. My understanding is that she knew nothing of this.' Then she recalled Princess Rebekah, as she now called her, telling her that many of her kind were involved at some point and in some way. 'Thinking about it though, I reckon she's written to you about the Ziggurat. I don't really know why I think that though.'

'Well we now all know about the Ziggurat, so I am not sure I follow why. One thing has occurred to me though, is the evidence dowries itself once, because that's all that is needed.'

'Well, we do indeed, however...' She then faced David. 'You know about the key, but what you don't know is that it unlocks a secret compartment in the Ziggurat that tells of my time there while it was being built. It is another piece of unquestionable evidence. Evidence that will aid

231

acknowledgement from those who matter, and they will act upon my tale, if you can call it that.'

'You did mention that the other day. A letter from Matilda and the scroll in the Ziggurat will gain the trust of even the most sceptical individuals.

Over the next four hours, they chatted about Rebecca's time in the past, and David's life as a parliamentarian. In what seemed like the blink of an eye, they were pulling up outside their hotel. After booking in and leaving their overnight bags in their individual rooms, they headed over to the museum.

Chapter 30 – British Museum

As David opened the large glass entrance door to the museum, Rebecca felt a tad of apprehension. Still in the back of her thoughts, she was wondering what Matilda had to say and what her role was. She then nodded as the penny dropped. She realised David had already read up on this woman and to some degree was an advocate for Matilda and her stories. She nodded again realising her letter, whatever it said, would add more weight.

Someone was waiting for them at the reception, which surprised Rebecca a little. However, David mentioned he had rung ahead to advise them of his arrival.

'Please follow me, David, Rebecca,' an elderly gentleman said.

As Rebecca followed, she couldn't help thinking this man looked like he'd just stepped from a Jules Verne novel, complete with his long wispy grey hair and huge curled moustache.

'We at the museum are so curious and have so many questions.'

'I am not altogether surprised,' David said and glanced at Rebecca, shaking his head ever so slightly. Then as they arrived by some large ornate oak doors, David asked, 'Would you mind if I take a few minutes with my colleague, Rebecca?' As soon as they were on their own, David nodded to Rebecca.

'It is your call, Rebecca. However, I think at this stage it is best if we keep the contents to ourselves for now at least. We can answer any questions when we are ready.'

'That is exactly what I was thinking. I have no doubts the people who run this place will have a million questions. However, as you say, keep it to ourselves at this stage. Besides, they will find out soon enough.'

David turned and opened the door to an enormous room. In the centre of the room was a large table with eight men sitting in elaborate looking chairs. Noticing they all had a similar appearance to the first man, made Rebecca grin to the point of nearly laughing. More importantly, though, she was aware most of them were frowning at her as if they were not expecting to see her with David. Annoyingly, she could physically taste the element of derision towards her.

She nudged David and whispered, 'I am going to say something. I am not having this.'

Wide-eyed, David nodded, having clearly picked up on the same mood as her.

Rebecca approached the table and glanced at all of them with an air of certainty. 'My name is Rebecca and I am here with David to read this letter, on our own, I might add. Importantly, I have no doubts you are all curious what is inside, however, your Victorian-style disdain of a woman being present means you will have to wait to find out what is inside. In the meantime, I suggest you do some research on the Suffragist movement. We are equal now, irrespective of age.' She then brushed her hands together as if she was dusting crumbs away. 'You can now stop sneering down your pompous noses, or you may never know the contents of this letter.'

One of the men stood up and waving his hands dismissively in Rebecca's direction, while looking directly at David, said, 'Are you going to let this common female talk to us like that?'

With his eyes wide, David walked over to the table, banged his hand down loudly, and glancing at each of them, said, 'I suggest you get in the twenty-first century. To my mind, none of you will ever know of the contents of this letter. So, you can take your curiosity and bury it under your out of date impertinence.' He then again looked intently at each of them.

'Then another stood and said, 'I will speak with the Prime Minister and we will force you to show us the contents.'

Having already spoken with PM Mary Scotland, regarding the letter and keeping its contents secret, he turned with a grin on his face. 'Good luck with that. Now, give me my letter,' he said holding his hand out.

A few seconds passed as each of the men looked at each other. Then four left the room while the fifth pointed to a large bank-style walk-in safe on the far side of the room. He then, after glancing back at the last three remaining men, opened the safe to a vault of locked drawers. Without making eye contact and saying anything, he handed David a key and pointed to box number 3838.

David took the key, and then without speaking, indicated for the man to leave them. He then glanced at Rebecca as he opened the drawer. He took the letter out, which was enclosed in some kind of see-through material bag, and whispered, 'I recognise Matilda's Germanic handwriting.' He then indicated for them to leave the vault. As he passed the table, he waved the letter and said, 'addressed to David Wilson, and Rebecca Ferguson.'

Rebecca now totally on board with David, followed him out of the room. Although she was desperate to find out what was inside, right now, she was happy to wait until they got back to the hotel.

Just as they were about to leave the building, the youngest of the men at the table came over. Looking directly at Rebecca, he said, 'I apologise for our behaviour. I am forever telling them to get into the current century, to the point where I am now considering working elsewhere.'

Rebecca nodded. 'Apologies accepted. Please do not give in. Change the future for those who follow. Stay and make a difference. What is your name may I ask?'

Smiling a little easier, he said, 'Martin Hewison.'

Shaking her head in disbelief, she asked, 'Hewison as in the Deer House Hewison family in Cumbria?'

Pulling his head back a little, he said, 'yes, how do you know that. Not like it's a common name, but even so.'

Before she could stop herself, Rebecca said, 'I know your mother, or perhaps Grandmother, Judith.' Instantly wondering how she was going to explain this away. Then an idea came to her. 'Well, I don't know her personally, I know of her having done some historical research on the orphanage she ran during World War Two.'

Shaking his head slightly, he responded, 'When you said you knew her, I did wonder. Of interest, Judith was my grandmother. I would be interested in any information you managed to find out. It would seem the house is surrounded in mystery.'

Nodding, Rebecca thought, *no surprise there then.* 'If you give me your phone number, or email, I will be glad to shed some light on the house.' She chuckled inwardly, thinking *you wait.* 'I should add, it is where I live now.'

236

After exchanging emails, David and Rebecca headed back to the hotel. Picking a table in the corner of the restaurant, they ordered some coffee.

'So, shall we?' David said staring at the letter.

Rebecca nodded. 'I am astonished by its condition. It looks newish.'

'The museum, I would suspect have a way of preserving this type of thing.' He then carefully lifted the seal and opened the letter. Glancing at Rebecca, he beckoned her to look. Having carefully opened a sepia coloured piece of paper that was around the size of A4, he peered at the page appearing dumbfounded. 'There's nothing, not a word, just a blank piece of paper.'

'It will be invisible writing I suspect, knowing Matilda. She was a bit cagey about everything. We need to use ultraviolet light. I bet this hotel has an ultraviolet to sterilise their cooking utensils, being posh and all.' She then got up and headed over to the food bar. 'Do you have an ultraviolet light in the kitchen that I can use for a moment or two?'

'I will just ask for you, Madam.' Seconds later, he returned with a lamp. 'Will this serve your purposes, Madam?'

'Thank you so much,' she said and returned to David.

After finding a socket behind David's chair, they plugged it in and switched it on. Both sat silently as they read the words. David then rummaged around in his briefcase and produced an old-looking book. This will help us translate her words into English. I used it for her novel and knew I might need it today.

Rebecca, ich danke dir, dass du in mein Jahrhundert gereist bist und mein Lebon gerettat hast. David, nimm alles, was Rebecca sagt, als die Wahrheit. In Rebekah's Ziggurat steckt eine Botschaft.

237

Matilda, Konigan von Schottland und daruber hinaus.

After a lot of scribbling, David eventually wrote down the message in English.

Rebecca, I thank you for travelling to my century and saving my life. David, take all Rebecca says as the truth. Both, there is a message hidden within Rebekah's Ziggurat.

Matilda, Queen of Scotland and beyond.

'Well, no debating that, and just another piece of evidence to present to those who might have a negative viewpoint.' David then carefully placed the letter back inside the envelope. 'So, Rebecca, you knew Martin Hewison's grandmother? I am guessing you met her on one of your many jaunts.' He then narrowed his eyes. 'Hang on, doing the maths, that must have been around the time of King George.' He shook his head. 'No point in asking.' Again, he shook his head, stood up, and said, 'right, I am going to get a lunch menu if you fancy.'

Still grinning, delighted how this was all panning out, she nodded. While David was getting the menus, she started going through everything in her head. All along, she'd thought she was in for a battle getting anyone to listen to her tale and importantly, act upon it in the right way. Now, she was seeing that her task might prove easier than she'd initially thought. She and David spent the rest of the afternoon chatting about her time in the past. They'd already agreed not to mention the future, especially as they were likely to be talking about that non-stop all day tomorrow.

To her delight, Rebecca's parents turned up at the hotel as they were already in London. Although Rebecca's task occasionally came up, the conversation was mostly about David's standpoint on human rights, equality in the workplace, and his hopes for the future. More than once, Rebecca was a tad surprised, not by her mother's strong views, but more the

238

way she firmly voiced her opinion. After supper, Rebecca bid her parents farewell and said goodnight to David.

Chapter 31 – Prime Minister and...

The following morning, Rebecca woke bright and early. Thinking about how well she'd slept, she was certain this was because she went to bed feeling the weight of the task in front of her had become that much lighter.

After a long shower, she headed downstairs to meet up with David. As she sat there drinking some coffee, she knew she should be feeling at least a tad anxious, what with meeting the Prime Minister and all. The odd thing, she was in fact completely relaxed and ready to take the whole episode in her stride. The more she thought about her emotions, the more she realised her relaxed mind was down to a number of things. For sure, she had all the evidence showing she had actually travelled through time, right back to the beginning of the civilised world. It was more what had happened of late, whereby everything was just lining up perfectly and everyone was buying into her story.

It was just a little before nine when David's driver collected them.

'How are you feeling, Rebecca? You seem very at ease.'

'Absolutely fine, thank you for asking, David. I was thinking about how chilled out I felt over breakfast and I believe it's because everything is set up perfectly.'

On the way, they chatted about Matilda's letter. In what seemed like a few minutes, they arrived outside the big black door at 10 Downing Street. In awe and grinning inwardly, even then Rebecca still felt relaxed. However, when the Prime Minister, Mary Scotland answered the door personally and greeted Rebecca like a long-lost friend, her emotions started to dance a little.

'Come in you two. I've been so looking forward to this gathering. I don't want to call it a meeting. Those things will come in all good time. I want to keep this informal. Come on through. I am guessing you've had breakfast, so perhaps a cup of tea for you both,' she said and radiated a smile.

Rebecca had never been one for voting in elections, however, this woman had inspired her. On the way down the elaborate hallway, she thought, I like this woman, we could be friends, and I am so glad I voted for her.

'Sit down, let's talk,' she said pulling a chair out for Rebecca. 'I would like to say right here and now, and hopefully, relax the mood. I buy into your story, Rebecca. That is in spite of it being a ludicrously outrageous tale and all. Time travel is a thing for the cinema, however, journeying thousands of years into the past and future, well. That said, David has told me of all the unequivocal evidence you have. So, let's go.' She then squeezed Rebecca's hand just as her mother often does.

Over the next couple of hours, Rebecca told her story, starting with the spiral staircase. Along the way, she showed Mary all the evidence she had to back her tale up, and that included the first photo she found of her and Meredith all those years ago.

'So, you suggest you have some answers to our problem. I believe you said you have a tablet affair that tells how we can fix the ozone and rid the planet of the horrid plastics.'

'I do indeed,' Rebecca said and then spent the next few minutes explaining to the PM how it works.

241

Taking a piece of fancy headed official notepaper, Mary started writing. 'I think this is the order in which we need to proceed. First off, visit the Ziggurat with some influential people. Thereby, we will have their buy-in once they witness you producing this note from four-thousand years ago, hidden in a secret compartment. Then meet up with some scientists to go through the information you have on this computer affair. Then we hit the press just before we go to the Global Warming Summit.' She then seemed to think for a moment. 'Can you give me a few minutes, please? I just need to make an urgent call.'

After Mary left, David turned to Rebecca. 'That could not have gone any better.'

'That is what I was thinking. I like her, a lot.'

Moments later, Mary returned. 'Right, all set up, we are going to see the Queen. Then we go to the Global Summit, and after, maybe the press, if it's not already out by then.'

Shaking her head in disbelief, Rebecca asked, 'When?'

'Now, right now, the car will be out front in a moment. We need the buy-in from the boss and if she says jump, most of the world will jump.'

'Err, okay, I think.' Rebecca was thinking *I am going to see the Queen.*

'Sweetie, you'll be just fine. She'll like you, besides, you met her father.'

With her mouth open, Rebecca suddenly realised she met Queen Elizabeth when she was with Judith. In the recesses of her thoughts was this idea that Elizabeth might just recognise her, especially after they'd seemingly made eye contact. She took a deep breath and said, 'Let's do it.'

With her thoughts away with the fairies, Rebecca didn't even notice them enter Buckingham Palace. Getting out of the car and being escorted by a member of the Queens Guard, complete with bearskin, suddenly hit her like a canon. *Oh my gosh,* she thought, *we are doing this.*

In what seemed like seconds, they were entering a large elaborate hall. Mary, David, and Rebecca followed the guard to a small room at the end of a long corridor adorned with paintings of Kings and Queens through the ages. They entered a room that had a much more informal feel about it. However, nothing could have prepared her for what was about to happen.

As she walked towards some informal chairs by a large fireplace, the Queen stood up and looking directly at Rebecca, said, 'I never forget a face.' She then shook her head ever so slightly and offered for all to sit.

Rebecca curtsied and sat down, realising the Queen was still staring at her.

'Mary, David, I need to ask Rebecca a question. Deer House, Judith and Christopher, Sir Leonard, my father. You know all these people; of that I am sure.'

Aware Mary and David were both sitting with their mouths open, Rebecca glanced in their direction and smiled. 'Yes indeed, and we have met, albeit in passing.'

'Passing indeed. I was a child, as were you. You are still within your youth, unlike me. How can this be?'

Rebecca then spent the next thirty or so minutes explaining the outline to her story, once more starting right from the beginning. Surprisingly to Rebecca, neither David nor Mary said a word.

'What a fabulous tale you have to tell. It is, however, one that may take me a while to understand.'

243

'She stays true to her story, Ma'am,' David said. 'I have heard it three times in two days and never once does it get boring or does Rebecca deviate.'

'Sorry, David,' Rebecca said.

'It is not a problem. I could hear your story a hundred times and would never tire.'

'Me neither,' said Mary.

Rebecca, along with David and Mary, then explained all about the tablet and that they had a way to fix things. Often, Rebecca emphasised the urgency, what with the clock ticking and mindful the deadline had already moved four-hundred years. This was again something she reiterated over and again.

'Well, Rebecca, I know you have travelled to the past, having witnessed it with my own eyes. I know not how this can be, nonetheless, the truth it is. So, I suggest you follow Mary's plan and call on me when I am needed to ensure that people listen. If nothing else, I can accommodate the leaders from the Commonwealth countries and with ease action what needs to happen.'

As Rebecca, David, and Mary were leaving, The Queen called Rebecca back.

Curtseying again, she said, 'Ma'am, at your service.'

'Rebecca, it is I who is at your service.' She shook her head. 'The first time we met, albeit briefly, your intrepid fearlessness left a lifelong impression on me. When problems arose, especially in the early days, I thought of you. The second you walked through the door I knew it was you.' She then glanced away for a second. 'All those years ago, although perhaps minutes for you, I knew you were different and... I just knew something was not as it should be and have kept this within my thoughts until today. When this is all over, I would love to sit and talk with you. Just us two, no one else, so I can see inside your mind, and understand how it works and why you can be of such steadfastness even though you know your tales face a barrage of disdain.'

'Thank you, Ma'am.'

'Thank you, Rebecca, for answering the questions I have carried for seventy years. I will be in contact with you shortly. Go now and follow your light, as I know you will. Remember, I am here and am your advocate. For this reason, your journey should have fewer bumps.'

Chapter 32 – A Time Twist

Returning home that evening, Rebecca was surprised to receive a phone call from David. He had been contacted by Mary, who having previously spoken with the Queen felt a trip to the Ziggurat was of the utmost importance. Therefore, with her agreement, he'd like to arrange a four-day trip, leaving on the 3rd June, which would be in two days. Somewhat taken aback, but nonetheless excited, Rebecca agreed.

When she came off the phone, she called her mother and then Duncan. Both suggested it would be a brilliant opportunity and felt it would add more substance to her story and thereby make her mission even easier. Her mum did ask a lot of questions about her meeting with the Queen, which Rebecca was kind of expecting.

After a slightly restless night, Rebecca woke the following morning invigorated. Sitting in the kitchen having some breakfast, she was at a loss what to do first. Her sensible side was telling her to pack her bags, whereas part of her brain was suggesting a walk down to the woods and sort her bags later. Just as she was about to head outside for a meander, something was telling her to go back and pack her bags now. Having made her mind up to go for a walk, she stood there battling with this logical thinking for a few seconds. Unusually something from deep within the carefree part of her brain was telling her to give the walk a miss.

She banged her eyes, put her laptop down, and headed up to her bedroom. As she entered her room, she nearly tripped over one of the four wooden boxes her father had found in the summerhouse when it was converted. Oddly, it was right in front of the door and the only thing she could imagine was that her mother had been tidying up. Picking the box up, she placed it with the other three and started packing her bag.

All the way through packing, not having a clue what to take, she ended up stuffing all her walk in the wood clothes into her rucksack. She then sat there trying to work out why she was being so indecisive. Right from the moment, she'd thought about going for a walk something had been nagging deep down in her subconscious. Glancing at the four wooden boxes, a thought suddenly occurred to her, maybe her mum had left the box there after all. Sitting on the edge of her bed, with her elbows on her knees and head in her hands, she just stared at the top box. Right from her first time with Meredith, and all the people since, she'd never known one of them to physically move something in her world. For sure, there had been things like the key mysteriously appearing in the painting of Meredith, but nothing like this. Feeling thirsty, she decided to nip downstairs and grab her drink. On the way back, she stopped by the paintings of Meredith and Millicent, something she hadn't done for ages. Everything seemed just so, which she found a little surprising, but didn't know why she felt like this. Just as she was turning away, she was sure she'd seen Meredith drop her hanky, almost as if she was alive in the painting. Without turning back, she shook her head and mumbled, 'now even by my standards, that's plain daft.' Weirdly, part of her didn't want to look back at the painting. She thought about this and reckoned it was because if Meredith had dropped her hanky in the painting, it would put a completely new angle on a world she was still coming to terms with. Slowly, she turned. 'What is this all about,' she muttered, seeing Meredith's white hanky lying on the floor by her feet. As much as her sensible side wanted to suggest she just hadn't seen it before, this was a painting and there's no way the artist would paint a hanky lying on the floor.

247

Peering at the hanky, suddenly the message came through loud and clear. Hurrying upstairs, she was certain she had one of Meredith's hankies in her room and was fairly sure she'd placed it in one of the boxes. *That'll be it*, she thought as she turned the corner at the top of the stairs. Rushing along the corridor, she nearly slipped on the new carpet.

Blowing her cheeks out, she reckoned to any onlookers, running around like this, she'd look like Tommy when he was at that twit age.

She grabbed the box, placed it in front of her, and opened it, not knowing what she was looking for, or what to expect. She then shook her head, and thought, par-for-the-course then.

Delving around in the box, she couldn't see the hanky anywhere. Just as she was about to fetch another box, a thought appeared in her head, almost as if she was looking at a photo. As she was moving the bits and pieces about, something had left a mark on her subconscious. Pulling out a few papers, she spotted an unfamiliar, unopened envelope, and to compound her thoughts, it was addressed to her. The thing that came as a big surprise is that it wasn't Meredith's handwriting. Instead, it was swirly, rather modern-looking handwriting.

She sat there for a few seconds staring at the envelope. Right, let's see what this is all about and where it may lead. With her curiosity taking control, she opened the envelope and as she did, she was aware it had a modern feel to it. When she pulled the letter out, she knew something odd was going on. The letter had an almost artificial feel to it, almost as if it was made from some sort of synthetic paper. Immediately, her attention was drawn to the bottom of the letter, signed off, your descendant 2138.

'What is going on with the number thirty-eight keep popping up,' she muttered as she started reading.

248

Rebecca, the clock has again changed. Instead of three hundred years, there is now less than two hundred years until humanity takes its last breath. Time is moving rapidly and may change again. Take this letter with you and show it to your scientists. This material will be invented in forty of your years, made from recycled plastic. Within the envelope is the process for producing this product. It will help a little in our time. However, it is pointless unless you can set the ship sailing. Go with speed.

Your descendant 2138.

Rebecca sat back holding the letter. Hurrying downstairs, she looked at Meredith's painting and as she expected, the hanky was back in her hand. 'Thank you, Meredith,' she mumbled. She then went back upstairs and finished packing, although this time she was a little more focused. She placed the letter along with her passport, the diagram, and the key in a lockable pocket inside her bag. She sat back, went through her tick list, and once she was sure she had everything, gave David a call to tell him about the letter from Matilda.

'Thank you, Rebecca. Although I should be shocked that you were sent a letter from someone who is not even born yet and will live generations into the future, I have learnt with you to expect the unrealistically unexpected.'

Chapter 33 – Mesopotamia again

The following morning, Rebecca woke excited by the prospect of visiting Rebekah's Ziggurat once more. With an odd surge of nostalgia running around in her thoughts, she climbed into the car David had sent to pick her up. It was eight in the morning and she was due to meet up with David at London's Heathrow Airport for a late afternoon flight.

Heading to board the plane, she was not expecting to go through a part of the airport that had an almost undercover, clandestine feel to it. To then compound her emotions further, the plane was clearly a private one, the likes you'd expect to be used by the rich and famous.

Now onboard, David introduced her to three women, and two men. Two were scientists, two were archaeologists, and the fifth person was someone she already knew, Martin Hewison. 'Hello, Martin. I did not expect to see you here. When I met you at the British Museum, I left feeling I owed you more of an explanation as to how I knew of Judith.'

'It is okay, I spoke with David and I now know your story, albeit, he only gave me a brief outline. Interestingly, I knew the second we met there was something special about you. Your spirit and tenacity resonated from you, portraying an inner strength, the likes of which I have rarely if ever come across. When I got home, I called my father, Judith's son and he said he had a letter for me. He went on to say that he was not to give me the letter until our paths cross.' He then shook his head, clearly, a tad confounded. 'So, the letter, as I am sure you've guessed, was from Judith.' Again, he shook his head.

'So, she told me all about you, your time in the past with her and the journey you now face.'

This was not what Rebecca expected when she set eyes on Martin and she wasn't sure how to respond. She thought about it for a few seconds, along with the letter from Matilda. It was now clear to her all the people she'd met through the ages were doing their utmost to help her mission succeed. She glanced back up at Martin. 'Sorry, I was just putting bits of the puzzle together inside my head. You know, although I should be surprised, I am not. The way this journey, as you described it, is knitting together, things like this have almost become the norm.' She then glanced toward David and the others who were listening intently. 'I guess, when you consider the importance of my mission, it is no surprise all those involved through the years are playing their part in making certain I accomplish all that is set in front of me. I should say, now set in front of us all.' She again glanced at the others. 'All the way along this path I've been following, my journeys have more often than not, involved me helping the people I meet. There were times when I had to stop time taking an alternative direction.' Seeing most of the others were looking at her, wide-eyed and wanting to know more, she decided to give them some details. 'I think the best way to explain what I meant by time taking a different route is to share an example with you. So, I learnt by way of a message that a plague carried by workers from Ireland was heading for an area north of Liverpool in the sixteen-twenties. If they'd arrived, the virus would have wiped out many families in that area. That includes my mother's forefathers.' She then paused as something occurred to her.

'Please carry on, this is better than any film I've watched recently,' one of the scientists said.

'Let me stop you right there, Malcolm. A fanciful story this is not.' David then wide-eyed shook his head in Malcolm's direction. 'Please continue, Rebecca. It helps most of us understand your world and we can then hopefully help you succeed.' He then turned to the others and in a very strong, ministerial like manner, he said, 'As bizarre as this story may seem to you, let me assure you it is not. Just because time travel was, I say again, was, a thing for the films, it is now a fact. Please continue, Rebecca.'

Rebecca felt assured by David's words, and surprisingly unconcerned by Malcolm's untimely film comment. In fact, she did suspect he was perhaps making light of his own inability to comprehend what was going on. 'So, where was I, oh I know. Something just occurred to me. I said just now that it was mostly me helping others, in reality, had I not got the message regarding the plague I would be a different person. This I know for a fact.'

'You are going to have to explain that,' one of the ladies said. 'By the way, my name is Kaitie and I am one of the archaeologists. I am intrigued, as I am sure we all are. This is a completely new world for us. Hey, two hundred years ago, if you told someone one day we'd be sitting on a jet as we are, they'd lock you up and hide the key.'

The idea of a hidden key made Rebecca laugh out loud. 'So sorry, Kaitie. I was not laughing at you; just you mentioned a hidden key, something I will come on to later. Anyways, so, I went to sixteen-twenty-three and failed to stop the plague. I then ended up in the eighteen-fifties with a woman named Meredith. She showed me my reflection in a pool in the stream. I was still me, but here's the thing, I was a different person, even down to the colour of my hair.' She wagged her head in an upward motion. 'It was because my mother's forefathers had been wiped out and, well. So, I had to find my way back to the sixteen hundred's, and this time stop the plague. I did by the way, as I always seem to. That I suspect is because I get help from all the others of my making through the millennia.' She then spent the next couple of hours answering questions about her time in the past. When she moved onto her time in the future, the whole mood changed. She could see, even Malcolm was now listening intently to her every word.

'So, you see my learned friends, we have a huge uphill task in front of us that will be met with disdain,' David said, glancing at Rebecca. 'Let me explain. I recall reading about the time Stephenson's rocket was first announced. People said the inventor was mad because passengers would suffocate at twenty-five miles per hour. Imagine telling someone from the fourteen hundred's that they could phone America. What's a phone and what's America. Oh, and by the way, Rebecca can travel through time, without any gadgets or fancy machines.' David kind of laughed nervously and then glanced around at the others.

'I would love to think with all this evidence and that includes what we will find in the pyramid, we will be heard. However, I just can't see the whole world responding. No more plastic, no more burning phosphorous fuels, ever. I mean really, that's going to happen overnight! We know it is something that obviously needs to happen, however.'

'Excuse me,' Rebecca said. 'First off, it is a Ziggurat and not a pyramid.' She then chuckled. 'In all seriousness, one thing is always certain. I never fail and that is not born from arrogance. It specifically comes from the fact that I never fail. I alluded to it before. There have been many like me; they all failed this one ultimate mission, to stop humanity following this road to damnation. This, our generation, are the first with the wherewithal, knowhow, and technical ability to succeed. Now the clock is ticking, and we do not have room or time for faint hearts.' She then glanced around at the others. Either you are on board as a passenger, or you are going to take your turn at flying this bloody thing, so to speak. In or out, speak now.' Rebecca shook her head inwardly gobsmacked by her own words and forthright manner. The more she thought about it though, she realised it was needed, especially as everyone, was although showing their own individual look of determination, there were signs that one or two weren't quite on board.

'Well said, Rebecca.' David glanced around at the others and said, 'as Rebecca said so clearly, you are in or out.

Although, seeing the look on your faces, I can see you're all in, or nearly in.'

They all continued to chat, although Rebecca with her newly found advocate, Kaitie, spent most of their time talking about Rebecca's experience four-thousand years ago with the original Rebekah.

'You know, I am Jewish,' Kaitie said, 'and one of our matriarchs is the Rebekah you speak of. Profoundly lovely to know history portrays her correctly. A woman of strength, guile, and beauty, it would seem she was.'

Flicking her eyes from side to side, Rebecca said, 'oh boy, she had something about her you couldn't measure. If she said three plus three was thirty-eight, you'd believe her.' Rebecca shook her head. 'There's that blinking number again, thirty, unbelievable how often it comes up, eight.' She then nodded, seeing Kaitie appearing quizzical. 'Thirty-eight has come up so often in the last few days.' She then explained and suggested she was now beginning to wonder what it in fact meant. Oddly, just speaking about it, she realised it related to the date it could all come to an end. Somewhere though, in the back of her thoughts, she reckoned it could well be more than just a date message.

The two continued to chat. Next thing they knew, the cabin steward was advising them to ready for landing.

Chapter 34 – Rebekah's scroll

Arriving at the most extravagant, temple-like hotel in northern Syria, a country torn by conflict for many years, Rebecca was a little taken aback. For sure, this area was now at peace, but the unrest had been ongoing for a number of years. Sharing a room with Kaitie helped her settle in quickly. At supper that evening, the two chatted about this part of the world. They particularly focused on what had gone on so recently, and how rapidly they were rebuilding. When they were joined by the others, the conversation turned to the days ahead.

'We are travelling in four-by-fours tomorrow, with an armed guard escort. I must emphasize, we are assured we are safe, and their presence is purely a guard of carriage.' David then glanced at the others. When any dignitaries travel in these parts, a guard is a standard. Even with total peace, it is the way it has always been.'

Rebecca nodded. 'When I travelled, albeit by camel, we had armed guards, and that was four thousand years ago. I soon learnt that was their custom. If you think about it, back home if the Queen goes anywhere, she has armed guards. It is just something that happens when we are in the presence of important people,' she said and glanced at David.

'That's it, blame me,' David said and laughed.

The remainder of the evening passed quickly and before she knew it, Rebecca was being woken by a maid with coffee and some kind of biscuit. Recognising the biscuits as being similar to those she'd been given by Rebekah relaxed her mood completely.

After another coffee with the other folk downstairs, they headed off in two rather fancy off-road vehicles. Along the way, Rebecca felt like she was back to where this journey unfolded. She leaned over to Kaitie and said, 'you know what, this has not changed one bit in four-thousand years. It looks exactly the same, excepting the road.'

Around four hours later, they drove past an oasis that Rebecca instantly recognised. 'We are so close, about five miles. If we aim for those mountains, she said, leaning over the driver's shoulder and pointing. 'There is a slight slope to the left of where the road is going. We may need to go off-road and over that slope.'

'How do you know?' Kaitie asked, shaking her head.

'I recognise this area as if it were yesterday. I know that sounds daft, but I know what I know. What you need to understand, I am not recalling something that happened four thousand years ago. For me, it was a couple of weeks ago. My memory is good, however…'

As the jeeps surmounted the sand dune, in spite of the draining heat, Rebecca shivered from head to toe. She then noticed Kaitie staring at her with her mouth open. Rebecca lent across and tapped her on the chin. 'Close your mouth, Sweetie, there's barely enough air as it is.' She then chuckled.

'I am so in. Next time you go anywhere in the past or the future, book me a ticket. Oh, my golly gosh. Time travel is real; move over Dr Emmett Brown, Rebecca is here, without a flux-capacitor.'

'Oh, I wish I could take you with me.' She squeezed Kaitie's hand knowing she'd found a life-long friend.

256

Seconds later, the two jeeps, plus the army vehicle pulled up aside the steps Rebecca had seen when they were being constructed. As she got out of the vehicle, she couldn't fail to notice that not only her driver, Kaitie and the other passengers were staring at her, but also one or two of the soldiers alwell.

David walked over. 'Where do we start looking with a building of this size?'

Rebecca shook her head, and asked, 'have you got a knife, David. In fact, does anyone have a knife or something similar? One with a strong blade.' She then produced her diagram, something she'd hidden away. Holding it up and lining everything just so, she noticed everyone, including all the guards now staring intently.

'Who is in trouble, Rebecca?' Kaitie asked and grinned. She then delved into her rucksack and produced a small kit bag that had an array of digging implements. 'Will one of these suffice, Madam?'

Grabbing a pointed trowel, Rebecca said, 'this is perfect.' She then walked out fifty steps from the base of the stairway. Turning towards the structure, all she could see in either direction or upwards was what looked like one huge slab. She narrowed her eyes, before glancing at David, and then Kaitie. Again, she held up the diagram.

'It looks like this structure is made from one colossal slab,' David said with a quizzical look on his face. 'Good luck with finding your secret recess.'

Turning away, Rebecca rolled her eyes, even more determined to go to the exact point. Closing her eyes, and recessing into a kind of semi-conscious state, she visualised herself back with Rebekah. She then opened her eyes, stepped towards the structure and with the trowel, started digging. Not put off by just scraping at what seemed like solid brick and knowing she was in the right area she moved the trowel an inch to one side. As the sand started to crumble under a little pressure, she glanced over her shoulder at the others.

With all in attendance now undoubtedly focused, she continued to dislodge the sand until she cleared all edges. She stood back and asked Kaitie if she had a small hammer.

Kaitie again rummaged in her backpack and produced a small rubber mallet. 'Will this do the job?'

'Perfect,' Rebecca said, taking the mallet and tapping the bottom right-hand corner of the slab. Within seconds, the ornate R started to appear. Once it was completely visible, she pressed the middle of the letter and stood back. As she knew it would, nothing happened.

'Press it again,' said a voice at the back.

Holding her hand up, Rebecca said, 'we must be patient, it will move.'

After what seemed like an eternity, which was actually only a couple of minutes, as Rebekah said it would be, there was a grumbling sound from behind the slab. Rebecca stood back, as a millimetre at a time, the slab started to free itself and move forward. She glanced around at the others and seeing one or two of the expressions nearly made her laugh out loud.

Now three-quarters of the way out, the slab to the left moved inward a little and turned slightly to the left. Moments later, the slab with the R on it turned ninety degrees to the right.

With chills running a mock with her emotions, Rebecca plunged her hand into the recess. Feeling nothing, she leant forward and immediately spotted the box Rebekah had placed in the space right at the back. Feeling remarkably relaxed, she leant inside and removed the box. She then turned and placed the box on the sand behind her. She again glanced at the others before delving into her bag and taking out the key. She then took a deep breath, inserted the key, turned and with one click, it was unlocked. She then stood back and grinning, said, 'I've seen the scrolls, who would like to look first?'

Stepping forward, Kaitie glanced around at the others and asked, 'Would anyone mind if I dived in first?'

Ushering Kaitie to go ahead, David said, 'I am sure we will all get to see the contents.'

Bending down, Kaitie glanced at Rebecca, opened the box, which made the most peculiar whooshing sound, instantly filling the air with an odour known only too well to Rebecca.

Certain she was among advocates and feeling able to speak freely, she said, 'I know that smell, it is almonds, and pretty much every time I am doing anything to do with the past, it's there.' She shook her head, inwardly beginning to wonder if the odour was, in fact, resonating from the other dimension that had cropped up so often of late. She then knelt down beside Kaitie who seemed to be waiting for her. 'Let's do this, Kaitie,' she said, nodding.

Kaitie fully opened the box and peered inside. 'I was half expecting to see some sort of cake in here, what with that smell.' She then carefully removed the scroll. With the others either now sitting, or leaning over, she unfolded the parchment. 'This is going to need deciphering, but hey, Rebecca, you're a wiz with that.'

David stood up and said, 'Now the soldiers have erected a marquee affair, perhaps we should head under cover, away from this incessant heat.'

They all headed inside, and on the way, David tapped Rebecca on the shoulder and gave her a thumbs up. Shaking his head, he said, 'Although I bought into your tale right from the get-go, today's events and the way you knew exactly what to do proves your time travelling adventures unequivocally.' He then shook his head again.

Sitting down at a wooden table, Rebecca unrolled the scroll. She looked at it for a few seconds and then delving into her memory and bizarrely able to recall exactly what Rebekah wrote, she started scribbling on a pad. Mindful that she was supposed to be deciphering hieroglyphics, she slowed herself a little. After around thirty minutes, which seemed like forever, she said, 'Done, ish. I might have a few mistakes, but this is as near as damn it. Sorry, Mother.'

'Why sorry, Mother?' one of the others asked.

'My mum hates me swearing and that includes words such as damn.' Rebecca then rolled her eyes.

Leaning over her shoulder, David asked, 'May I?' He then shook his head as if he was reflecting. 'I suppose you got the diagram of this structure from Rebekah, four thousand years ago?' He then shook his head again.

Rebecca nodded, and then handed him her note pad. 'Please feel free to read it to everyone, David. I knew what it said before I deciphered it.'

David then read out Rebecca's version of the scroll. He looked up at all and said with an urgent tone, 'We need to get back to London quickly and start the ball rolling now. If we don't, our children won't have a future and that's a fact. I am going to see if I can bring our flight forward. No need for us to stay here another three days watching the sun go up and down.'

Chapter 35 – Scientists

David managed to change the flight arrangements and bring them forward. In what seemed like minutes, Rebecca was climbing back on-board and heading home. As the plane took off, she looked at the landscape wondering if she'd ever be back. Feeling a little emotional, she sat quietly staring out of the window. After a while, Kaitie came and sat next to her.

'Are you okay, you're unusually quiet?'

'Yeah, fine, just feeling philosophical about leaving this place where the journey I am on started to unfold and help me truly understand my life's destiny.'

'That is very profound, I must say. You must feel rather odd, I'd suspect.'

They sat chatting for a while and eventually everyone was listening intently to Rebecca's every word.

She surprised herself how much she enjoyed speaking freely to everyone about her time in the past. This pleased her no end knowing she so easily convinced all these educated individuals who not only accepted her tales of time travel as real but also had become advocates for her mission.

Kaitie again asked if Rebecca would take her on her next trip.

'You know, I would love to. It would be so good, although that would depend on where we ended up,' she said and giggled.

261

'What was it like? I mean there you were as a fifteen-year-old minding your own business and bingo you find yourself back in eighteen whenever it was. How did that feel?'

Rebecca shook her head a little. 'Minding my own business and me in the same breath is a non-starter.' She then chuckled. 'I just see something in front of me that I feel needs investigation and go for it. Yeah, for sure, I get goosebumps on my goosebumps, but I have never felt alarmed or as if I am doing something I shouldn't. Not once have I felt in danger. I think overall, I have always reckoned it was something I was meant to be doing, my destiny if you like. Even that first time back in the summerhouse with Meredith, a complete stranger, from another century, who was calling my name, I just thought, okay, this is interesting.'

Nodding, and clearly on Rebecca's page, Kaitie said, 'perhaps that is why you've been given this task. You mentioned another dimension when we were at the pyramid, and I guessed you were referring to the place the others who you speak of either come from, live, or exist, whatever label you'd put on it.'

'Yeah, I am not altogether sure.' She then spent the remainder of the flight home chatting to Kaitie about her understanding of the journey she was on and occasionally mentioning the other dimension. 'Yeah for sure, I am my mother and father's daughter, the twit's sister, Duncan's wife and a mother one day. However, I now believe my very existence is to change humanities habits and thereby save our children's future. The way time keeps moving the goalposts, humanity won't be here in fifty years. The thing that annoys me most is I believe some scientists know what's coming but won't or can't speak out for fear of causing a worldwide panic. Also, even more annoyingly, they say nothing purely because it's unlikely to happen in their lifetime.'

'My goodness, that is rather philosophical.' She paused. 'I think you might be right.' She then nodded and said, 'I am guessing the twit is a younger brother. Hang on a minute, your name before you were married was Hewison, is that right?'

'Yep, where we going with this? she asked and narrowed her eyes.

Is your brother Tommy Hewison by any chance, plays football or soccer as my aunt would say in the States, for Liverpool?'

'Yep, afraid so, bloody twit was always using me as target practice when he was younger. That nuisance football of his was the scourge of my school days. Wherever I went, his ball was flying towards me.'

'Being a Liverpool season ticket holder, you will so have to introduce me. He is well cute.'

With her eyes wide, Rebecca said, 'wash your mouth out now. Cute and my bro do not go together in the same country, let alone the same sentence. Only kidding, I will, of course introduce you when we get a chance to take a breath that is.'

Just as they were disembarking the plane, David said, 'I have arranged a meeting tomorrow with the PM and some renowned international scientists. They are flying into London as we speak. In fact, on the request of Mary, most of the big worldwide players have sent their senior scientist. I hope this is okay with you Rebecca. I really do not think we are in a position to wait.'

After a relaxed evening with everyone, where once more Rebecca was the centre of attention, she headed off to her room. Lying in bed, she wondered what the following day would be like, what with so many top-brass scientists all undoubtedly having a strong opinion. In the end, she dozed off feeling relaxed having reflected on how easy her mission had been so far. She woke the following morning, again thinking about the day ahead and reflecting on everything that Meredith,

Matilda, and Rebekah had put in place, she was sure her journey should be straightforward.

The meeting was set for twelve noon, although arriving in the designated room in some posh hotel, Rebecca was more than a little surprised to see so many faces sitting in chairs facing a small stage area.

David came over, and said, 'While you guys were chatting last night, I put together a presentation showing slides depicting every piece of evidence. This will help to validate your story to those who are understandably sceptical. For sure, there will be cynical individuals, as you'd expect among our learned friends. So, with that in mind, I will take the stage first and explain all I know and show them all they need to know. Then, when we both feel comfortable, you can join me and explain your side of the story. We can then go through the information on your tablet. I've managed, after a bit of fiddling about, to transcribe all the tablet information onto paper and have produced a file for everyone. This way, each individual can take the information back to their respective governments and get the ball rolling.'

'Thank you so much, David. I was wondering how we'd go about all this.'

'Your job, Rebecca is to spend time in the past and future and tell us what we should do. My job is to make sure everyone listens.'

As Rebecca sat there listening to David speak to the guests, she found herself feeling like she was watching her life story on stage. When it was her time to join David, although a tad nervous, she pushed back her shoulders knowing this was her one chance to be counted and everything had led her to this point in time. She then spent a couple of hours going through everything with David, although, she was doing most of the talking.

264

After the event, there was a long line of people wanting to ask Rebecca questions. Although she was more than happy to chat about her time in the past, she found this a bit overwhelming. At one point especially, she was being asked two or more questions at once. As if David had recognised this, he came over and politely intervened, taking her to one side.

'Bit much, all these questions I suspect. I am going to inform everyone that we need to leave now, which we do as we have a meeting with the PM.'

Rebecca nodded. 'Thank you, David. It was all becoming a bit too much.'

After David had made their excuses, the two of them headed off to Downing Street to meet up with Mary, which still felt all a bit surreal for Rebecca.

'Hello, Rebecca dear. I've heard you had the most advantageous time in Syria. David also explained the meeting with the science fraternity went to plan. On the back of the information you have shared, and the views David has expressed, I have spoken to many world leaders. We have arranged, as a matter of urgency, the annual Global Summit gathering to be brought forward for the eighth. That's two days time, which gives you, David, and me all day tomorrow to work on our presentation. Although, David, it would seem has done most of that already. I have spoken with Queen Elizabeth and she has given her full support. While you were on your way here, I took calls from the respective leaders in the US, Canada, China, Russia, Germany, and France who also offered their full support. I dare say I will be receiving calls from all the other one-hundred and ninety-five countries over the next few hours. It would seem each representative scientist sent back the same message. That being, act now or we fail.'

The following day passed in the blink of an eye for Rebecca, as she, Mary, and David correlated all the information. Most of the time, having now all agreed Rebecca's story was now irrefutable, their focus was on the wind turbines, and the plastic-eating cray-lobster crossbreeds.

Chapter 36 – Global Summit and the Press

Waking up in her London hotel room, Rebecca's mind was going in circles. She'd always reckoned there was a reason for her ability to travel back and forth through time. Of late, she realised her very existence had become magnified by the importance of what she'd seen in the future and what she'd learnt from others of her kind. She knew if today's meeting went as planned, it should result in the continuation of the human race. She also knew, if her story wasn't accepted and acted upon, humanity would end abruptly. To compound her emotions, tucked away in the back of her thoughts was the notion that if she succeeded it could perhaps be her journey's end. The very thought of not seeing the people who had become a part of her life left her feeling a little tearful. She pushed this thought to one side and got herself ready for the day ahead.

Arriving at a huge arena in South London with Mary and David, created a surge of adrenalin and excitement, oddly though, she also felt an unusual amount of trepidation. She glanced at David. 'I am a little anxious, but I am not sure why.' Just then a thought occurred to her. Seeing Tommy in her minds eye running out to a full house at Anfield made her feel a little easier. She mumbled, 'if the twit can do it, so can I.'

'Well, you have the backing of the British Government, the Queen and importantly, some of the world's leading scientists. In addition, you have a solution by way of your computer

267

tablet, which is clearly from the future. Nonetheless, I understand your feelings. I get like that every time I attend such meetings, especially if I have to speak. I think though, as you mumbled, if the twit, I am guessing that's your brother, can do it, so can you.' He then nodded, which kind of made Rebecca feel he too gained some solace from this.

Mary tapped Rebecca on the arm and added, 'so much so, we as a country have already started a huge programme working on the wind turbines. Norway, Germany, and Sweden have started a colossal investment programme mimicking the crossbreed, plastic eating lobster. In addition, Canada, and the US, along with Russia and China have started working on the turbine solution. I am assured other countries are ready to follow suit imminently. In essence, today's summit is really only a show of hands from other smaller countries to follow the already agreed programme of investment. This is the first time all one-hundred and ninety-five countries have attended.'

'So, in effect, my plan is live?' Although obviously delighted with this news, Rebecca's head had been so focused on convincing people her tale was true, she now felt a little odd. For sure, she didn't feel thwarted, it was just she'd built herself up for a battle and there wasn't going to be one.

'It is indeed,' Mary said. 'Today's event is really as I said, only a show of hands. Importantly though, it is so the wealthier nations can establish which smaller countries may need financial backing. The scientists believe to make this work absolutely, there needs to be a global network of turbines.'

'After, there will be a press conference to announce a worldwide ban on the use of non-degradable products. Also, the use of fuels sources that damage the atmosphere, and so on. For sure this is going to be a challenge for the smaller nations, however, for this to work there must be one-hundred percent buy-in.'

268

Although Rebecca had hoped for this kind of ultimate reaction, never in her wildest dreams did she expect it would happen this seamlessly and with such pace. Knowing there would be a worldwide press conference was a little unnerving. It was one thing talking to individuals, and being part of a group at this summit, but speaking directly to the world's press was something she just wasn't prepared for. 'So, this press conference, how will that work?'

'Rebecca,' Mary said, 'you will, over the coming months and years face many questions, many of which will relate to your ability to do something most thought was impossible, travel through time. As a result, we made a joint decision to keep you at the back during this meeting with the press. I hope you are okay with that. We felt it might be best for you. Obviously, you can be involved as much as you want, especially as it's your baby. However, we felt all the questions would relate to you and your abilities, rather than the international bans that must be adhered to.'

Rebecca was in fact rather relieved. She'd worked out on the plane back from Syria that many of the questions related to her abilities, rather than the job in hand. 'I have the rest of my life to answer questions about my time-jumping. Today must be about saving our planet.'

Arriving in the conference hall and seeing national flags of every shape and colour made Rebecca feel if she did nothing else with her life, this was enough. In fact, the more she thought about it, the more she realised she'd never top this and again reckoned this could finally be the end of her time in the past or future. The conference itself was relatively straightforward with a handful of leaders from the bigger countries explaining what was to come if we didn't act forthwith. Some amazing graphics had been created to show where we would end up if we didn't act now. Much of the focus was on us changing direction regardless, with no ifs or buts. What did surprise Rebecca was there being no mention of her in any aspect of the agenda. This was something she was delighted by although a tad put out, even though she knew why and recognised it was for the best.

As if Kaitie, who was sitting next to her at the back, had sensed her mood, she nudged Rebecca and whispered, 'it was decided to keep you and your time-travelling out of this for fear it would raise too many eyebrows. Instead, the big players decided to share today's information as a fait-accompli. In essence, you will act or else. Indeed, to add to this, one or two countries that were ostensibly digging their heads in the sand were pre-warned there would be huge financial restrictions put on them if they did not adhere to the set-out programme of events.'

After, at the press conference, Rebecca sat with Kaitie towards the back of the venue, which she rather liked. There was, however, a few times following challenging questions from the press when she felt like standing up and asking them how they would react if they'd seen Earth without man and so on. However, she refrained, and a lot of this was because Kaitie, who seemed to be in tune with her emotions, whispered for her to let it go.

That evening in the hotel, with most of the senior representatives still discussing pragmatic financial solutions at the conference centre, she, Kaitie and a couple of the others who made the trip to Syria sat together engaging in a well-deserved relaxed evening meal.

Peter, one of the scientists who'd made the trip to Syria asked, 'How do you feel, Rebecca, sitting at the back without any input, especially as this is all down to you?'

'I felt a little odd initially, Peter. It is my baby. In fact, it is what I was put here for, my destiny, bit cliché but hey. However, if they'd introduced me to the world press as a time traveller, something that is impossible I might add, their focus would have been on me and not the job in hand.'

270

'That's very gracious, Rebecca. However, time travel clearly is possible and humanity was doomed had it not been for you. I've been an archaeologist all my life. I wanted to be one when I was a child and have been part of groups who've uncovered some amazing history. You, on the other hand, have been there and seen it all first hand,' Melissa said and shook her head. 'If you don't mind me asking, how did you feel the first time you climbed the spiral stairs and ended up in eighteen-fifty something. That must have sent a chill up your spine. Make a great film by the way. Maybe when you've finished your book someone might just do that, who knows. Although, thinking about it, it wouldn't be a fantasy science fiction film, more like a documentary of events.' She then laughed out loud.

'Funny you know, I can remember it as if it were yesterday. For sure, my emotions, and nerve endings were dancing around a maypole. Oddly though, it was as if it was meant to be and I felt strangely comfortable.' Rebecca narrowed her eyes. 'During every one of my journeys over the last few years, I have always known I am going somewhere. Although I am obviously excited with a palpable adrenalin rush, at the same time, I always feel relaxed, almost as if it's normal, which clearly it isn't.'

'How so?' Kaitie asked.

'I get a gut feeling, no more, no less. For sure, there are times when I smell almonds and such like. However, generally, I head out of my front door and think here we go. Even in the early days, before I'd found the key that led to the summerhouse and the stairs, I got this feeling something was afoot. I still get it now.' She'd had a strange feeling when she left the arena and spotted a huge ancient naval ship moored on the River Thames. It made her feel as if she was going to jump somewhere, although when David started speaking to her the feeling vanished. 'You know that huge galleon moored outside the arena? Well, I took one look at it and thought here we go.'

Shaking her head, Kaitie said, 'you didn't though, did you?'

'No, although the way it works, I could have jumped and been back before any of you noticed. I once spent thirty years on the other side and came back a minute of my own time later.' She shook her head, unable to believe her own words. 'I got married, had two children, and lived a full life.' Again, she shook her head.

Kaitie was just sitting with her mouth open.

Rebecca tapped her on the chin. 'Imagine telling your mother, at the age of, I think I was about twenty-one ish. Anyways, I had to tell her, oh yeah, by the way, Mum, blah, blah, blah.'

The group spent the rest of the evening sitting around chatting mostly about Rebecca's time in the past. Rebecca felt increasingly comfortable around these people and knew along with Kaitie, they'd be in her life forever.

Chapter 37 – New York

The next month passed so quickly for Rebecca going to various meetings with various scientists, the PM, and a number of world leaders. Mostly, the meetings were to check on the progress of the wind turbine installations across the globe. Just before she was due to visit New York with her family, she received a call to say the Norwegian company had successfully bred the lobster/crayfish species and confidence in its success was high.

On the 13th July, she boarded the plane at London's Heathrow full of optimism. With Roxy sadly unable to attend due to her commitments in Asia, Kaitie was able to jump in at the last second, something that delighted them both. During the journey over to New York, most of the conversation was about Rebecca's endeavours over the last few weeks.

'I was hoping it would go well for you, Rebecca,' her father said, 'but I never imagined for one second it would be this straightforward. It is one thing the world accepting you can travel back and forth through time. To then act upon your suggestions so quickly is way beyond anything I think any of us could have hoped for.' He then glanced at the others.

'It is interesting that you mention that, James. Obviously, for me, the first I knew of Rebecca's abilities was when I met her on the plane going over to Syria. You know, I found it easy to accept her story as the truth, although I couldn't tell you why, I just did. Aside from all of the unquestionable evidence and the buy-in of other senior global individuals, it was her enthusiasm and downright doggedness that got me believing.'

'Thank you, Kaitie. Your buy-in essentially helped me hugely. What with you being an academic and all.' She then glanced towards her father. 'Dad, believe me, I keep pinching myself. I went into this expecting a battle. I think the thing that shocked me most was the implementation of an overnight worldwide ban of non-biodegradable substances and the use of fuels that contaminate the atmosphere. I wouldn't have previously thought that was possible. To compound my sentiments, I then learnt all the wealthy countries would financially help the poorer ones at any cost, well, I can tell you, that came as a shock.' Rebecca shook her head, still unable to believe this all went through so seamlessly.

'Well, all I can say, it's a good thing it did go through so easily, not like we have time on our hands to discuss the matter. Strikes me, all the big players knew they had no choice. It was either stump up the money or fail.'

All the way through the conversation, Rebecca often noticed Tommy looking over as if he were listening. He had his headphones plugged in and was playing some football game, so she reckoned he wasn't.

Just before they landed, he pulled out his earphones and said, 'I so knew there was something strange about you, even when we were young. Time traveller indeed.' He then pulled a silly face in that twit like way and asked, 'How many goals will I score next season?' He then got up and collected his bag. However, surprisingly to Rebecca, he got Kaitie's first and with a smile she'd rarely seen, he handed it to her. 'Here you are, Kaitie. If you would like, I can carry the bag from the plane.'

As they walked down the steps, Rebecca nudged him and said, 'keep your eyes off, she's my friend, Twit.'

274

In what seemed like the blink of an eye, they were all heading back to London. Throughout their few days in New York, Rebecca couldn't fail to notice how well Kaitie and Tommy were getting along, so much so, she wondered if Kaitie would end up becoming her sister-in-law. This made her laugh out loud.

'What's so funny, Sweetie,' her mum asked.

'The twit and Kaitie have become inseparable.'

'I know, to think he has never had a girlfriend to speak of and now, well, wedding bells. You mark my words. I know you two and I knew within days of Duncan's appearance where it was going. Same for Tommy, I think. Not heard a single slang word or term from him since we got on the plane.'

While in the taxi on the way home, Rebecca received a phone call from David. 'Hello, Rebecca, I hope you had a good holiday. So, there's some great news from a laboratory in Siberia. Evidently, they have been tracking a particular weakness in the ozone layer for years. Over the last ten years, it had been weakening by an average of... Well, I was given some gobbledygook numbers, but in essence one percent a year. In just thirty-eight days, they have seen the weakness positively shrink by twenty-three percent. Their Prime Minister, Afanasi Linotile asked me to pass on his thanks, describing you as a world saviour. In fact, at some point, he would like to meet up with you to see if together you could put in place a plan to uncover other travellers like you who have perhaps kept under the radar for obvious reasons.'

Reckoning his suggestion was an exciting idea, Rebecca agreed to meet up with Afanasi as soon as possible. As she sat there in the back of her car, something Meredith had suggested a while ago now made perfect sense. In fact, the more she thought about it, the more she realised others she'd met during her time in the past had said something similar whereby in her time the world would start to see her type as the way forward.

The very prospect of finding some twelve-year-old, who had the same ability as her, and was scared to speak out, perhaps living in a remote place in Russia, in reality, energized her. 'Well, that's me sorted for the next few years,' she mumbled.

'Doing something other than fixing the planet, I suspect by your expression, Rebecca. So, what plans will now keep you occupied?' Duncan asked with an obvious look of intrigue on his face.

Rebecca then explained all about what had been agreed with the Russian Prime Minister. Everyone was pleased, but in particular, her mother delighted in the concept. Thinking about this briefly, Rebecca fully understood her reaction, while reflecting on all her mother had gone through as a child. This very thought hit her senses with a thud of realisation that there could actually be many like her walking around, frightened to speak out, or worse still, ridiculed when they had.

Feeling a little jet-lagged, Rebecca decided on an early night. The following morning, with Tommy off at training camp, her father, and Duncan away on business, Rebecca sat chatting outside with her mother over breakfast. Just as the conversation turned to Meredith, Rebecca had a call from David asking if she was free to travel in two days to Moscow for a meeting with the Russian PM.

'Mum, it seems ironic that we were talking about Meredith.' She then explained what Meredith had told her previously about the world accepting her kind as the way forward and here she was, heading off to Russia in two days.

Appearing a little upset, Elizabeth said, 'well, about time if you ask me. To think there could be others like you, or particularly like me, who can't speak out, dotted all around the world. And because of you, they will now have a voice.'

Nodding, Rebecca said, 'my exact thoughts, Mother. I immediately thought of you, and what you went through after you mentioned your tale. Who knows what these others may know?'

Chapter 38 – Russian PM

The next two days flew by for Rebecca, as she unpacked her New York case and replaced the contents with suitable clothing for her trip to Russia. David, who had now been given a new job title, Minister of Global Affairs, was due to travel with her on the trip, along with Kaitie. This pleased Rebecca no end because Kaitie was someone who she now saw as a close friend. Vitally, she had also shown a tangible understanding and firm grasp of Rebecca's ability to travel through time.

As they left Moscow airport, the greeting and onward travel to the Kremlin appeared to Rebecca's mind to have a distinct clandestine feel. When she climbed aboard a long black tinted-windowed limousine, it was suggested this was purely to avoid the waiting press. She had for some time, been aware that at some point she'd have to face the press. This was something she wasn't too enamoured with or looking forward to, not knowing what to expect. So, although she initially raised her eyebrows at the reception they had received, she was now actually grateful.

'Bit of a cloak and dagger reception, Rebecca,' Kaitie said and rolled her eyes. 'What was that James Bond film?'

Grinning and thinking this is one of the reasons why I like this girl, Rebecca said, 'do you mean, From Russia with Love?'

On the way into Moscow city centre, Rebecca found herself looking at every girl she passed wondering if they could be like her. 'I wonder if there are more like me, or if it's one per generation, which is what I have kind of been led to believe?'

She then thought about why she believed this concept. 'I think, over the years, just from what others have said about our kind, I just assumed it was one of us every now and then.'

'Well, I am sure in time, we will find out. You'd think though, that if there were more of you around, why has this all fallen to you?'

'Hmm, just you saying that is perhaps subconsciously why I feel the way I do. Thinking about it now, it just occurred to me, perhaps I was the only one receptive enough to hear the message.'

As the car approached the huge gated entrance to the Kremlin, there were dozens of paparazzi. All waving cameras at the window to the point where Rebecca thought the glass would break.

Now inside the gates and with a little normality returning, David handed Rebecca a letter. 'I had this letter passed to me to hand on to you. It is from Malcolm, Duncan's friend at the Liverpool Gazette. I perhaps should have given it to you on the plane, but I wanted to see how things were once we arrived. It is about a press article that ran in a national newspaper in Brazil. Subsequently, the whole world's press now knows about your time travelling exploits.' He shook his head. 'I thought with Russia supposedly restricting freedom of speech, or so we've been led to believe over the years, that perhaps the press here would pay you no attention. How wrong I was, on both counts.' Again, he shook his head. 'I should have known better really. A close friend of mine visited Russia for the Winter Olympics a couple of years back and said it was no different here to the UK, US or anywhere else. Shamelessly, being a parliamentarian and all, I should have known better. Sorry, Rebecca, had I told you, you could have been prepared for that barrage of camera abuse.'

'It's just fine, David. I knew one day my news would get out and I have been ready for that some time. It is no wonder, time travel indeed, really,' she said and flicked her head in an upward motion.

Rebecca, along with the others, were shown to their accommodation. Entering an enormous, lavish room, more like a film set, she couldn't help mumble, 'fit a family of ten in here.' Noticing the porter glancing at her from the corner of his eye, she said, 'I am always talking to myself.' Then seeing the odd expression on his face, she said, 'Do you speak English?'

'Yes, Madam, I do. Is there something I can help you with?'

'No, I am just fine, thank you for asking. I noticed the way you looked at me when I was muttering.'

Sheepishly, he nodded without saying anything.

'It is okay, you can talk to me. I won't bite.'

He then smiled. 'I was not expecting you to speak with me in such a tactile way. In this job, I would normally move bags and no more. This building has many visitors, mostly dignitaries, all of which have little time for the likes of me.'

Rebecca shook her head. 'Why ever not, like them, you are a human being, with feelings, thoughts and, well, underneath we are all the same.'

'Thank you, Madam.' He then seemed to think for a moment. 'Madam, can I ask you a question?'

'Yeah, fire away. I can always say no,' she said and chuckled.

He then seemed to go deep into thought, almost as if he was choosing his next words. 'I have seen stories within the press suggesting you are able to travel from one year to the next. Is this true?'

She nodded. 'As inconceivably bizarre as it is, I can travel back and forth through time, seamlessly covering generations and in some cases, millennia.'

Now grinning, he put the bags down and said, 'my sister, Nadia, is like you. Sadly, she is locked away in an asylum in Kamchatka. Perhaps...' he said, and then stopped abruptly.

Rebecca seeing his hesitancy, touched his arm gently and said, 'I will get her freed. Give me the exact location and I promise you she will be freed by the end of the day.'

Appearing a little startled, he smiled but at the same time narrowed his eyes.

'Worry not; I am here to meet with your Prime Minister to discuss exactly this. Our intention is to set in place a global search for others like me and here we are. What is your name, and will you write down your sister's name also?'

Nodding, he started to write. 'My name is Dmitri, and my sister is Nadia, as I said earlier. She is fifteen years old and only told her schoolteacher she had spent time with a Russian Tsar's named Saint Nicholas the Passion Bearer. He lived in the eighteen-eighties, perhaps I should point out. The very next day, Nadia was interned. She has now been locked away for two years.'

Again, Rebecca touched his arm. 'Leave it with me. I will come and find you soon with a solution.'

Now on a mission, Rebecca headed out of the door and down a huge sweeping staircase with Meredith's aunt and all she went through right at the front of her thoughts. On a mission, she marched up to the reception desk. However, the receptionist's indifferent attitude towards her got her back up. She tapped on the desk in front of him, and in her most assertive tone, demanded to speak with the PM.

281

'Madam, I would suggest you lower your voice and soften your tone.'

'I am here as a guest of Afanasi and must speak with him now as a matter of urgency.'

Frowning and without taking his eyes away from Rebecca, the slightly surly receptionist picked up the phone and said something in Russian. Within a few seconds, his whole demeanour changed. Nodding, somewhat subserviently, he lowered his eyes and said, 'There will be someone down shortly to take you to the Prime Minister.' He then pointed towards a smartly, almost military style, dressed woman and said, 'my colleague will take you up now.'

Rebecca followed the woman up the stairs and into a stately room. Afanasi looked up from his desk, lowered his glasses and just as her father did many years ago, waved Rebecca towards him with one finger. Although this kind of made her smile, it also really annoyed her at the same time. She flicked her eye brows upwards and slowly walked towards his desk. Without waiting to be asked to sit, she sat down in the chair opposite him. 'So, you invited me here to find others like me and yet you have one girl of my making locked up in an asylum in Kamchatka.' She then shook her head, 'and while we are on the subject of how to behave, your desk clerk obviously learnt his people skills from you. Beckoning me towards you with your finger, almost as if I am some kind of naughty school child is not a good way to win me over.'

'I do so apologise, Rebecca. Sadly, rightly, or wrongly, this type of churlish behaviour is usual for someone in my position. I do not agree with it, but advisors would have one believe it is expected. It effectively maintains distance, evidently.' He then rolled his eyes. 'I must say, your fearless approach is a breath of fresh air. However, I would expect no less from someone who travelled to the cradle of civilisation, came back and subsequently made the world believe her story.'

282

'I have always been like that. As I often used to say to my mum, we need to stand up to these men. As for the twit on the desk, well he will always be going home alone with a smelly attitude like that. Rolling his eyes at me is not how to behave. Anyways, that's enough about me. There is a girl, Nadia who has been locked away for two years because she told her teacher she spoke with Nicholas the Passion Bearer.' She then handed him the asylum address and Nadia's details. 'Can we get her released today because if we don't, I am on the next plane home?'

Blinking a couple of times, Rebecca realised from his reaction that she was perhaps the first person to speak to him like this since his mum. He studied the note, and then made a call. Seconds later, someone entered the room. He spoke to them in Russian and then turned to Rebecca. 'She will be on her way home within minutes. I have also requested she visit with us. Can I ask how do you know of this girl?'

Rebecca then explained about the man who showed her to her room. 'I now find myself wondering how many others there are around the world, like Nadia, who have all been incarcerated.'

'Exactly my thoughts,' he said just as his phone rang. After a few seconds, he came off the phone and continued. 'She is now on her way home to her mother, and the two of them are happy to visit us tomorrow. There have been suitable arrangements made for her rehabilitation.'

Offering him her hand, she said, 'thank you for acting so quickly. I must now go and find Dmitri and tell him of the good news.' She shook Afanasi's hand and headed back to reception. This time as she approached the front desk, the man who was so brusque earlier was now acting somewhat sheepish.

'Madam, how can I be of assistance?' he asked lowering his head slightly.

283

'Well, for a start off, you can try acting like one normal human talking to another human. Good old-fashioned eye contact would be a good starting place. I need to speak to Dmitri, the bellboy, as a matter of urgency.'

Seconds later, Dmitri appeared at the front desk.

'Come and sit with me,' Rebecca said, indicating towards some palatial chairs by a large elaborate window.

Shaking his head, he said, 'Madam, those seats are for guests.'

'Well, you are my guest, so come and sit.' She then sat with him and explained about his sister's imminent release, emphasising she will be arriving here, with his mother, tomorrow. She stressed that she would make certain that he would get a good opportunity to have some time with his mother and sister.

'Thank you, Madam. That will be such a lift for our mother. She has not been the same since Nadia was locked away.'

Chapter 39 - Nadia

The following morning, Rebecca woke feeling quite odd. While she was in the shower, between wondering why every tap seemed to be made from solid gold when half the planet was starving, she considered her emotions.

She'd intended on wearing one of her work suits to meet Afanasi. Now having already crossed paths, she decided to dress in something a tad more comfortable, so put on a t-shirt and jeans. However, just as she was about to head downstairs, she thought about David and Kaitie, and the way her dress sense might make them feel. After a quick change, she made her way down for breakfast more suitably dressed.

She entered a room she'd previously believed would be some kind of breakfast bar and was more than a little taken aback by the grandeur of this tennis court-sized room that was fit for the highest echelons of society. To her mind, it was way over the top, but she got how things worked at this level. She was also a little surprised to see, not only David, Kaitie and Afanasi, but also Dmitri sitting at the table.

It would seem Afanasi had taken notice of yesterday's conversation and jumped up to pull Rebecca's chair out, even though there was a waiter in attendance whose job was to do exactly this. 'Please sit Rebecca, would you like tea, coffee, or something else?'

'Morning everyone,' she said, glancing around the table. 'Coffee would be nice, thank you, Afanasi. Nice to see you were able to join us, Dmitri. How long is it since you've seen your sister?'

Clearly, a little uneasy, Dmitri glanced around at the others.

'Feel free to speak, Dmitri. The world has changed thanks to Rebecca. No more standing on ceremony or waving iron fists toward each other. Humanity has this lady and her type to thank for its very salvation. All one-hundred and ninety-five countries are finally working as one, for a common goal, deliverance. We must now make sure we stop listening to the noisy minority who tell bad stories. Instead, we must act as one with care for our fellow human, irrespective of their beliefs, preferences, or country of origin. If we can rid the planet of pollution to save our lives, we can rid the planet of poverty to save our souls. These past few weeks must stay in our focus for all time.'

'Well said, sir,' Rebecca said. 'Let's hope all world leaders see it this way and act accordingly. Words are cheap, actions cost, and the wealthy must pay. With the money it costs to send a phone satellite into space, we could feed a small country.' She then nodded. 'So, Dmitri, when did you last see your sister?'

'It was when I left to work here in Moscow. She was just ten, and even then, we knew she was different. She was born fearless, with a naturally gallant way about her. She never accepted things for the way they appeared. Often, she would look beyond the obvious and see things in a different way. Even the harsh winters we faced, she'd say, without them, we wouldn't have the snow tiger. Everyone she touched was left with a smile, and that is not just other men and woman, animals too. Often, I would hear her saying hello to the shrubs, bushes and even the creaky old doors.'

Feeling all goosy, Rebecca rubbed her arm. 'She sounds just like me. I still say hello to the groaning doors and fruit-bearing shrubs. I know now, as I have always done, that people

286

would laugh if they could hear me, but I didn't care and still don't.'

Dmitri touched her shoulder and said, beaming a huge smile, 'Nadia and you are one of the same people. I am so looking forward to you two meeting. She always said she was meant for greater and richer things, and so it may prove.'

Oddly, Dmitri's last comments didn't sit well with Rebecca and suddenly her antenna was up.

After breakfast and knowing Nadia and her mother would not be here until late afternoon, she fancied going for a walk outside. With her room on the second floor, she was able to see the paparazzi had gone and reckoned it might be her only chance to see Red Square.'

After popping down to see Kaitie, it was agreed that the two could go for a walk, albeit, there would be security nearby. Rebecca and Kaitie then spent the next few hours wandering around, taking endless photos of the amazing buildings that most people have only ever seen in films or through photographs.

'From Russia with Love,' Rebecca said.

'It sure is an amazing place. The grandeur is beyond anything I expected. Simply stunning, yet in the west, for many years we are fed this grey soulless exposé.'

A couple of times, Rebecca noticed individuals with big cameras heading their way, and just as quickly, they were gone. In what seemed like minutes, it was time for them to head back in doors. On the way, Rebecca kept thinking about Nadia, and how her mental state might be considering she'd been locked away for two years. 'I am a little concerned for Nadia's state of mind you know. If she is indeed the free spirit her brother talks of, it must have been an absolute nightmare for her.' Still in the back of her mind was just one-word Dmitri said, richer.

287

'I was thinking the same. You know, it got me to thinking about something you said about Meredith's aunt and how she accepted her fate knowing she was part of a bigger plan. Hopefully, Nadia will feel the same now. That is providing she is like you and can actually travel through time.'

'I never considered that, but hey, all things being well, we will know within a couple of hours. It's two now and she is due here by four.' She then thought for a moment. 'I will know if she is of my making within seconds. I don't know why I'll know; I just know that I will.'

As they headed back to the Kremlin, Rebecca was feeling a little odd. On one hand, she was looking forward to meeting someone who may share the same abilities as her, but forever, she'd thought she was the only one of her kind, certainly for this generation. For years, convincing people her stories were more than dreams, even those closest to her, had always been an uphill battle, one she oddly enjoyed. Right now, it seemed she had the buy-in of the whole planet. However, finding someone else who could see the past as she does was a completely new world, and one she didn't know how she'd react to or deal with. Right from her earliest memories, she'd known she was different and was happy being that way. She knew people would more than likely mock, laugh at, or come up with the dream notion for her tales, and she was kind of happy that way. She'd never cared what people thought and still didn't now. To have someone else like her, living proof that her journeys through time were real was a game-changer. Over the last few weeks, many of those she'd met had bought into her story. Some though, she felt, were just going along with the idea simply because they had no choice, especially as her tale affected humanities future. She was fine with this, realising in this modern day of technology, the notion that someone, without any fancy gadgets or machinery, could move freely through time was borderline laughable. As she entered the gates, she knew she had to be open to this girl and take it for what it is, a surreal experience. After all, for years, she'd

288

evidently told a similar story. Something though just wasn't sitting right in her gut, and she trusted her gut, a feeling that had ultimately led her to Meredith all those years before.

Sitting down in the reception room and looking at this frail, drawn faced girl who couldn't make eye contact was not a nice experience. Inwardly, Rebecca was shaking her head, not feeling any kind of vibe from Nadia. Even when she spoke via a translator, the girl couldn't make eye contact, and this bothered Rebecca. For sure, Nadia had been locked away for two years. However, this was her opportunity to speak out without fear. The fact that she couldn't was not sitting right with Rebecca.

'I need a couple of minutes outside if that's okay. Kaitie, would you come with me please?'

Kaitie followed her outside. 'I know what you are going to say. It just isn't sitting right with me. As horrible as it is to say, I actually think this girl is missing a few marbles.'

Nodding, Rebecca said, 'Yep, in a nutshell. Sad, and I will give her a chance to convince me, but I think I'd know if she was for real.'

'Let's see how it goes.'

The two went back inside and joined up with the group. Over the next few minutes, Nadia told her story. The thing that instantly caused a problem in Rebecca's head was this girl kept changing her story and couldn't recall any details. Even several years after her first meeting with Meredith, Rebecca could bring to mind every second, even down to how she felt.

'Nadia, how did you feel the first time you realised you had travelled through time?'

After Rebecca's question was translated, the girl glanced towards her mother. Again, without making eye contact with

Rebecca she said, 'I do not remember.' She then hesitated and again glanced towards her mother. 'I thought it was funny.'

'Is that it, funny, that's all you felt?' Rebecca knew there and then that the girl was not of her making. Of all the emotions she felt, a mixture of exhilaration, trepidation, a little fear and importantly a gut feeling she was doing the right thing, never did she think it was funny or anything remotely similar. Deciding she'd give this girl one more chance, she asked, 'so when you found yourself back in your time, what were your immediate thoughts? Importantly, who did you tell first?'

Suddenly the girl's demeanour changed a little. She looked up and said in a very uncharacteristic way, 'I sold my story to the local newspaper.'

That was it for Rebecca. The last people she thought of telling was anyone from the blinking press, and to compound that thought, this girl had asked for money. She glanced around the room, nodded to Kaitie and Afanasi and said, 'Okay, that's me done. Sorry, Dmitri, I believe your sister's story is exactly that, a story.' She rolled her eyes towards Afanasi. 'I am going outside for some fresh air.'

As she walked outside, she breathed out heavily. Although part of her initially wanted to believe this girl, and there were feelings of sympathy for her having been locked away, she was now feeling rather cross. For her mind, every journey she had been on was life changing and part of a bigger plan. Never was it funny or an opportunity to earn money. To now think that this girl's brother had seized an opportunity to get his sister out of the asylum and in all probability earn a few dollars along the way angered her no end.

Right, she thought and headed back inside the building. She opened the door just as the others were getting up to leave. 'I need a few more minutes, please. Dmitri, did you know my story before I got here?'

He narrowed his eyes, and uttered, 'Umm, yeah, I think so.'

'You think so? Either you did or you didn't. And as for you, Madam, your tale is sad, and that's all. You thought you could make a few dollars selling your story and it backfired. Both of you are scammers.' She then turned to Afanasi. 'Just send them back home.'

She then tapped Kaitie on the shoulder and indicated to head outside. As they walked into the courtyard, she turned to Kaitie. 'I am so flipping cross.'

'This is going to happen a lot. People jumping on the bandwagon having seen your story and so on.'

'I know, and because of this, it's going to be impossible to track down any others like me. I'll end up meeting with so many fraudsters, well.'

During supper with David, Kaitie, and Afanasi, they initially discussed Nadia, and all agreed at this juncture it might prove impossible to track down others like Rebecca, especially now her story was known worldwide.

'I think we may need to leave it for a couple of years so the dust can settle. Then start looking again.'

'I think you are right, Afanasi. You know, if there are others like me, they will creep from the woodwork, not come out trying to make fame and fortune from it. It's a gift and one that is a design process by greater powers to save mankind. I was the one who was in the right place at the right time. She then remembered something Rebekah said to her. 'The original one of my making, Rebekah of Mesopotamia, told me that every generation would have one girl of my making. If that is true, there is no point in us looking.' In an odd way, this thought kind of pleased Rebecca. The idea of traipsing around the planet meeting up with others who may be of her gene was not top of her list. In fact, she was just about done with all of this and was ready to head back to the summerhouse with Duncan. Then possibly, once settled down, think about starting a family.

Chapter 40 - The Future

Rebecca arrived home after a long delay at Moscow Airport, which David had suggested was the norm when travelling to and from Russia, with their security being the best in the world. Over supper that evening, she told her mother, father, and Duncan all about her time in Russia.

'Seems like you didn't much enjoy your time there, Rebecca?' Elizabeth said, narrowing her eyes.

'Oh, far from it. I loved the country, the people and in particular, the Russian PM was a lovely man. The sights were amazing. Some of the buildings are almost fantasy-like. I must say though, after the last few hectic weeks, I am so glad to be home and get back to normality. Although, I suspect we may have the press snooping about.'

'That won't happen,' Duncan said. 'I spoke with the PM, Mary Scotland, and there is a nationwide ban on press approaching you. I am not sure if you know, but while you were away, every newspaper ran a front-page story about you. Somehow, your actual name and our home were not included.'

'How did they manage that, Duncan?'

'Well, the press agreed prior to running the story, you, our family, and our home would be kept out of any relating articles. This was because of what you'd done for mankind. It was concluded by all you'd earned the right to anonymity.'

'I am glad about that because I am so ready to get back to normal life.'

Her dad grinned and said, 'normal and you rarely go together in the same sentence.' He then chuckled.

Rebecca then spent the weekend with her family, along with Kaitie, which included a trip to Anfield to watch Tommy play football. This is just what Rebecca needed, the opportunity to shout at her twit of a brother in a nice way. The next couple of weeks continued this way and by the time her father and Duncan were both heading off for a meeting in America and Elizabeth had decided to go to France with Ruth, she was ready for some Rebecca time.

'Are you sure you won't come with us,' her mum asked.

'Thanks, Mum, I really am looking forward to some time on my own. I just fancy spending a few days down in the woods sketching and such like.'

'Hey, maybe you can catch up with Meredith,' her mum said and giggled in that delightful way.

Once everybody had headed off, Rebecca grabbed her pencil and pad and made her way down to the woods. On the way, she was feeling totally chilled and looking forward to getting back to some kind of normality, Rebecca style. As she sat down on the trunk, memories of her early days here rumbled around in her head. It suddenly occurred to her it was rare that she'd sat here without anything happening. Thinking about this she guessed her mission was complete and that meant her time in the past was perhaps over. Then again, she'd thought that before, and muttered, 'never say never.'

The next two days passed in a similar way. It was now Wednesday and as she was heading down to do some more on her book, she felt that oh so familiar sensation. Because she had kind of made her mind up her time in the past might be over, this gut feeling came as a bit of a surprise. Entering the

294

summerhouse, that sensation seemed to magnify. The thing was, unlike her previous jaunts into the past, there was no smell of almonds. Racking her brain, she tried to recall ever going anywhere via the summerhouse without this smell first filling her nostrils. She headed upstairs to fetch her laptop but remembered it was still in her bedroom in the main house. 'Damn it,' she muttered. As she opened the front door, she instantly knew she wasn't going back for her laptop. Around the outside of the summerhouse was a large glass-like fence. She walked over to the glass panelling and was unable to see an exit. It seemed to be one long continuous sheet of glass-like material. She headed around the back, hoping she'd find a way out. As she walked around the side, she could see a group of people wearing the most bizarre clothing, the likes of which she'd expect to see in a star trek episode or something similar. With her thoughts jumping from one idea to the next, she now had an idea of what might be going on. She walked over to the fence and waved at the people. Oddly, it was as if she was invisible. She mumbled, 'been here before.' She stood and listened as a young guy, dressed in what appeared to be a one-piece, dusty green suit affair, addressed the dozen or so people.

'This is where Rebecca's story started. That was twelve-hundred years ago. Thanks to Rebecca, humanities saviour, the Earth is thriving with mankind. Because of her vision and intrepid nature, she made the world listen. Subsequently, we now live without the need for an indulgent, planet-destroying lifestyle. Furthermore, she opened the door for others of her making to come forward and stop humanity from once again taking the wrong turn and then derailing mankind's very existence.'

Just then, she felt a tap on her shoulder. Sensing who this was and without turning, she said, 'Rebekah, Meredith, it is so good to have you here with me.'

She then turned and greeted each of them with a kiss on the cheek.

'Your work is complete, Rebecca. Our types are free to speak out and the planet, along with humanity is all the richer for it.' Rebekah then squeezed her hand.

'All of us, who passed before you, now know our life's mission was a success. You, above all, had the tenacity to get this job done. For that, we who now live in the other dimension can look on with peace in our hearts, minds, and soul. We may see you again.'

Then, unexpectedly, the two of them seemed to evaporate into thin air, and as Rebecca turned, she knew she was once more back home.

Chapter 41 – Another Dimension

Heading back into the summerhouse, Rebecca wasn't quite sure how she felt. She'd been positive for some time her mission would be a success, especially after the early news that the wind turbines were working. The mention of another dimension though was once again playing on her mind. Since the first time Meredith had suggested she was an apparition, she'd wondered what that had actually meant. Since she wasn't too keen on believing in ghosts, well not the way films portrayed them, she had wondered if Meredith had visited her from elsewhere. Having heard this other dimension mentioned a few times, she now felt the need to know a little more. The stumbling block in her thoughts was how she was going to find out what they were referring to earlier. Now back in the main house and staring at her laptop, there were no words. Instead, her mind was elsewhere trying to imagine Meredith, Rebekah, Matilda, and many others that were there with them, all watching mankind.

At university, Sam, her tutor had suggested she read a novel about the spiritual path we are all on, and now that book was kind of making sense. It had suggested all of mankind were here to learn the true meaning of goodness, integrity, and truthfulness. Once any individual truly understood, they would move to a higher plain. At the time, she wasn't sure how to interpret this other than it made her think about the Ten Commandments. Now though, she was beginning to interpret this in a similar, but somehow different way. Focussing her thoughts, she'd initially believed the book she'd read was designed to make people think about their impact on society and their fellow man, similar to the Old Testament.

With her jumbled thoughts a little clearer, she was as certain as she could be there was another dimension, even though the very idea was at best bizarre. Suddenly a light bulb went on in her head, reanalysing the idea of another plain where people could live was no more outlandish than her travelling through time. With that concept in her head, she was able to focus on her book. She now felt certain if she were meant to see this other dimension, it would happen, as with everything else that had occurred, she would somehow find a way.

The next couple of days passed quickly for Rebecca, with most of her time taken up with writing and editing her novel. Feeling sure she had reached the end, she decided to go for a walk in the woods. For sure, she knew there might be more to add to her book, but for now, she felt she'd gotten her message across, although there may be more to come. With her pad and pencil, she made her way through the woods to her favourite place. As she arrived and once more perched herself in the best position, she started doodling a couple of youthful pixies playing among the crocuses. As her mind wandered off to another world, out of the blue, she could see herself standing with Meredith and Rebekah looking on a thousand years into the future, outwardly invisible to the others. 'Hey, maybe that's the other dimension,' she muttered. She should have known what was coming next. Whenever she talked to herself hereabouts, Ethernal would appear. *Well, not appear,* she thought, *but I'd hear his voice and sense his presence.* There was silence though. 'I wonder if he moves in that other dimension also.'

'I do, and you've always accepted that I am here, but not.'

'What does that even mean?' she muttered.

'It means exactly what it says. You've always accepted I am by your side, even though you have never seen me, just felt

298

my presence. Of interest to you, there is only one of your making for each generation. There have never been two on this Earth at the same time. So, the alternate dimension that has proved a conundrum for your thoughts is exactly what you want to believe it is. Moreover, it should represent a place you would consider full of goodness. Your mission has been a success, as I knew it would be the first time we met. Your spirit is the strongest I have known and therefore, we trusted you to succeed.'

In a flash, Rebecca's focus was on one word, we. 'You said, "we trusted". Who do you mean by we?'

'We, as in all of us who watch, which includes Meredith even though she is not of your making, both Rebekahs, Matilda and many others who have followed or preceded your path, either as a traveller or as your spiritual guidance and direction.'

'Spiritual guidance, can you explain what that means. I have my own perception of this, but I am intrigued to know your interpretation.'

'Meredith, Judith, and your beloved Tabitha are the best example of one who has followed this path. Your parents, Kaitie, and Roxy are on this path. Your brother, Tommy, will follow this path once he learns from Kaitie.'

'What do you mean by that, learn from Kaitie?' Rebecca's thoughts were already running away with her, especially as she'd only heard this morning that Kaitie and Tommy were going out for a meal. 'Tell me what that means,' she exclaimed. There was silence and she knew she would have to wait to find out what he meant by that.

Chapter 42 – Baby Girl, Kaitie and the Twit

Over the coming weeks and months, there were no more jaunts for Rebecca. She did have an exciting visit to London to receive the Most Noble Order of the Garter from Queen Elizabeth. This was a grand affair, enjoyed particularly it seemed by her mother and father. However, when Roxy, who had flown home especially for the event, referred to her as Lady Rebecca and laughed, it made her feel a little uncomfortable. Then to top this, as they headed back to the car, the twit curtsied, opened the door, and said, 'your carriage awaits, Me Lady.'

'Thank you, Parker, you twit.'

On the way home in the car, she had to listen to Kaitie and Tommy acting like two teenage lovebirds. If she'd been in any doubt about what Ethernal had meant when he suggested Tommy would learn from Kaitie, she now knew.

When they arrived home, her dad had arranged the setting up of a fabulously decorated garden marquee. As she entered to a fanfare of music, she didn't know which way to look next. Everyone was there from a couple of old school friends, her school English teacher, Sam Pochard who'd flown over from the States, Ruth, Amanda, half of Tommy's blinking football team, along with Kaitie and Kaitie's parents. This instantly started bells chiming in Rebecca's thoughts, certain she knew what might come later. She didn't have to wait too long to find out as Tommy came over and tapped her on the shoulder.

Again, with a twit like curtsey, he said, 'If it is okay with your ladyship. Seriously, Sis, this is your day and I am so proud of you. When you went up to get your award, I nearly shouted out just like you did when I scored my first goal for the Pool. Anyways,'

'Anyways, you never use that word.'

'I got it from Kaitie, who reckons she got it from you. So, as we are on the subject of Kaitie, would you mind if I asked her to marry me tonight. I know it is totally your day and all.'

'Wonderful, especially under her guidance you'll stop kicking your football at me.' She then laughed and gave him a cuddle.

Tommy being Tommy pulled away and yelped, 'ger roff.' He then pulled Rebecca back and as he cuddled her, he said, 'thank you for everything you have taught me over the years. I love you, even though you're still a moving target.'

The rest of the afternoon went wonderfully well, albeit, Rebecca had spent too long speaking with her old English teacher who was the first to tell her to write a book. As they headed into the evening, Rebecca started thinking, get on with it, Twit. She noticed him across the room speaking with Kaitie's father and reckoned she wasn't going to have to wait too much longer. As she caught his attention, she pulled a silly face, rolled her eyes, and mouthed, 'get on with it.'

He stuck his thumbs in his ears, wiggled his fingers, and mouthed, 'moving target.' He then noticed Kaitie's dad watching him. At a loss for words, he kind of pointed towards Rebecca without saying anything. She then saw Kaitie's father pat him on the shoulder and laugh.

Rebecca's laughter was then broken by the sound of her mother tapping the side of her glass. She stood up on the stage and turned to everyone. 'Well, what a wonderful day. As you all know, Rebecca received the highest award from the Great

301

British Monarchy today, and rightfully so, saving the future for our children's children. As if this day could not get any better, we have another wonderful announcement.' She then turned to Tommy and beckoned him up on the stage.

He got up on the stage and in true Tommy style, took his jacket off, and undid his shirt to reveal a Full England international shirt. This was immediately met with a rapturous round of applause and lots of cheering from his teammates who started singing; "you'll never walk alone," the Liverpool Football Club anthem. Once the din had settled down Tommy took the microphone and said, 'I got the call up for the Euro's squad yesterday. However, that is not why I am on stage. You guys sang the perfect song for me. Today it means more than just a football song.' He turned to Kaitie and asked, 'Kaitie, will you be my wife, so I never have to walk alone?'

Rebecca turned to Kaitie who was standing next to her, and with tears in both their eyes, Kaitie nodded to Rebecca. She then climbed up on the stage and as Tommy knelt in front of her, she held out her left hand.

The rest of the evening went off brilliantly with Rebecca going from one person to the next. Towards the end of the evening, her mother came over to her, quickly followed by her father.

'I am so proud of you, my daughter. The strength of character you have shown over the last year has been more than we could have hoped for in our daughter. Both you and Tommy have done us proud.'

'As a father, we have hopes for our children's future. Never did I expect or believe I could learn so much from you. You have shown your mother and me a new way to live our lives, as one. With our new addition, we have the perfect family. So, I thank you.'

Mum, Dad, it is me who must thank you. Through all the difficult twists and turns, you have been there for me and made this path I follow an easy one. So, I have some more news for you both.' She then beckoned Duncan over. 'Mum, Dad, Duncan. By March of next year, Mum and Dad, get ready to be grandparents.

This time the end.

However, there is this other dimension, so who knows if Rebecca will call me again…

Thank you all for sharing this journey with Rebecca and me. I hope like me, you may now see life and the world around you through a different set of eyes. Be gracious, consider your actions, and above all, be kind. It is free.

Steve – Stephen M Davis

PS keep your eyes open next time you're walking in the woods, who knows what or whom you may see.

I can be contacted through My Website:

stevedauthor.com

Or via my author email:

stevedauthor@gmail.com

Printed in Great Britain
by Amazon